Welcome to the Future . . . of Madness and Murder

It is a new century built on chaos. Citizens have divided into violent warring factions. Environmental self-destruction has taken its toll by the millions. And two tattooed corpses chained together have been dragged from the Bay . . .

Some things never change.

Only Tanner, an ex-cop turned smuggler, knows the Chain Killer's labyrinth. But only the punk urchin Sookie can lead him there—to a terminus called The Tenderloin. Here the Angel of Death resides. Here the ultimate crimes of the future are born . . .

And only here can they be stopped.

DESTROYING ANGEL

DESTROYING ANGEL

ANGEL

RICHARD PAUL RUSSO

ACE BOOKS, NEW YORK

This book is an Ace original edition,
and has never been previously published.

DESTROYING ANGEL

An Ace Book / published by arrangement with
the author

PRINTING HISTORY
Ace edition / July 1992

ISBN: 0-441-14273-7

Ace Books are published by The Berkley Publishing Group,
200 Madison Avenue, New York, New York 10016.
The name "ACE" and the "A" logo
are trademarks belonging to Charter Communications, Inc.

PRINTED IN THE UNITED STATES OF AMERICA

10 9 8 7 6 5 4 3 2 1

For Karen, Lee, and Patty;
friends who helped through rough times

ACKNOWLEDGMENTS

I'd like to thank the Centrum Foundation and the Cannon Beach Arts Association for their support during the writing of this book.

I'd also like to thank the following people for their comments and suggestions on different parts of the novel: Frank Milan, Alison Pride, Kelly Jurgensen, and Ursula LeGuin.

My thanks, also, to Sally Wies, who read the nearly final draft and made several invaluable suggestions.

Finally, special thanks to John Buckley for his encouragement and advice, and for his friendship.

ONE

TANNER WATCHED THE children playing among the methane fires of the neighborhood dump. Overhead, a sick green and orange haze muted the late-afternoon sun, the green curdling through the orange. It was hot, and Tanner was sweating.

The children chased one another, stumbling through the garbage, weaving in and out of the fires. Soot stained their faces, their tattered clothes. One of the girls periodically barked a patterned sequence of noises; each time she did, all the children abruptly changed direction.

Tanner walked on, away from the children. He skirted the dump and headed down a crowded, narrow street. Stone buildings rose on either side, radiating the damp heat of the day, echoing the sounds of car engines, shouts and laughter, bicycle bells, hammering, and the distant wail of a Black Rhino.

Half a block further on, Tanner entered the Carousel Club, which was hot and smoky, and dark except for several globes of emerald light that drifted randomly near the ceiling. He walked to the back of the main room, along a narrow corridor, then up a flight of stairs to the second floor.

There were a dozen tables in the second-floor room, most of them occupied, and another three outside on the small balcony overlooking a slough that fingered in from the bay. Paul sat at one of the balcony tables, gazing down at the slough, and Tanner walked over to the table. Paul looked up, his face gaunt and sallow, dark crescents under his eyes.

1

"You look like shit," Tanner said, sitting across from him. There was no breeze, so it wasn't any cooler than inside, and a faint stench drifted up from the stagnant water.

Paul smiled. "Thanks." He shook his head. "Just got off twelve hours in ER."

That was where Tanner had met Paul several years before—in the emergency room of S.F. General, back when Tanner had still been an undercover cop, bringing in the casualties of drug and gang wars for Paul and other doctors to patch up. Tanner wasn't any kind of cop anymore.

Tanner looked out from the balcony. Directly across the slough was a junkyard with several hundred wrecks piled four and five high. Atop one of the highest piles, a young girl sat cross-legged on the caved-in roof of a rusted blue sedan, smoking. Tanner had the impression she was looking at him.

A waitress wearing a bird mask came to their table, took their order, and left. Paul took a pack of cigarettes from his pocket, pulled one out, and lit it.

"I thought you quit," Tanner said.

"I've unquit."

"And you a doctor."

Paul shrugged. "Hell, I figure it can't be much worse than breathing this air."

Tanner looked up at the orange and green sky, decided Paul was probably right. He turned back to Paul, but he was gazing down at the dark, still water of the slough. Long shadows lay across its surface, with a few small, bright patches where the sun broke through between the buildings and reflected off the water.

"So what's wrong?" Tanner asked.

Paul shrugged. "I'm thinking about giving it up."

"What?"

"The clinic, the ER work, all of it." He paused, shook his head. "I'm burning out."

Yeah, no shit, Tanner thought. And I'm not far behind you. Quitting the force had only given him a temporary postponement. "What will you do?" he asked.

Paul smiled. "Hang out my shingle. Do nose jobs and liposuctions and neuro-genital enhancements. Make myself a god damn fortune."

Tanner laughed.

Drinks came. Tanner sipped at his, gazing across the slough at the girl in the junkyard. A pang went through him. There was something painfully familiar about the girl. He did not think he knew her, but she reminded him of someone. Who? He did not know. Her cigarette was gone, and now she was moving her hands and arms through the air in slow, complex patterns. Tanner still thought she was looking at him, and wondered if she was trying to send him a message. A cosmic bulletin. A spiritual communiqué snaking through the wrecked automobiles and the stinking water. Whatever it was, he wasn't getting it.

The girl stopped moving. She remained completely motionless for a few moments, then turned her head, looking toward the bay. The girl glanced back at Tanner, then scrambled down from the pile and disappeared into the heart of the junkyard.

Tanner leaned over the balcony rail, looked toward the bay, but didn't see anything unusual.

"What is it?" Paul asked.

"Don't know."

Then he heard the sound of a boat motor, and a few moments later a Bay Security boat appeared, headed slowly up the slough. Its lights were not flashing, but several Bay Soldiers stood on deck.

On the opposite bank, several men and women emerged one at a time through a gap in the chain-link fence just down from the junkyard. The first two were uniformed cops, the others in street clothes. Tanner recognized the fifth one through—Carlucci, from Homicide. Tanner had always respected him, though they had hardly ever worked together and never got along well enough to become friends. Carlucci was sharp, and you could depend on him. Tanner wondered if he'd made lieutenant yet.

One of the uniforms stopped, turned back, and said something. Carlucci shrugged, shook his head. Then all six spread out along the bank and began searching the water's edge.

Tanner felt sick. He knew, suddenly, what they were looking for, and what they would find.

The Bay Security cutter had dropped anchor in the middle of the slough, and all the soldiers were watching the cops search. Bay Security didn't have any authority here, but they wanted in on it. It was their territory, if not jurisdiction, and if bodies had been planted in the water, it affected their reputation. Tanner didn't feel any sympathy for them. They were parasites.

One of the plainclothes cops called out. He squatted at the edge of the water, looking down. The others came over, all looking down now, then the plainclothes cops moved away to make room for the two uniforms. The uniforms got the shit work as usual, Tanner thought.

The two men bent over, reached into the water, and pulled up a section of rope attached at one end to something just underwater—probably a metal stake embedded in the bank— and at the other end to something heavy and deep in the slough. They began to pull in the rope.

It was slow going. Twice, whatever was at the other end of the rope caught rocks or debris on the bottom, and the cops had to work it free. Then, as it neared shore, flashes of white skin broke the surface of the water.

Soon they had the bodies laid out on the muddy graveled bank. The cops surrounded them, trying to block them from the view of the Bay Soldiers. Tanner, though, had already seen enough.

There were two bodies, a man and a woman, both naked, back to back and chained together at the wrists and ankles.

"Jesus Christ," Paul said. "I thought that was all over with."

Tanner did not reply. He watched Carlucci and the others shifting their feet, smoking cigarettes, trying not to look at the bodies as they waited for the coroner's assistants to arrive. They should have had the coroner's men with them, Tanner thought, they should have known what they were going to find. Probably they hadn't wanted to believe it.

It had been two and a half years since the last set of chained bodies had been pulled out of water somewhere in the city. Working Narcotics, Tanner had never been directly involved with any of the investigations, but he'd pulled up a pair of bodies himself—two women he'd dragged out of Stowe Lake in Golden Gate Park—and he was glad that now he wouldn't have anything to do with it. Now it was someone else's nightmare. Wasn't it?

He looked away from the cops, finished off his drink.

"I could use another," he said.

Paul nodded. Tanner looked for the woman in the bird mask, signaled to her for two more drinks. She bobbed her feathered head and moved out of sight, deeper into the club.

Tanner looked back at the cops standing on the opposite bank. One of them tossed his cigarette into the water, where it sizzled for a second and sent up a tiny puff of smoke. No, Tanner thought, he didn't miss that work one bit.

TWO

SOOKIE WATCHED FROM the front seat of a two-door Sony, the middle wreck in a pile of five. She had a view of the water, the men, the naked bodies they had pulled from the slough. Drive-in movie, she thought. Sound turned low. She wished she had popcorn.

I'm thirteen, she thought. I'm not old enough to see this. She smiled, squirmed in the seat. Sit still, she told herself. She wanted a cigarette, but the smoke would give her away. Or they'd think the junkyard was on fire. She imagined sirens, giant streams of water, a helicopter dropping water bombs.

The men weren't doing anything. Talking, but she couldn't really hear it. Sookie looked at the bodies. Their skin was gray; no, white; no, gray-white. A strange color. She wondered if they were real bodies. Maybe it *was* a movie. But she didn't see any cameras. Didn't you need cameras to make a movie? Sookie wasn't sure.

The chains on the wrists and ankles were beautiful. Bright silver, shining brighter than the sun now. She couldn't see the sun, it was hidden by the buildings. Sookie closed her eyes, tried to imagine what the chains would look like on her own wrists and ankles. Pretty.

She opened her eyes, looked across the water and up at the people on the balcony. The man who had been looking at her. What a strange place! A giant bird wearing a short skirt served them drinks.

Some other men came through the fence, and then she couldn't see the bodies anymore. Flashes of light, someone

6

was taking pictures, but they weren't movie cameras.

Sookie felt dizzy and sick to her stomach. She was thinking about being dead and naked and people taking pictures of her like that. She closed her eyes, sighed, and lay back in the seat. She didn't want to watch anymore.

TWO

THREE

A FEW MINUTES after Tanner left the Carousel Club, a hot rain began. He ducked into a bakery to wait it out, knowing it wouldn't last more than half an hour. The bakery was hot and crowded and noisy. Tanner felt quite comfortable in the midst of it all, lulled by the heat, the smells of baked goods and strong coffee, and the rush of Spanish voices surrounding him. In the back of the bakery, a parrot squawked incessantly, producing an occasional word or phrase in Spanish.

He bought a cup of coffee and sat by the window, watching the rain spatter against the glass. Middle of July, highs regularly in the upper nineties, and rain every morning and afternoon—it was going to be one hell of a summer. Most of the country in extreme drought, and San Francisco was turning into a goddamn tropical rain forest. He missed the fog, the *real* fog, which he hadn't seen in ten years.

Eyes half-closed, Tanner sipped at the coffee and gazed out the window. Across the way, the narrow alley between two buildings was choked with green ferns streaked with brown and rust, the leaves shaking violently as a girl chased a dog through them. Bromeliads filled the air above the ferns, dangling in colorful clusters from windows and makeshift trellises crafted from scrap metal and plastic pipe.

He thought about the two chained bodies that had been pulled from the slough. Chained bodies in water. How many had there been? Thirty-seven over a two-year period. But none in two and a half years. And now . . . had it begun again? He

8

did not want to think about what that meant for him.

Lights came on up and down the street as night fell. Tanner finished his coffee when the rain stopped, and went back out onto the street. Time to go home.

He caught a bus and rode it to Market Street, getting off at one of the border checkpoints for the Financial District. The bus, with no access authority, turned around and headed back south.

Tanner stood at the edge of the checkpoint, looking at the bright glow of the Financial District. An enclave of towering structures of gleaming metal, bleached stone, and mirrored glass, the Financial District was the only part of the city that looked like it belonged in its own time. The rest of the city was still back in the twentieth century, or worse.

The shortest and safest route back to his apartment was through the District, but Tanner was in no mood for the ID checks and body searches. Instead, he took a more circuitous route that was almost as safe, and a lot more alive.

He walked a few blocks west along Market, then turned right into one of the city's three Cuban corridors. The street was crowded and noisy, brightly lit and filled with the smells of curry, black bean soup, bacon, and Cuban bread. Street soldiers wearing green and red scarves and armbands stood on the corners or walked casually through the crowds.

Several blocks from Market, the Cuban Corridor linked with the Chinese Corridor. Here, Tanner had a choice of streets, the Corridor encompassing nearly all of Chinatown. He cut over to Stockton, and the smells changed, shifted to seafood and incense. The street was even more crowded than the Cuban Corridor, pedestrians, cars, scooters, and bicycles moving in chaotic, halting patterns.

On the other side of Columbus, as Tanner neared the edges of the Corridor and Chinatown proper, the crowds thinned. The noise level dropped; fewer street soldiers were visible. And then the Corridor ended.

Tanner lived just a block and a half off the Corridor, but that block and a half was nearly silent, and much darker, without a single street soldier in sight. He walked quickly, but without fear, and he thought of what his father used to tell him: Don't look like a victim. He sometimes wondered if his father had forgotten his own advice.

He unlocked the outer gate to the grounds of the six-story apartment building, made sure it was securely latched, then walked through the overgrown garden to the building entrance. The plants were out of control again, damp leaves and branches crowding the walkway, streaking his clothes with moisture. Tiny insects whirled silently through the misty halo of the porch light.

Tanner keyed in the building code, his personal code, then unlocked the door bolts with his key. He stepped into the lobby, door and alarm locking automatically behind him.

The lobby was dimly lit, the air still and warm. Tanner stood motionless for a minute, listening to the building sounds filter to him from above—a faint, low hum; whispers of deeply pitched voices; a muffled rattle of glass; the whistle of a teakettle.

He opened his mailbox, but it was empty. Third day in a row. He wondered if it meant anything.

Tired, he climbed the stairs to the fourth floor, seeing no one in either the stairwell or hall. His apartment was at the far end of the hall, on the right; the door had a dozen boarded window frames without a single bit of glass. Occasionally he thought about replacing the glass, but not often enough to actually do anything about it.

The apartment was fairly good-sized for one person—front room, den, hall, bedroom, and kitchen—but more and more often recently it felt *too* large, and half-empty. He wandered from room to room, the empty feeling washing over him again, leaving a dull throb in its wake. It had always seemed the right size, warm and comfortable, whenever Valerie and Connie had spent time here. But that was long over, and they had not been here in more than a year. Well, hell, that had been his own choice, hadn't it?

He stopped at the den window, looked down at the street. Cones of light from the street lamps cast blurred shadows of trees and old cars. Apartment lights glowed dim and orange, dull rectangular eyes in the night. Oscar, the blind neighborhood cat, incredibly still alive after two years without sight, stumbled along the opposite sidewalk, head weaving stiffly from side to side. He bumped into a garbage can, hesitated for a moment, then turned into a narrow alley.

Bodies.
Another rain began.

After he ate, Tanner climbed to the roof, carrying an aluminum lawn chair. He hoped Alexandra would be there, but the roof was empty. The rain had stopped and the moon, three-quarters full, shone through the night haze with an amber cast.

Tanner set the chair at the roof's edge and sat. The night was unusually quiet. Traffic sounds were light, and he could hear the breeze rustle through the dense foliage that grew between the buildings and in the yards of the neighborhood. A damp earth smell, laced through with the odor of rotting fruit, rose to the roof, drifted across him.

Tanner gazed toward the south and the Hunter's Point launch fields, though he could not see even the tops of the rocket gantries from here. There was a freighter scheduled to go up tonight, and a part of its cargo was a contraband load of gourmet foods—primarily swiftlet nests—for one of the big investment firms in the New Hong Kong orbital. Tanner had brokered the deal, with most of his commission going to small packets of cash pressed into half a dozen different hands to make sure the shipment got through. In return, he was getting a shipment of prime, zero-gee pharmaceuticals. After a small sell-down—he had to make a living—the rest of the pharmaceuticals would be going to free clinics like Paul's.

The bright orange flame of the rocket launch appeared in the southern sky, followed a few seconds later by a barely audible rumble as the ship, carrying his load of contraband, rose into the night. Tanner watched the flame rise, growing small and faint, until it disappeared far above him.

He remained on the roof another hour, motionless, watching the night sky, thinking, trying not to think. Then he picked up his chair and returned to his apartment.

Tanner dreamed:
He climbs the hot, dark stairwell, Freeman just in front of him. His heart beats hard, and he sweats, smells mildew from rotting hall carpets. He feels for the knife in his boot, but isn't reassured by its touch. He wishes they could have

risked carrying guns, but these assholes will surely search them before running the deal. Tanner feels like his ass is hanging out a window. Even knowing they have backup out on the street below isn't much help. Backup in the Tenderloin? A joke.

At the top of the stairs, Freeman stops, looking at Tanner through dreadlocks hanging over his eyes. The building's too damn quiet, Tanner thinks. Too damn hot. And too damn dark. A single bare bulb glows at the other end of the hall.

"You ready?" Freeman whispers.

Tanner nods. His throat is dry.

"Let's nail these fuckers," Freeman says.

They walk down the hall, stop in front of a cracked wooden door with a huge black number nine painted across it. Freeman knocks once, once again, then quickly three times.

The door opens, and a big bearded guy looks out at them from a room almost as dark as the hall. He doesn't let them in. Tanner smells tuna, and something thick and sweet.

"Money?" the guy says.

Freeman takes a wad of bills from his jacket pocket, holds it up long enough for the guy to get a good look, then puts it back. The bearded guy nods, opens the door a little wider, then brings up a gun and sticks it against Freeman's forehead.

Jesus.

"Eat this, nigger." He pulls the trigger and blows away Freeman's face, spraying blood and flesh and bone all over Tanner.

Jesus fucking Christ.

Tanner runs.

He nearly reaches the stairwell when another explosion sounds. Something hard and compact slams into him, knocks him off balance, still running, he doesn't know what it is. Then he *does* know, and hot pain erupts in his side, sends him flying blindly around the corner and crashing down the stairs. . . .

And Tanner wakes:

He sat up with a sharp intake of breath. Sweat rolled down his sides, the base of his spine. The adrenaline rush left a tingling in its wake.

It was not the first time. The dream, the nightmare, had repeated over the years—not regularly, not often, but often enough. A nearly exact replay of what had happened two and a half years ago, of a drug bust gone completely to shit. A replay of the way Freeman had been killed.

Tanner got out of bed, went to the open window, and looked out, rubbing at the thick scar on his side. He could see the flicker of flames a few blocks away—dump fires or burning cars. Not a neighborhood cookout.

He hadn't had the dream in several months, and he knew why he had tonight—those fucking bodies. And Tanner knew he wasn't going to be the only one with nightmares.

A few cops would, at first. Then, as the news spread through the city, and especially when other bodies were found—and Tanner knew there would be other bodies—the nightmares, too, would spread. And what would make the situation worse was the unknown. Years ago, the cops never had a clue. Never an idea who was doing the killing, or why. When the killings had stopped, the hope had been that the killer himself had bought it. Now, though, it didn't seem that way. There was the possibility of a copycat, but Tanner doubted it. Carlucci would know. Maybe Tanner should track him down, ask.

Christ, he thought, just forget it. It wasn't his problem. Except for that damn two-and-a-half-year-old message. He did not want to think about it, but unless this was just a fluke, it *was* going to be his problem. And he knew he wasn't going to forget it.

Tanner looked at the clock—12:53. He wondered if he could stay awake until dawn. Better than dreaming again. He stood at the window and watched the flickering glow of flames in the night.

FOUR

TANNER PUT IT off for three days. Then, all it took
was a phone call to Lucy Chen, who told him where Carlucci
held his morning coffee-hashes.

It was a place called Spade's, a spice and espresso bar in the
Tundra run by Jamie Kingston, a black ex-cop who'd had half
his left leg blown off by his partner during a race riot outside
City Hall. Tanner walked in just after six in the morning, and
the place was packed. A dozen sparking ion poles stood among
the small tables, adding a clean burn odor to the heavy smell
of espresso. A deep, thumping bass line pounded beneath the
babble of voices.

Tanner worked his way through the tables and ion poles,
then spotted Carlucci in a booth against the back wall. Two
women uniforms sat across from him, drinking green-tinted
iced tea from clear glasses. Carlucci had a coffee cup in his
hand and several stacks of paper laid out on the table.

Carlucci saw Tanner approach, stared at him for a few
moments, then nodded toward an empty stool at the end of the
main bar. Tanner sat on the stool, ordered a double espresso,
and waited.

He was half through the espresso, and already regretting
it—a burning pain had begun in his stomach—when Kingston
emerged from the steaming kitchen and headed along the
bar, smiling at Tanner. It had been more than a year since
Tanner had last seen him, but Kingston still wore black leather
knickers that revealed the scarred flesh of his right leg, and the

gleaming metal of his cyborged left. On his feet, both the real and the artificial, were leather sandals.

Kingston took a pastry bar from under the counter and set it in front of Tanner.

"On the house." Kingston leaned against the counter. "Been a long time, Tanner."

Tanner nodded. "How's the leg?"

Kingston's smile broadened into a grin. "Same as always. Better than the real thing."

Kingston's leg was a legend in the Tundra. Rumor was he could disconnect the leg and convert it into a scattergun in less than ten seconds.

But Kingston's grin vanished, and he leaned forward, his face just a few inches from Tanner's.

"You're waiting to see Carlucci."

More statement than question. Tanner nodded again.

"What the hell for?" Kingston was angry now, and Tanner had no idea why. "You aren't a cop anymore."

Tanner wondered what he was missing, but he didn't say anything. He didn't have to justify himself to Kingston.

"Tanner." Carlucci's voice.

Tanner turned, looked at him. The two uniforms were gone. Tanner looked back at Kingston. "Go," Kingston whispered. Tanner picked up his espresso, brought it to Carlucci's booth, and sat. Carlucci was looking through one of the stacks of paper.

"What's eating Kingston?" Tanner asked.

"None of your business. Got nothing to do with you." He looked up. "Tanner the civilian. How's life out in the hive?"

"Buzzing."

Carlucci snorted. "Yeah. I hear stories about you. Most of them good, I guess." He sighed, shaking his head. "Your leaking heart is the reason you couldn't ice it as a cop."

Tanner didn't respond. Probably there was some truth to what Carlucci said. But only some. Besides, Carlucci wasn't exactly a cold-hearted bastard himself, and he was still a cop.

"All right," Carlucci said, "so why are you here?"

"I was on the Carousel Club balcony Thursday. I saw you pull them out of the slough."

Carlucci suddenly looked more tired, worn down, and he didn't say anything for a while. He finished his coffee, waved at the barman for another. He rubbed his eyes, then looked back at Tanner.

"Yeah, and so? You here to give me some lunatic theory?"

Tanner shook his head. "Been getting theories again?"

"Up the fucking ass. Mannon thinks it's more than one guy. Fuentes is convinced the guy's a Roller gone over the edge. Tinka believes it's a woman. And Harker still thinks the killer's a fucking alien. And those are cop theories. You should hear the shit we're picking up on the street. The newshawkers are having a fucking feast." His pager beeped beside him; he glanced at the readout, then reached down and touched something to silence it. "No theory, then why?"

"I pulled two of them out of Stowe Lake myself, remember? I just want to know if it's the same guy."

Carlucci slowly nodded. "Oh yeah, it's the same guy, it's the same motherfucker. Strangled. Chained together with the bands fused to the skin. A benign virus injected into Homicide's computers that froze the system and then gave the location of the bodies." He paused. "And the angel wings."

Tanner nodded to himself, picturing the tiny, silver-blue angel wings tattooed inside the nostrils of the victims. "Any progress?" Tanner wasn't sure why he asked the question. He knew the answer.

Carlucci gave a bitter laugh. "Progress, shit. There wasn't any progress for two years, you expect something in three days?" He shook his head. "They've got two of the slugs upstairs working on it full time, but that's not going to do any good."

Tanner shuddered, thinking of the slugs, imagining them in their cubicles above the station, hardly human anymore, their bodies distended and distorted by the constant injections of reason enhancers. They were supposed to be able to solve almost any problem, but they'd been useless with this one.

"That's all you want? To know if it's the same guy?"

Tanner shrugged.

"You want to come in on this from the outside?"

Tanner firmly shook his head, knowing he should be nodding, that almost certainly he *was* going to have to come in at some point. "No. But do you mind if I stay in touch on it?"

Carlucci sighed. "All right. Just let me know if you pick up anything substantial on the street, and don't bug me every other day about it. It's not going to move any faster than it did before, even if the mayor doesn't want to hear that." He glanced at the main bar. "I've got more people to talk to, so if there isn't anything else . . ."

Tanner looked at the bar, saw Deke the Geek on a stool, staring at him. Deke flipped him off, grabbing his crotch with his other hand.

"Old friends?" Carlucci said.

"Yeah." He turned back to Carlucci, slid out of the booth, and stood. "Thanks. See you around."

Carlucci nodded, then said, "Hey, Tanner."

"Yeah?"

"Do you have to use a police van to make your shipments?"

So, Carlucci knew. "Makes things a lot easier," Tanner said.

"I'm sure it does. It's a damn good thing you're discreet." Carlucci shrugged. "All right. See you."

Without looking back at Deke, Tanner left.

Outside, it was already hot, though it was still early. The sky, however, was clear, and almost blue. Tanner crossed the street to the Tundra's open space park. There were no trees in the park, only stunted clumps of mutated plants that had managed to emerge after the defoliants had been dropped onto the Tundra two years before.

Tanner sat on a stone bench that was still slightly damp from an early-morning rain. He didn't feel like moving, didn't want to do anything but sit in the growing heat and let it work through him. His shipment from the orbitals wasn't coming down until the next day, and he had nothing else going until then. He closed his eyes and tilted his head back, directly facing the sun.

A burst of shouts and the roar of board motors brought Tanner upright, eyes open. From the other end of the park, a girl was racing toward him on a motorized board, hand working the rear control line, weaving along the concrete path. Fifty feet behind her was a pack of thrashers in pursuit. The girl was grinning.

As she got closer, Tanner recognized her—it was the girl from the junkyard. Once again a pang of familiarity went through him, then faded when he could not lock it down. People moved out of the girl's path, and she swung wide around him, throttle full open, then shot out of the park and into the street, moving skillfully among the cars.

The thrasher pack went past, following her into the street. Two of them crashed into cars, tumbling to the ground, the boards spinning their wheels. Brakes squealed, people yelled, the thrashers yelled back. The girl, two blocks past the park, turned a corner and was gone from sight. Those thrashers still on their boards, seven or eight of them, followed her around the corner, and they, too, were gone.

Tanner watched and listened, but nothing happened. He tilted his head back, and closed his eyes once more.

FIVE

SOOKIE WAS FLYING. Chase scene. The stolen board hummed along slick and smooth. She'd picked a good one. She laughed, thinking of the thrasher she'd tumbled to get the board.

The other thrashers. She didn't look around, but she knew they were behind her, she could hear the motors. The shouts. The swearing. Wind lifted her hair, flapped her shirt. Sookie took another corner, wheels skidding across the pavement, fishtailing. She leaned, throttled up and straightened, then jumped the curb and shot along the sidewalk. Clattering wheels. Zoom!

People on the sidewalk scattered, some yelling at her, arms waving. *They* didn't know. Zap. Sookie swerved, went off the curb, hit the street. She angled across, wheels caught for a moment in a drain grate, then jarred loose as she tumbled from the board. She rolled back onto her feet, righted the board, and jumped back onto it. Sookie throttled up, flying again.

She shot down an alley. Holes and rocks. Broken windows, splintered wood. The thrashers were closer now, at least a couple of them. Sookie weaved in and out of piles of trash, emerged from the alley and turned onto the street, bouncing between a parked car and one in motion. Halfway down the block, she heard one of the thrashers go down, screaming.

Underground. She had to get underground. She looked ahead. Two more blocks, a few more turns. Sure.

She wanted a cigarette. She laughed. What a crazy idea! She flew. One block. Then two. She turned hard right, swung an

19

arcing left through traffic and into another alley. She twisted
the throttle, hoping to get just a little more speed. She felt
terrific, terrific! Yow. The alley was clear, the ground almost
smooth. She ducked under a loading platform, veered to the
left.

At the mouth of the alley, Sookie cut back right, grazing the
brick corner as she jumped the curb, shot down the sidewalk.
Almost immediately she cut hard right again, into a narrow
gap between buildings, toward concrete stairs going down.
Sookie cut the engine, squatted, and grabbed the board as
she flew off the top step and dropped. She hung on as she
hit the lower steps and rolled, tumbling, sprawling across the
bottom. Ignoring the pain, Sookie scrambled to her feet and
pushed through the broken vent screen, into the darkness of
the building.

The basement was quiet and black. She couldn't see a thing,
but she knew where she was. She coiled the control line and
attached it to the board, tucked the board by feel onto a shelf
above the screen, then set off across the basement. On the far
side of the basement floor was a hatch leading to underground
rail tunnels. As she approached the far wall, still unable to see
anything, Sookie dropped to hands and knees, moved forward
until she felt the hatch.

It wouldn't open. She adjusted her grip, pulled harder. Nothing. What was going on? Once more, on her haunches, pushing
with her legs. Still nothing.

Sookie released the handle, stood. She wondered if something was happening down in the tunnels. Belly races? Sub-
terranean barbecue? It made her hungry, thinking about food.
Why hadn't anyone told her?

There had to be another way out. She didn't want to go
back through the screen; not yet, anyway. Thrashers. She got
out matches, used one for a light.

The basement was nearly empty. A few shelves on the
walls, the floor hatch, a cabinet, a pile of broken glass. And a
wooden door in the corner. Was it there before? She couldn't
remember. Another match, and Sookie approached the door,
pulled at it. Solid but unlocked. A cracking sound, and the door
jerked loose, swung open. Behind the door was a short, narrow
passage, another door. Sookie smiled, thinking of secret passages, hidden treasures. Electric ghosts and wailing mutants.

She proceeded along the passage, lit a third match, pushed open the far door, stepped through.

She stood in a much larger room, ceiling above ground level, grimy windows high above her letting in just enough light for her to see. Strange, old, tall machines filled the room. Cables snaked along the floor between the machines, huge pipes hung from the upper walls and ceiling. And then she saw them, glinting in the feeble light—silver chains.

Hanging from hooks driven into the concrete walls were dozens of sets of silver chains attached to wide silver bands. Sookie stepped toward a set, reached out and touched the cold, smooth metal. Just like on the naked bodies. Beautiful. And again she wondered what they would look like on her own wrists and ankles.

A thrum, a rumble, a high, oscillating whine. Sookie turned, stared at machines coming to life. All of them? She couldn't tell. She saw wheels spinning, belts rolling, rods moving up and down. The floor vibrated beneath her feet, the pipes above her shook and hissed. The vibration increased, joined by a steady pounding.

Then, in the back of the chamber, obscured by all the machines, a deep blue glow appeared. It grew, spread across the back wall, cast wavering shadows among the machines. The glow brightened and moved forward.

Sookie went stiff, unable to move. She wanted to run, toward it or away from it, she wasn't quite sure.

The glow moved through the machines, like gliding on air, and as it approached, Sookie could make out a huge, vague form within it. She caught a glimpse of a hairless scalp half metal and light. Other flashes of metal. And, she thought, feathers. The edge of a wing. A voice emerged.

"You, girl." Man or woman? She couldn't tell. It was smooth, sounded like it came from a machine. "Girl."

Sookie turned and ran. Through the door, along the short passage, into the basement. She tripped over the hatch, sprawled on the floor, scrambled to her feet. She pushed her way through the screen and into daylight, started up the steps. The board. She came back down, started to push through the screen when she felt a breath of hot air wash across her from within, heard the scraping of metal on stone. She pulled back out and ran up the steps to street level.

On the sidewalk, Sookie stopped to catch her breath. She scanned the street, searching for the thrashers, but didn't see any—only cars, bikes, pedestrians. She looked down at the broken vent screen and watched, waiting for something to appear. Nothing did. She lit a cigarette, turned away, and started down the street.

SIX

TANNER'S FOOTSTEPS ECHOED off
concrete in the police garage, then were drowned out by
the roar of an engine, tires squealing, and finally the crash
of metal against cement and the shattering of glass.

"God damnit!" someone shouted from inside the office in
the far corner. "Is Walliser drunk again?" Tanner recognized
Lucy Chen's voice. Somebody else inside the lighted room
laughed—Vince Patricks, probably. On the other side of the
garage, a car door opened, slammed shut.

Tanner approached the small office, and soon the awful
stink of Lucy Chen's boiling tea overwhelmed the smells of
gasoline and smoke. He stopped in the doorway and looked
inside.

Lucy was sitting at her desk, head bent over a pot, breathing
in the fumes of the boiling tea. Behind her, at the other desk,
Vince Patricks leaned back in his chair, feet propped on the
drawer handles. Wall space not filled with locked key cabinets was covered with magazine and newspaper photos taped
over one another like a collage—Vince's perpetual project.
The photos were all of old men and women wearing idiotic
expressions. Vince taped up his photos, Lucy brewed her tea.
They both figured it was a fair arrangement.

Tanner said hello, and Vince nodded, smiling. Lucy looked
up.

"Want some tea?"

Vince laughed and Tanner shook his head. Lucy scowled
at them, then poured herself a cup of the vile stuff; bits of

slimy black herbs slopped into the cup along with the thick, dark liquid. She put the pot back on the burner and adjusted the heat.

"Hey, Tanner," Vince said. "Want in on the body pool? Only ten bucks a shot. Day the next bodies are found, which shift, how many, and which body of water. Sex of the victims as a tiebreaker."

"You're a fucking pervert," Lucy said.

Vince grinned at her, then raised an eyebrow at Tanner.

"No, thanks," Tanner said. "I never win."

"You talk to Carlucci?" Lucy asked.

Tanner nodded. "Yesterday."

"Get what you want from him?"

Tanner shrugged, didn't say anything.

"Lucy gets what she wants from him," Vince said.

Ignoring him, Lucy got up, unlocked one of the key cabinets, and removed a set of keys. She tossed it to Tanner. "Seventeen-A," she said. "And Tanner?"

"Yeah?" He knew what was coming, part of Lucy's ritual.

"Bring it back with a full tank."

"Sure, Lucy. Thanks." He pocketed the keys and headed toward the back of the garage.

Inside the office, Vince said something Tanner couldn't make out, and started laughing again. "Fuck you," Lucy said, followed by more of Vince's laughter. Tanner smiled to himself. A team. Some things really didn't ever seem to change.

Tanner drove the police van through the pelting rain. Paul sat beside him with his head against the window, eyes half-closed. The van bounced over the cracked highway, swerved around potholes. Tanner kept the speed down, unwilling to risk going more than forty. They were halfway between San Francisco and San Jose on U.S. 101, the back of the van loaded with pharmaceuticals.

Tanner turned on the radio and tuned in to a talk show.

" . . . *should put more slugs to work on it, you know, cart in a few from other cities or someplace. We've got to stop this maniac and fry him before he kills more people.*"

"*You really think that would make a difference, William? They've had slugs on this since the killings began.*"

"Yeah, what, two or three of them? I say get a whole bunch, fifteen or twenty, stick 'em together in a big room, and pump 'em full of that brain juice. It's worth a shot."

"And how about you, William? Do you have any ideas about who the killer is or why he's doing it?"

"Sure, I've got ideas, and I'm working on them. When I have them worked out better I'll go to the police, but I need to keep them to myself for now."

"Okay, William, I understand, and thanks for the call. We're going to take a short break here, but when we come back we want to hear what you think about the return of the Chain Killer, especially if you have any ideas about who it is."

Bouncy music came on, then crashing sounds, and a voice-over talking about Charm Magnets. Paul turned down the volume so it was barely audible, and said, "How can you stand to listen to that?"

"The radio?"

"Talk shows."

"I learn some things from them. About people."

"They depress me."

"Most of what I learn about people is depressing."

Paul nodded, but didn't say any more. He sighed and turned the volume back up.

" . . . name's Silo."

"All right, Silo, what's on your mind?"

"The cops are just giving us bull SCREEE! *about these killings."*

"All right, Silo, you're going to have to watch your language there. This is *radio. We're in modern times here, but not* that *modern. So, what, you think the police are witholding information?"*

"They're not telling us everything the killer does to 'em, to the bodies. I know. After he kills 'em he SCREES! *'em in the* SCREE! *and then he . . ."*

"O-kay, so much for Mr. Silo. Remember, folks, keep it clean or I'll have to cut you off, too. All right, Milpitas, you're on the air."

"Hello? Hello?"

"Hello, this is Mike on the mike, you're on the air, Milpitas. What's your name?"

"Meronia."

"All right, Meronia, what's on your mind?"

Paul reached forward and switched off the radio. "Listen to it some other time," he said. He put his head back against the glass and closed his eyes.

The rain had stopped by the time they pulled into the Emergency entrance of Valley Medical Center. Tanner hit the horn, and a minute later Valerie, in her hospital whites, came through the double doors. Paul opened his door and Valerie squeezed in behind his seat, then crouched on the floor between them. Tanner pulled out of the drive and swung around toward the rear of the hospital.

"It's been a long time since you've had anything for us," Valerie said.

"I get what I can when I can."

"I realize that. I was just saying."

He drove along a narrow, looping roadway and stopped beside the laundry annex. He turned on the van's overhead interior light, rolled back the wire barrier, then he and Valerie crawled into the small open space between the seats and the stacks of cartons.

Valerie whistled, gazing over all the boxes and crates. "You got some shipment this time. How much is ours?"

Tanner touched a stack. All the cartons in the van were labeled AGRICULTURAL IMPLEMENTS. "Here's a list." He handed her a folded sheet of paper.

Valerie spread the paper and read it by the overhead light. She whistled again. "Beta-endoscane. Nobody but the richest of the private hospitals are even getting a crack at this stuff." She continued reading, nodding once in a while, then refolded the paper and tucked it into the upper pocket of her hospital coat. From a larger, lower pocket, she removed a roll of bills and handed it to Tanner.

Twenties. He unclipped the roll and started counting.

"I know it's not even close to black market, but it's all we can come up with for now."

Tanner finished counting, then, trying to keep the disappointment out of his voice, said, "That doesn't matter. This is fine." A week ago it *would* have been fine—enough to pay the rent, buy food, and work on the next shipment. Now, though, he had a feeling he was going to have extra expenses. A lot of them. He was going to have to sell more of what remained in the van.

Paul stayed with the van as Valerie and Tanner unloaded through the side door. They carried the cartons into the annex, through storage rooms filled with linens, the warm and damp laundry room, and along a connecting corridor that led down into the hospital basement, where they stacked the cartons in an unmarked closet. Tanner knew the procedure by now: Valerie and the other doctors would work out a distribution plan later that day, trying to keep the shipment itself quiet.

Valerie made sure the closet was securely locked and bolted, then they swung by the doctors' lounge, picked up three cups of coffee, and returned to the van. Tanner gave a cup to Paul, then he and Valerie sat together on folding chairs just inside the annex.

"So how have you been?" Tanner asked.

"Oh, I've been fine. Still spending too much time at the hospital, but that's nothing new."

"No." He smiled. "And Connie?"

Valerie smiled back, shaking her head. "She's sixteen, and she's a pain in the ass sometimes. But she's a good kid at heart."

"Yes, she is."

"She asks about you," Valerie said. "How you're doing, if I've seen you. She really cares about you, Louis. She never asks about her father." She put a hand on his knee. "She'd love it if you were to come by and see her sometime, take her to a movie or something." She paused. "She doesn't understand why you and I aren't still together."

Who did? Tanner thought. But he didn't say anything. Neither of them did for several minutes, sipping at their coffee. The sun came in through the window, lighting up dust particles in the air, fluttering motes of bright silver. Someone had once told him that dust was primarily made up of the skeletons or shells of microscopic creatures. Dust mites.

"So," Valerie finally said. "It's starting again in the city."

Tanner looked at her, confused for a moment. Then he realized what she was talking about, and nodded. "Looks that way."

"How are the nightmares?"

Tanner shrugged. "They'd stopped."

He thought she would say more about it, ask something else, but she didn't. He finished the coffee and stood.

"I need to go."

She walked back to the van with him, kissed him lightly before he got in. "Take care of yourself, Louis."

"You, too."

"Good-bye, Paul." She waved.

"Bye, Valerie."

"Thanks again," she said to Tanner.

Tanner nodded and started the engine, then slowly pulled away.

"You made a serious mistake," Paul said, "when you stopped seeing Valerie."

"Christ, don't start."

Paul shrugged, then said, "Back to the city?"

"No. Make some phone calls, another couple of stops, sell some more of this stuff."

"You're going to sell more?"

"Yeah. I'm getting greedy. Just call me Uriah from now on. And help me find a pay phone that works." He drove on without saying any more.

SEVEN

THEIR LAST STOP before Paul's clinic was the free clinic in the Golden Gate Park squatter zone. The police markings on the van served as an unofficial pass, getting barriers moved and chains retracted so they could access restricted roads. Tanner drove slowly along the road fronting the Academy of Sciences, the stone walls of the buildings glistening from a recent bleaching. Schoolchildren in uniforms walked in tight formation, or clustered in well-defined groups on the steps in front of the building. Across the concourse of leafless trees, next to the manicured grounds of the Japanese Tea Gardens, the remains of the De Young Museum were covered with flowering vines.

They had to go through one more barrier, then Tanner swung the van around and behind the De Young ruins and stopped at the edge of the squatter zone—drab tents patched with faded swatches of colored fabric, shanties built of warped plywood and irregular sheets of metal or plastic, lean-tos erected over slabs of concrete. The zone filled a large meadow and sent out dozens of tentacles into the least dense sections of the surrounding woods, the trees and brush cut down to make more space for tents and shanties and to provide firewood. Mud-slick paths wound among the dwellings, the paths crowded with adults and children and animals.

The medical clinic was housed in an abandoned park maintenance building. A long line of people stretched from the clinic, snaking past the van. Seeing the police van, the people shifted and turned to one another, whispering and gesturing, though they didn't leave.

"They must have something special going on," Paul said. "Line that long. Inoculations, maybe."

"Maybe I should stay with the van," Tanner said.

Paul gave a short, hard laugh. "*One* of us better."

Paul got out of the van and walked toward the clinic. The people in line tensed, staring at him as he walked toward the building. Tanner sat behind the wheel, the heat building up inside the van despite the open windows. But he did not feel like moving. The people in line stopped staring at the van, but they did not seem to relax much. They looked like they had been in line a long time, and many of them tried to get off their feet without sitting in the mud, which wasn't easy. Most of them looked ill as well as exhausted.

Tanner glanced over the treetops and could just see the top of the hill rising from the island in the middle of Stowe Lake. It had been a long time since he had been on that hill, and he wondered if he was going to have to do something similar again. He hoped to Christ he wouldn't, but he did not have a good feeling about it.

A few minutes later Paul returned to the van with Patricia Miranda, one of the clinic's volunteer med techs. Tanner had met her two or three times before, and she shook his hand with a smile.

"This van." She shook her head, then turned to the people in line. "They are not police," she said, loud but calm. "They have medical supplies for the clinic." Then she repeated it in Spanish. The people in line visibly relaxed, though their wariness did not disappear altogether.

"What's going on?" Tanner asked. "Fever inoculations?"

"No," Patricia said. "Wish it was, though it's probably too late for most of them. No, we managed to get several thousand sets of nose filters. A lot of the people here had enough money once to get plugs implanted, but most haven't had a filter change in years, so we're trying to do them all."

Tanner sniffed, twitching his nose at the thought. He was due soon himself. He looked up at the hazy sky, thinking about the crap that got into his lungs even with the filters.

"Tanner, Patricia wants me to help out here for a while," Paul said. "You want to just go on without me? I'll give you the keys to the clinic and you can just drop the stuff."

"How long you think you'll be?"

"An hour, hour and a half tops. I've got my own shift at the hospital tonight."

"I'll wait. There's something I want to do, if it'll be all right to leave the van awhile."

Patricia nodded. "It'd probably be fine, but I'll get a couple of people to watch it."

They unloaded cartons, leaving only Paul's share in the back of the van. Then Tanner locked the van, and Paul and Patricia went into the clinic.

Tanner walked through the heart of the squatter zone, along the slick, muddy paths. Most of the tents were makeshift, heavily patched, the walls sacrificed for the roofs; the shanties were not much more solid than the tents, providing shelter from the rain but little privacy. Clothes on people were as patched and torn as the tents, often revealing unhealed wounds and large streaks of fever rash. As he walked along, half-naked kids came up to him and begged, hands held out. But they were listless and halfhearted, as if they recognized that anyone walking among them would have little or nothing to give away.

Smelling smoke and roasting meat, Tanner came to a large open area between two groups of shacks. A fire pit had been dug in the center of the clearing, and a wide, blazing fire burned within it. Above the fire, on crudely made roasting spits, were several small, unrecognizable animals (raccoons? dogs?), and one much larger, headless beast that Tanner was pretty sure was a horse. Fifteen or twenty men and women stood around the roasting animals, talking and drinking from unlabeled bottles.

He worked his way through the shanties and tents, feeling more and more closed in by them as he went. Eventually the zone ended and he reached the denser foliage of the woods. Tanner pressed on, the way slightly uphill now, and a few minutes later emerged from the trees. He crossed a narrow strip of broken pavement and stopped on the bank of Stowe Lake.

Tanner stood at the water's edge and looked across to the island that filled so much of the lake. The island was a heavily wooded hill, its peak the highest point in the park. At the top, there were views of the entire park and close to half the city.

Also at the top was a small, muck-filled reservoir that had once held two naked, chained bodies.

Tanner looked up at the top of the hill, remembering. He had been alone that day, too, and it was alone in the muggy afternoon heat that he had pulled the two dead women from the water, naked but covered with green and brown muck. Chained together at the wrists and ankles, face to face, as if embraced like lovers.

He walked along the edge of the lake for a few minutes, then crossed one of the bridges to the island. He stopped at the foot of the long trail that curved around the island and up to the top of the hill. Tanner did not know why he was doing this, but he knew he would not go back until he did. He started up the trail.

It had been hot and muggy that day, just the way it was now. There had been a crazy run of other murders in the city, and Tanner and Freeman were on loan to Homicide to help out with the casework overload. But Freeman had called in sick that morning, and Tanner was working alone out in the avenues along the park when the virus came through the system giving the location of the bodies. He was given the option of waiting until one of the regular Homicide teams was freed up, but he couldn't stand the thought of the bodies staying in water any longer than necessary. It was irrational, but there it was. And so he had made this climb alone, knowing what he would find at the top.

He knew there would be no bodies this time, but that did not help his mood much. It was, he feared, only a matter of time. A slight breeze took the edge off the heat, whispering through the ragged eucalyptus trees that still survived. His view of the park and the city expanded as he climbed higher. He stopped at one point, almost at the top, and looked down at the sprawling squatter zone. Separated from the zone by only a narrow strip of trees were the Japanese Tea Gardens. He could see the wealthy tourists walking along the tended paths, sitting in the tea pavilion.

Next to the tea gardens was the De Young, and as he looked at it Tanner thought he glimpsed movement within the wreckage of crumbled stone and thick vines. He stared a long time, watching, but did not see anything more. Animals? Or people living in the ruins? It would not be surprising.

He resumed the climb. A few minutes later the trail widened to an open area at the top of the hill. The concrete reservoir was still there, still filled with more muck than water. A heavy, warm stench rose from it, worse than the stink of the slough the other day.

Tanner sat on the concrete rim and stared down at the muck-covered water. He wondered what else was at the bottom of the reservoir. Probably it would never be drained and cleaned out because no one wanted to know. Just like everything else. He picked up a stone, tossed it into the water. The stone hit the green muck without a splash and slowly sank. It was going to be one hell of a summer.

EIGHT

NIGHT. SMOKE IN the air. Sookie sat in the open window of her room on the upper floor of the De Young. She could see the glow from burning lamps, the flicker of the tent-city fires. Smelled the smoke, the cooking meat, the shit from the portable toilets. Heard the murmur of voices, singing.

She didn't need anyone, she could take of herself. She sniffed once. Crazy people, living in the tents. All jammed in together, crawling over each other. They had nothing. Sookie had lots of things.

Sookie lit a cigarette, then climbed down from the window ledge. She lit the set of five squat candles arranged on the plastic crate in the center of the room. The candlelight, quivering, cast shadows at the edges of the room.

The room was small, but the walls were intact. In the corner nearest the window was her bed—a sleeping bag on top of two thick layers of foam rubber. The walls were covered with yellowed newspapers. And along the walls were the makeshift shelves and boxes that held her things.

Sookie moved along the walls, taking inventory. She liked doing it, taking stock, checking things. Looking, picking up a few. Touching. The things she found in empty houses and apartments. She was good at finding things other people couldn't see. Finding good things other people thought were worthless. Her things.

Two plastic mushrooms. A light bulb with a tiny hole and blue swirls of color around the hole. A set of shattered headphones. Neatly wrapped bundles of computer cable. An L-shaped length of shiny copper pipe.

She stopped and picked up the large wood woman. The top half of the woman came off, and inside was a slightly smaller wood woman. It, too, came apart, another smaller woman inside. They went on like that, ten of them until, at last, Sookie would find a tiny wood woman that did not open. She loved opening the women, one after another, but she was always disappointed when she reached the last. She expected something more.

Sookie put down the woman, moved on. An energy band that blinked dim red light, slower and fainter each day. Three neuro-tubes. A jar filled with pieces of green broken glass. Six wooden chopsticks. A clear glass ashtray.

She knelt and pulled out the box of her own private things—the few items she had not found, that she had owned ever since she was a child, that she had taken with her when she had left the place she herself had never called home. Looking at them, touching them, always made her feel both sad and special. Now she just looked at them without touching. The silver metal bracelet with her other name engraved on the band: Celeste. A string of tiny red beads. A clear glass figurine of a cat. And a drawing she had made once of an angel. She had never hung the picture because it frightened her. It pulled her, held tightly onto her, but it also scared her. *My* angel, she thought.

Sookie shivered, put away the box. She moved around the rest of the room, faster now, hardly looking anymore. She finished at the bookcase next to the bed, filled with books and magazines. On the floor was the pocket dictionary she used to help her with words she didn't know. Sometimes, when she was in the mood, she was quite a reader.

But not now. She returned to the window, looked at the lamps, the glow of fires. Look what I have, she thought. She clambered onto the ledge, one leg dangling outside. Look. Sookie slowly, repeatedly banged her fist against the windowsill, and closed her eyes tight.

NINE

TWO MORE BODIES were found. Two men, this time, pulled out of Balboa Reservoir. The newspaper made much of the fact that it was the first repeat use of a given body of water. Tanner, reading the paper in a cafe on Columbus, doubted it meant anything. What the two new bodies did mean, though, was that now he *had* to go back to Carlucci.

He set down the paper and looked out the window at the early-morning streets. Here, close to the border of the Financial District, the streets were busy, filled with people and cars, delivery trucks and flashers, scooters and runners—an economy that thrived on the edges of the District, living off the workers who ventured a block or two out of the District during daylight hours. When darkness fell, the area narrowed, became a blazing finger of the Chinese Corridor stretching all the way to the Wharf.

Once, Tanner's father had told him years before, this area of the city had not been part of Chinatown. It had been called North Beach, and had been heavily Italian—which explained the two or three Italian restaurants and the few cafes like this one. But Tanner's father had never explained what had happened to the Italians.

Tanner drank slowly from his coffee, putting off what he knew he had to do. He had been afraid of this on the Carousel Club balcony, watching the two bodies being pulled from the slough, but he had hoped it was a fluke, an isolated blip, and not a resumption of the killings. So much for hope. Tanner wondered if he would still be alive at the end of the summer.

He glanced back at the newspaper. This time there was a lurid photo of the bodies. The newshawkers, taken by surprise when the first two had been pulled from the slough, were now on fire alert, shadowing the police.

Tanner flipped over the newspaper, hiding the picture, then finished his coffee. It was time to see Carlucci.

Spade's was half-empty when Tanner arrived. Between mealtimes. The ion poles were turned up, sparks flying, as if Kingston wanted to scare away potential customers.

Carlucci was alone in his booth, staring at the empty seat across from him, tapping at the table with a pen. Kingston was nowhere to be seen. Tanner slid into the booth, and Carlucci blinked several times, as if coming out of a trance.

"My day is fucking complete," he said.

"I need to talk to you."

"So talk."

"Not here," Tanner said.

"Terrific. Melodrama."

"I'm not screwing around."

Carlucci waited, staring at him. "Is it about . . . ?" He left it unfinished. Tanner nodded. "All right," Carlucci said. "Should've known." He wrote something on a piece of paper, folded it several times, then handed it to Tanner.

"Thanks," Tanner said. He put the paper in his pocket without looking at it, then got up and left.

At three-thirty that afternoon, Tanner stood beside a massive concrete pier support, the freeway overpass above him casting a wide shadow. Traffic above rumbled, but was muted, a muffled echo. Two supports down from him, several teenagers in whiteface and pulse-jackets gathered, huddled around a black cylinder. A sudden explosion of sound rocked the air, music blaring from the cylinder, and the crisscrossing bands on the jackets began pulsing colors with the beat.

Tanner saw Carlucci come around a corner, then cross the street carrying a paper bag. When he reached Tanner, he opened the bag, took out two cups of coffee, and handed one to him. They popped the lids and stood without speaking for a few minutes, sipping at the hot coffee and watching the kids down the way. Already a steady procession of customers had begun, mostly teenagers with a few adults to change the pace. As Tanner and Carlucci watched, they could see the exchanges—money for packets. The kids weren't even trying to hide it.

"Not my jurisdiction," Carlucci said.

Tanner understood. Carlucci was Homicide. If he followed up everything he saw happening on the streets, he'd never get to his own job. Unless it turned to murder, Carlucci would let the kids be, though Tanner knew he didn't like it.

"Would have been yours," Carlucci added.

Tanner nodded. They didn't say anything else for a while, then Carlucci finally asked, "So what is it?"

"You're not going to like this."

Carlucci snorted. "Figured that one out all on my own, Tanner."

"Three years ago," Tanner began. "One day, a message gets delivered to me and Freeman. Inside a sealed envelope, a single sheet of paper with just two words. 'Angel wings.' Then two figures. Ten thousand slash one million. And then the name of the man who sent the message. That was all."

"And who was that?"

"Someone who claimed to know who the killer was. Those two numbers. Ten thousand dollars was admission price for a meeting, and one million for the info."

"All right, cut the phony suspense. Who sent the message?"

"Rattan."

"Christ!"

"I told you you weren't going to like it."

Carlucci looked down at his coffee, grimaced at it. "So what did you do?"

"Nothing. We talked about it, tried to figure how to run it. If we went upstairs with it, we were pretty sure it would be killed. Pay ten thousand dollars to a scumbag who'd jumped bail and disappeared with a couple dozen felony drug charges outstanding? They'd argue that he couldn't know anything, that some cop had leaked the info to him about the angel wings."

Carlucci nodded. He stopped grimacing, now just sipped his coffee and watched Tanner, listening.

"So we thought about going after it on our own. We thought we could come up with the ten thousand from slush funds, and if it turned out Rattan's information was good, they'd have to buy it upstairs."

Tanner paused, looking at the kids. Business was complete—it didn't take long—and they turned off the cylinder, packed it away, and moved on. In a few minutes they'd probably be setting up shop elsewhere.

"We hadn't decided for sure. It would have been a hell of a job because we'd have to track down Rattan ourselves. He was offering to sell, but he wasn't going to come to us." Tanner paused again. "Then Freeman got killed. I had other things to deal with for a while." The scar on his back began to itch just thinking about it. "By the time I got back to it, I realized it had been a long time since any new bodies had turned up. So I held off, hoping the killings had stopped. After a few more months, it looked like they had. I left it alone."

"And then you quit the force."

Tanner nodded.

"But now the killings have started again."

Tanner nodded once more. Carlucci finished his coffee, dropped the cup and crushed it into the dirt with his shoe.

"Christ," Carlucci whispered. He looked at Tanner. "Why did Rattan go to you and Freeman?"

"Probably because he thought he could trust us."

"Was he right?"

Tanner shrugged. "Sure. We'd dealt with him before, you know how it goes down sometimes. And we wouldn't have screwed him over."

"Could you trust *him*?"

"In the right situation. We would have trusted him with this deal. It was worth the risk."

"You think his offer was legit?"

Tanner hesitated before answering. He and Freeman had talked a lot about that. The key issue.

"He might have been wrong," Tanner said. "But I think he *believed* he knew who was doing the killing."

"But he wasn't going to give that information to us for nothing," Carlucci said. "And never has." He looked away, slowly shaking his head. "Jesus Christ. Trying to find that fucker now is going to be a lot harder than it would have been three years ago."

No shit, Tanner thought. Three years ago it was felony drug charges. Now Rattan was also wanted for killing two cops. For more than a year he'd managed to stay hidden despite one hell of a hunt-down. He had to be so deep inside the Tenderloin he probably never saw the sun.

They both remained silent for a long time. Carlucci, gazing off into the distance, was probably doing a lot of the same thinking Tanner had done over the last few days. Tanner didn't think he was going to like Carlucci's conclusions any better than his own.

"I'm going to have to get back to you," Carlucci finally said. He was still gazing into the distance, along the line of shrinking highway piers. "I want to talk to a couple of people, but it'll stay tight, believe me."

"You're not going upstairs with this, are you?"

Carlucci turned to look at him. "Not a chance." He paused. "Rattan came to you and Freeman. Freeman's dead. And you're out." Paused again. "You'll come in and work this?"

"I'm going to have to, aren't I?"

Carlucci stared at Tanner for a minute, then said, "I'll call you." Without another word he turned and crossed the street, leaving Tanner alone under the freeway.

Tanner sipped at the coffee. It was cold. He drank the rest of it anyway, crushed the cup in his hand, then dropped it next to Carlucci's.

TEN

WHEN TANNER CAME out onto the roof, Alexandra was already there, seated near the far edge, cider machine hissing beside her, surrounded by half a dozen cats. Tanner carried his chair across the roof, watching the cats get up and move aside to make room for him. The moonlight glinted off paws and legs—all of Alexandra's cats had at least one metal prosthetic limb. Kubo had all four, and his paws clicked loudly on the rooftop gravel until he settled under Alexandra's chair.

She stood and bowed gracefully, folding her long, thin body nearly in half, her pale hair touching the ground. "Good evening, Mr. Tanner." She laughed, straightened, and sat back down.

"Hello, Alexandra." Tanner set up his chair beside her.

Alexandra poured two steaming mugs of cider and handed one to him. "How's the smuggling trade?" she asked.

"You should know," Tanner said. "Don't you have the stats for it?" Alexandra did statistical research and analysis for a corporate law firm in the Financial District. She spent half her time at the company doing research for radical underground organizations and her own personal interests.

"Black-market pharmaceutical trade is up eleven percent over last year," she said. "But I haven't been able to find a thing on black-market gourmet foods. Care to provide me with some figures so I can start a database?"

Tanner smiled and shook his head. He sipped at the cider, which was hot and strong, with a deep kick. The sky was

41

nearly clear, only a slight haze muting the stars and moon. A regular, almost explosive pounding sounded from the north, maybe near the water. Two green flares shot across the peak of Telegraph Hill, illuminating the jagged ruins of Coit Tower, followed by a short burst of gunfire. Then the quiet and the dark returned.

"People are funny," Alexandra said. It was her standard beginning when she wanted to talk about something she'd been researching.

"What now?" Tanner asked.

"These murders. The 'Chain Killer.' A lot of people in this city are scared out of their minds by this guy."

"Shouldn't they be?"

Alexandra shook her head. "Not the way they are. The numbers aren't right. Last year in this city, seven hundred ninety-three people were killed in race riots. About fifteen hundred were killed in the so-called drug wars. Three hundred seventeen died from tainted prescription pharmaceuticals. Eighty-nine died in the explosion in Macy's, one hundred fifty in the Unicorn Theater bombing. Ninety-three in the Shaklee Building fire, seventy-five in the Market Street gas leaks. And sixty-nine students mowed down at the USF anti-draft rally." She waved her hand. "I could go on. I didn't even bother digging up the numbers for other murders, or car-accident fatalities, anything like that." She paused, looking at Tanner. "Let's face it, sometimes life in this city is a horror show." She paused again. "So how many people did this 'Chain Killer' murder the first time? Thirty-seven over a two-year period. Add four new ones, and that's a total of forty-one in the last four and a half years. I'm not saying the killings aren't awful. They are. And I'm certainly glad I'm not one of those forty-one. But it's a relatively small number, compared to the others I just gave you. If this guy scares them so badly, they should be crapping their pants on a daily basis just at the thought of living in this city."

Tanner smiled. "Some people do," he said. He drank from the cup, looking at Alexandra over the rim. She seemed genuinely puzzled. "I know what you're saying, but you should know it's never that simple. It's more than the numbers. People don't understand these killings. Everything else you mentioned, people can understand why they happen. They don't like it, but it makes sense. Race riots? Awful, but comprehensible. The Macy's fire? Terrible, but only an isolated incident, and the cause was known. And people know you're asking for trouble if you walk in certain parts of the city after dark, or some parts any time of day. They *understand* that." He paused. "But people can't make sense of the Chain Killer. Nobody has any idea who it is, why he kills, no pattern to when or where. Which means that it could happen to anyone, at any time, so there's nothing, absolutely nothing they can do to protect themselves."

Three more flares went off on Telegraph Hill, but this time there was no gunfire. They watched as the glow of the flares burned brightly for a minute, then faded. One of the cats jumped onto Tanner's lap, metal claws digging through his pants.

"You could be right," Alexandra said. "I suppose it makes a kind of sense." She reached under the chair, scratched Kubo, then looked at Tanner. "You glad you're not a cop anymore? You won't have to deal with this."

Tanner gave a short, chopped laugh.

"What's that supposed to mean?" she asked.

"I'm not a cop, but I'm involved. I'm stuck in this damn thing."

"Why?"

Tanner just shook his head.

"You don't know who did it?"

"No."

"But you know something."

"Sort of. Really, Alexandra, I don't want to go into it." He held out his cup for a refill. "I just want to sit up here with you, have some cider, talk about other things, and enjoy the night."

Alexandra nodded. She poured fresh cider for them both, and they remained silent, drinking.

A series of multicolored flares filled the sky, this time to the south, sending up a brilliant, shifting glow. Several loud explosions sounded, then a column of flame rose into the air, fanned out, and showered back to earth.

"Wonderful," Alexandra said. "Probably the Purists at work again."

" 'Purify with flame, sanctify His Name,' " Tanner quoted.

With the buildings of the Financial District blocking the view, he could no longer see flames, but Tanner knew that buildings were burning somewhere south of Market.

"Enjoy the night," Alexandra said.

ELEVEN

THE FIRE BLAZED just a few blocks from the drive-in. The flickering glow interfered slightly with the picture on the screen that had been erected at the boundary of the junkyard. Sookie sat in the front seat of a big four-door Buick, watching the movie through the glassless windshield. Sound came from a dozen speakers scattered throughout the junkyard. Most of the top-level cars around her were occupied. Nearly a full house.

The movie on the screen was called *The Courier's Revenge,* and starred Sylvia Romilar as a corporate gene courier. It was a comedy, and Sookie had been laughing since the movie had begun. Everyone in the junkyard was laughing.

A knock came on the driver's door. Sookie leaned over, looked out the window—it was Dex, the food man, on his stilts. Racks hung from his neck, filled with boxed candy, popcorn, and canned drinks. Sookie bought a large carton of popcorn and a can of Twist, and Dex moved on.

On the screen, Sylvia Romilar, naked, was winding herself up in Saran Wrap. Empty boxes and rolls lay all over the floor of the tiny bullet train cabin. She flopped onto the bench seat, trying to wrap her arms. Sookie had no idea why Sylvia, whose name was Natasha in the movie, was doing this. That's what Sookie liked about Sylvia Romilar's movies—most of them never made any sense.

There was a dull thud on the roof of the car, then footsteps, the car rocking, and another thud. A man's head appeared upside down in the windshield.

45

"Hey, chickie," the guy said.

"Move it, asshole, you're blocking the picture." She shifted across the seat, trying to see the screen.

"Want some company, chickie?" He slid along the roof, blocking her view again.

Sookie slapped at him, he pulled up and away, and she slid back across the seat. "Go away!" She tried to pick up what was happening in the movie. Sylvia/Natasha was now crawling along the roof of the bullet train, still wearing only the Saran Wrap, her hair blowing wildly in the wind and shooting bright blue sparks.

The guy's head reappeared, then his body as he pulled himself through the windshield and into the car. Sookie shoved him and he lost his grip, landing half on the seat, half on the floor. He pulled himself onto the seat, next to Sookie, and she punched him in the ribs, swung at his face.

"Get out!"

The guy laughed, blocking her punches. "Hey, hey, *hey*, chickie! I just want some company, don't you?"

"No." She pulled back against the door, watching him. Slowly, she reached down next to the seat, felt for the gravity knife. She wasn't scared—the guy was a jerk, but harmless— but she'd had enough of him.

The guy was still grinning, and now he slid closer to her, until his thighs were pressed against her knees. "Hey, chickie, we're at the drive-in, let's have some fun."

He leaned forward, moving slowly, then his hand darted out and up under her T-shirt, fingers grabbing at her tiny breast. Sookie hit the charge, then brought the knife up and into the guy's arm.

The guy screamed, jerked his arm back. Sookie held tight onto the knife and it came free. The guy, still screaming, kicked wildly as he scrambled out through the windshield. His boot caught Sookie across the side of the head, knocked her into the steering wheel. The guy crawled across the hood of the car and dropped over the edge, landing heavily on the ground below. He stopped screaming, and Sookie could hear him stumble away through the junkyard.

Sookie cut the knife's charge and wiped the blade clean on her T-shirt. She put it back beside the seat. Then she groaned when she saw the popcorn scattered all over the floor of the car.

Another knock on the car door. "Sookie, you all right?" It was Dex.

Sookie leaned out the window and nodded. "Yeah."

"That your blood?"

"No. But I need more popcorn. Asshole ruined all mine."

Dex gave her a carton. "On the house."

"Thanks."

Dex moved on, and Sookie sank back against the door, looking out the far side of the car, gazing at the fire instead of the screen. What a week. Bodies in the water. Machines and a winged monster in that Tundra basement. Now this. Maybe it was time to go see Mixer again.

Sookie returned her gaze to the movie screen, settled back in the seat with her fresh popcorn, and tried to pick up the story line. On the screen, the bullet train was gone. Sylvia/Natasha, still in the Saran Wrap, sat inside a tiny shack, warming herself in front of a fire and smoking a cigarette. The fire popped loudly, and several large embers burst out, landing on her. The Saran Wrap ignited, began to melt and flame. Sookie laughed. She knew Sylvia would be just fine.

TWELVE

THE MEETING PLACE, on the outer edge of the old Civic Center, was appropriate, Tanner thought. From the concrete bench where he waited for Carlucci, he could see, a few blocks away, the upper reaches of the Tenderloin—razor wire on the roof boundaries, jagged television antennas and tiny satellite dishes, reflecting glass windows and armored balconies, vast networks of flowering vines, seeded catch-traps, and columns of steam rising through mist clouds that hovered above the enclave.

Across the plaza, a group of True Millennialists swayed and stomped in chaotic, circular patterns around a pile of broken concrete blocks and twisted metal pipe. Occasionally one of the group would leap away from the others and scream into the face of a passerby, then rejoin the circle. The True Millennialists claimed that during the years of changeover from the Julian to the Gregorian calendar a great fraud had been perpetrated, skipping a number of years of reckoning so that the True Millennium had *not* occurred at the official turn of the century. Instead, they claimed, the True Millennium was only now approaching, due in less than two years and destined to bring about the destruction of all civilization.

My kind of people, Tanner thought. A woman broke from the group, ran across the plaza, and stopped in front of him staring with widened eyes.

"Don't bother repenting!" she shouted. "It's too fucking late for that! Too much sin and not enough time. Hah!" She leaned forward, grinning at him. "The Chain Killer is one

of the harbingers. He is the Angel of Death." The woman
was trembling. Christ, Tanner thought, that's exactly what the
media would call the guy if they ever found out about the angel
wings. The woman whirled and sprinted back to the group.

"I'd heard you had a way with women." It was Carlucci,
who stood a few feet away, watching the True Millennialists.
He looked at Tanner without smiling, then approached the
bench and sat.

Tanner didn't say anything. He didn't even want to ask
Carlucci what he had come up with because he knew it wasn't
going to be good. So he waited in silence, looking up at the
hazy, discolored sun.

"Forecast is for two days without rain," Carlucci said.

"Is that supposed to be good or bad?"

Carlucci shrugged. A man without legs, hip stumps surgically attached to a motorized dolly, wheeled past them, beating at
his bare chest, mouth open in a silent scream.

"I talked to a couple people," Carlucci said. "They both
agreed this is worth pursuing." He paused, shrugging again.
"They also agree that you have the only real chance of getting
to Rattan."

"I wonder how much of a chance that is," Tanner said.

"That's a bad attitude."

"Yeah, well."

"We'll work together on this. Partners."

"You going into the Tenderloin with me?"

"No. You know I can't do that. I'll do everything I can from
out here."

"Logistical support."

"Something like that."

Tanner looked up at the rooftop boundaries of the Tenderloin. The steam columns, almost pure white and coherent when
they first emerged above the buildings, rose quickly toward the
sun, coming apart and breaking into a scatter of dirty colors.
What kind of real help could Carlucci give him from out here?

"So I go into the Tenderloin and find Rattan," Tanner said.
It wouldn't be the Tenderloin itself that would be dangerous;
it would be what he had to do to track Rattan. He smiled.
"Sounds so simple."

"Okay, so it's not simple, but yeah, that's what you do. Find
him, and if he's got the real stuff, make a deal."

"How high can I go?"

"Christ, as high as you have to. If it's for real, they'll come up with the money. The police and the city have a real public relations problem with this guy." Carlucci grinned. "The mayor says this guy's generating a very high 'hysteria quotient.' "

"Hysteria quotient? What bullshit."

"You got it. They're choking out a lot of that nonsense right now, running scared. We've got an election coming up in four months, though why anyone would want to be involved in running this city is way the hell beyond me. But that's also why they'll come up with as much money as they have to." Carlucci's grin transformed into a frown. "But one thing won't go. No way the murder charges can be dropped, not for killing cops. Never happen."

"Rattan won't ask for that," Tanner said. "He'll know."

"You give the guy a lot of credit for a cop killer and drug dealer."

"He's smart, Carlucci. How long you guys been trying to find him?"

Carlucci grimaced. "Fair enough." He looked over at the True Millennialists, who were now huddled around the mound of rubble, hardly moving, chanting in low voices. "Goddamn freaks." He turned back to Tanner. "You're going to need money just to get to him."

Tanner nodded. "I've got a little."

"Enough?"

Tanner shook his head. "Not even close."

"Day after tomorrow, go by the garage and see Lucy. She'll have whatever I can dig out of slush."

Tanner thought about asking Carlucci if he was giving Lucy anything else, but decided it wasn't worth it. Carlucci had a strong sense of family, and would probably resent any suggestion he was cheating on his wife, even as a joke.

The sun blazed down through the haze, enervating him. But it's a dry heat, he told himself. "Do we still have people inside?"

"A couple," Carlucci answered.

"Wilson?"

Carlucci shook his head. "She pulled out last year. Got blown and barely got out alive."

"Menendez?"

"He *didn't* get out alive."

"Koto?"

Carlucci smiled and nodded. "Yeah, Koto's still inside. He'll never come out. Loves it in there. Told me he wants his ashes scattered over the streets at midnight." The smile faded. "I'll tell you how to reach him, but don't go anywhere near him except as a last resort. Too many years invested to risk blowing him. You can go to Francie Miller. You know her?"

"No."

"She's good, she'll take care of you. Everything you'll need on her will be with the money."

They sat awhile longer in silence. Across the plaza, a trio of Rollers, headwheels spinning and flashing green lights, had faced off with the True Millennialists, and the two groups shouted back and forth, an exchange that to Tanner seemed almost ritualistic in its tone and cadence.

"You don't have to do it, Tanner. It's not your job anymore." He paused. "You don't have to do it."

Tanner gave him a half smile. "Sure I do. I have enough trouble sleeping as it is."

"Guilty conscience?"

"No. But I don't need one." He stood. "I'll see you, Carlucci."

"Stay in touch."

"Sure." He glanced over the True Millennialists. The Rollers were gone, and the Millennialists were now settling down on their pile of rubble, as if they were going to sleep. They seemed to be at peace. Then Tanner looked one more time at the armored upper reaches of the Tenderloin, sun glinting off metal and glass, and started for home.

THIRTEEN

TANNER BEGAN THE night in the Financial District. With the blaze of light from all directions it was nearly as bright as day, though the light was cleaner, white and sterile as it reflected from shining alloys, polished stone, darkglass, and bleached ferroplast. Streets and sidewalks were fairly busy even at this hour—between foreign market hours and the security of the checkpoints, the District never closed down anymore; it only slowed its pace a little at night.

Tanner was still uncomfortable from the checkpoint run. He had never become accustomed to the body searches, and without a permanent pass there was no way to avoid them. He'd had to put up with the searches even as a cop—only those stationed within the District got the passes. On the other hand, Tanner thought, he didn't really *want* a permanent pass to this place. He did not like the Financial District and did not like most of the people who worked here.

Tanner pulled his raincoat tight, though there was no rain yet—an attempt at regaining some comfort. The raincoat was a marvel, coated with some kind of semi-permeable membrane that kept the water out, but actively breathed, kept him almost cool even in the damp heat.

As Tanner moved through the crowds, he noticed the glint of metal on flesh all around him. A lot of men and women appeared to have metal prosthetic limbs or facials, but Tanner knew that most, if not all, were fakes. It had become a fad, a fashion trend. *Faux Prosthétique*, Alexandra called it. Money people had taken to wearing the metal add-ons and coveralls like jewelry or makeup—put them on in the morning, take them off at night. Very expensive—they had to be custom fitted to allow full limb function—but not permanent. Like rub-on tattoos, Tanner thought.

He climbed the steps leading to the massive glass doors of the Mishima building. Workers streamed in through the doors, the evening shift coming on for the opening of the Tokyo and New Hong Kong exchanges. Tanner noticed that none of them wore metal—Mishima Investments strictly forbade any fakes.

Tanner stepped through the high doors and approached the security desk. A visitor's pass complete with his photo was already prepared for him, and after a quick and polite identity check he was passed through to the elevators.

When he emerged into the open fifty-eighth-floor reception area, Tanner was enclosed by a solid hush of quiet. A wide expanse of pale carpet, sand walls, and low furnishings surrounded him. At the matte black reception desk on the opposite wall sat a tall, dark-haired woman with a silver metal face. Tanner had never seen her before, and the shining metal disturbed him. It was not a mask; the polished metal contoured to the woman's skull *was* her face. He wondered if it had been elective.

"Mr. Tanner." The woman's voice, emerging from between metal, segmented lips, was soft and cool. "Mr. Teshigahara will see you now."

The wall to her left swung open. Tanner walked toward the opening, and as he passed the woman he thought he heard a long, low hiss. He turned to look at her, but she was facing the elevator, silent and unmoving. He turned away and went through, the wall closing behind him.

Two of Teshigahara's office walls were all glass; through them was an expansive view of the bay and the Golden Gate. The wall through which he'd entered was fronted by a series of cherry-wood cabinets; behind their closed doors, Tanner knew, was a bank of television and computer monitors. In front of the last wall was Hiroshi Teshigahara's desk. Teshigahara sat behind it, immaculately dressed in black except for a white shirt. His thin, black tie was tastefully streaked with silver, nearly matching the streaks in his hair.

"Mr. Tanner," he said.

"Mr. Teshigahara." Always so damn formal, Tanner thought.

Teshigahara stood and walked to the largest of the windows, facing north. Tanner joined him, gazing out through the glass. Almost directly ahead, out in the bay, the bright lights of the casinos on Alcatraz pulsed in the night, their reflections flashing off the choppy waters around the island. The Golden Gate Bridge, intact once again, was a beautiful lattice of amber and crimson lights spanning the entrance of the bay.

"My friends in New Hong Kong would like me to express their appreciation for the shipment of swiftlet nests." He turned to look at Tanner. "They believe the vital qualities of bird's-nest soup are of even more value in the orbitals than on Earth."

"What do *you* believe?" Tanner asked.

Teshigahara smiled, shrugged, then said, "They are Chinese." He turned back to the view. "The nights are quite beautiful from here," he said. "The worst of the city is hidden by darkness and distance, or given a false sheen by the lights." He paused. "You have something for me?"

Tanner took a sealed manila envelope from inside his jacket and handed it to Teshigahara. TO BE OPENED IN THE EVENT OF THE DEATH OF LOUIS JOSHUA TANNER, the label read. A hint of smile flickered across Teshigahara's lips.

"It sounds so ominous." He looked at Tanner. "Are you going to die soon?"

"I hope not."

"A precautionary measure."

"Yes."

"Some items you wish attended to if you are . . . incapacitated."

"Yes."

"Are you going somewhere?"

"Not far," Tanner said. "Into the Tenderloin."

Teshigahara moved his head slightly, a gesture of dismissal. "Its dangers are greatly exaggerated," he said. "Outsiders are not killed in the Tenderloin, at least no more frequently than in any other part of the city."

"I know," Tanner replied. "It's not the Tenderloin. I am looking for someone."

"Ah." Teshigahara nodded.

Tanner half expected an offer of help, but Teshigahara made none. Instead, the small man crossed the room and laid the envelope on the desk before turning back to Tanner.

"When you have completed your task," Teshigahara said, "my friends in New Hong Kong will want to resume making use of your services."

"I'll let you know."

Teshigahara nodded once more, then said, "Good-bye, Mr. Tanner."

No offer of help, no wishes of good luck.

"Good-bye."

The wall swung open. Tanner walked through, glanced at the metal-faced woman, then headed for the elevator. Once again he thought he heard hissing come from the woman, but this time he did not pause, he did not look around. The elevator doors were open. Tanner entered, the doors closed, and he descended.

Chinatown. It was a long trip to the other end of the Corridor, where it abutted the east wall of the Tenderloin, and Tanner hired a scooter. The driver was a skinny old man around seventy or eighty, with long white hair braided down to his waist. He wore black leather jacket and pants, and black leather boots with clear thermoplast heels that sparked a bright blue and crimson pattern in the night.

As he rode through the Corridor, bouncing roughly on the back of the scooter, Tanner thought of Teshigahara's observation on the view from his office. Down in the streets a lot less was hidden. Flashing neon and sputtering amber lights lit the teeming crowds and street soldiers, illuminated the scarred edges of skin and fabric, cast pulsing and shifting shadows into the alcoves and gutters. They passed a string of stunner arcades, jerking bodies visible through tinted glass; hovering outside the doors were packs of street-medicos waiting to pick up some business. A thrasher pack was walking their boards through the Corridor, blood leaking from a gash across the leader's forehead. The high-pitched singsong of Chinese music battled with explosive pockets of neo-industrial metal, an occasional blast of slash-and-burn, and the general clamor of human voices.

The scooter dropped him at the door of Joyce Wah's restaurant at the far end of the Corridor. Alexandra stood in the doorway, watching him. She wore an ankle-length raincoat of black swirled with opalescent red.

"I know, I'm late," Tanner said.

Alexandra smiled. "I knew you would be. I just got here a few minutes ago myself."

Inside, they were met by Tommy Lee, Joyce's partner. He scowled at Tanner, said, "I wish I could kick you out, you son of a bitch."

"Is Joyce in tonight?"

"No. Home sick. So why you don't just leave?"

"We'll eat upstairs."

Tommy turned and stalked off.

"He doesn't like you much," Alexandra observed.

Tanner smiled. "We had a disagreement a couple of years ago. If it wasn't for Joyce, he'd probably poison me."

They climbed the narrow, tilted stairs and sat at a window table with a view of the Tenderloin's eastern wall directly across the street. A young woman brought cups and a pot of tea to the table. Alexandra spent a few minutes looking through the menu while Tanner gazed across the street at the wall of buildings that formed one boundary of the Tenderloin.

There were no longer any regular street entrances into the Tenderloin. Buildings had been erected across the streets along the outer boundaries, filling the gaps so a nearly solid wall of buildings—broken only by narrow alleys—formed a rectangular perimeter, ten blocks long and eight blocks wide. The streets opened up again inside the boundaries, but you would never know that from the outside.

Lights were on in nearly all the windows, and would stay on through the night. Like the Financial District, the Tenderloin never closed down. In fact, the Tenderloin ran faster at night, like a colony organism on speed. Which was why Tanner was going in at night.

The young woman returned, took their order, and left. Tommy Lee came through the room, glared at Tanner, then headed up to the third floor.

Alexandra laughed. "My grandfather told me once about a restaurant in Chinatown where one of the major attractions was a terribly rude waiter. People actually went in order to be insulted by him."

"Poor Tommy. Born out of his time."

Tanner looked back out the window. Across the street and down a block, two large freight trucks were unloading into one of the Tenderloin's underground docks. The trucks blocked traffic, and men and women worked furiously with the stacks of crates. Horns blared, lights flashed.

"So you're going into the Tenderloin," Alexandra said.

"Yes."

"That should be fun."

Tanner smiled, still watching the trucks being unloaded across the street.

"You going to stay inside, or go in and out?"

"I'll stay, at least for a few days. I'll be looking for someone."

"I know a place," Alexandra said. She waited a moment, then said, "My sister lives inside."

Tanner turned to look at her. Alexandra had a pained, distressed expression on her face. "You've never mentioned a sister," he said.

Alexandra nodded, turning away from him. She did not say anything for a minute, then finally spoke again, her voice hardly more than a whisper. "Identical twin."

Tanner did not respond. He watched the muscles in Alexandra's face and neck tighten. She sighed and nodded again.

"I don't talk about her because she doesn't want me to." Another pause. "You'll have no trouble telling us apart. Her growth hormones went skizzy on her when she was about ten. She's a foot and a half shorter than I am, and her bones have been rotting away since she was fifteen." She paused, pressed her face against the window. Rain had begun to fall, spattering the glass. "But her face is just like mine." She picked at loose slivers of wood on the windowsill.

The waitress brought their food: shrimp chow fun, war won ton soup, rice, and pot stickers. She checked the tea and quietly left.

"I've talked to her," Alexandra said. "She has an extra room, and she'll be expecting you. Here's her address." She slid a card across the table. Tanner slipped it into his shirt pocket.

"Thanks." He hesitated, reluctant to press her, but he felt he needed to know more. "So tell me," he finally said. "What's she like?"

Alexandra slowly shook her head. "Hell, that all depends on your timing, I guess."

"What do you mean?"

"She's got a lot of weird stuff going on inside her. The hormone stuff. And drugs—painkillers, mostly. And an occasional bout of depression. Most of the time she's all right, but when you get the downside of all those things hitting her at the same time, well, she can be just a miserable bitch." She paused, looking at Tanner. "But basically she's a good person, Louis. Remember that, even if she's in a foul mood."

Tanner nodded. "I will."

They ate without talking much. Water from the rain washed down the window in sheets, distorting the lights and images of the street. The food, as always, was delicious, though relatively mild. Tanner had given up spicy food, as much as he liked it, back when he had been a cop. His digestive system had become too sensitive, easily irritated, and he had wanted to make damn sure he never developed ulcers. He had watched his mother suffer for years with them; whenever he thought of her he always pictured her mouth, lips ringed with chalky white from antacids. It had seemed strange when lung cancer killed her in the end, especially since she'd never been a smoker.

When the food was gone, they stayed and drank more tea. Tanner chewed on the fortune cookie, smiling to himself. Stale. Every time he had eaten here the last fifteen years the fortune cookies were stale. His fortune read: "Monkeys will guide your life. Feed them well." As always, it meant nothing to him. Alexandra would not read her fortune. Instead, she made a great show of chewing and then swallowing the narrow strip of paper, washing it down with tea.

"It will transubstantiate within me," she said. "Become a mutated neurotransmitter that will fire my brain to Nirvana." She smiled. "Or fry it into slag."

"You probably won't be able to tell the difference."

"Probably not." She stopped smiling and gazed at him silently for a long time. The restaurant was quiet, and the rain was loud against the window, slapping at the glass. "It's like watching myself decay," she finally said.

"Your sister?"

Alexandra nodded. He thought she was going to say more about it, but she just shrugged, shook her head. She gestured

across the street, then said, "It's a funny place." Tanner nodded. "Watch yourself in there." She paused, gave him a half
smile. "And say hi to my sister."

"I will."

Tanner stood on the sidewalk in the rain, gazing across the
street at the light-filled wall of buildings. The dark, narrow
alleys, misted with rain and shadows, appeared to be the only
way through, but Tanner knew better. Trying to get in through
the alleys wouldn't get you killed, but you would end up back
outside in less than ten minutes, without a nickel, without half
your clothes, and completely dazed and confused.

He glanced back and up at the second-floor window.
Alexandra was still there, watching him. She did not wave,
and neither did Tanner. He turned away, pulled his coat tighter
against the rain, and started across the street.

FOURTEEN

SOOKIE STOOD IN front of the basement door, breathing heavily. Wasn't the same basement, but she was scared anyway. No machines here. No machines, no winged freak with metal skull and metal voice. An empty basement. Maybe.

She stepped back, leaned against cool concrete, lit a cigarette. Fingers shook. Save it, she told herself.

The ground rumbled and she turned, looked up at the street to see a Black Rhino thundering down the road. Chunks of pavement kicked loose, people scattered, and a string of Chikky Birds on roller skates moved along in its wake, dodging the new potholes and chunks of street. Smoke and streaks of sparkling blue electricity shot out from under the vehicle.

Sookie shook her head and turned back to the basement door. Just go. You want to see Mixer? Then go. Go. GO.

She crushed her cigarette, grabbed the doorknob, pulled. Dark and dust. Sookie slipped inside but didn't shut the door. Light, where was it? She fumbled along the wall, found the switch, flipped it. Nothing.

Oh, man. It's okay, you know this basement. She had known the other basement, too. Sookie stood against the wall, let her eyes adjust. There was dim light from outside, too. Eventually it was enough.

She could see the rows of empty metal shelving, the rolls of dirt and dust. And the hatch. She went back to the door, got her bearings, then closed it. Sookie moved quickly now, feeling her way along the rickety metal shelves, then dropped to her knees next to the hatch.

The hatch came up easily. A soft glow of light rose from below. Sookie dropped through, landing on the wooden platform, and let the hatch slam shut. She sat on the platform and breathed deeply. Completely underground, out of the basement, she felt safe again.

The tracks beside the platform hummed quietly, not quite silent. Picking light was green. Sookie grabbed a luge cart from the rack, checked the neutrality, then set it on the tracks. She stretched out onto it, feetfirst and belly up. Shoes into stirrups, head into the support, propped up so she could see ahead. Hands on brakes and controls. She cut the neutrality, and the cart shot forward.

Light, shadow, light, shadow—she moved quickly along the low, narrow tunnel. The tracks dipped steeply, diving deep to go below a flooded tunnel. Power downs cut her speed, stop and go, then rising as she approached the Tenderloin. A hard left, and the tracks headed away, curving back around toward Market Street.

Alone on the tracks. Alone again. Mixer. Time, all right. She needed something.

Sookie was counting the light/dark shifts after the hard left. At twenty-three she braked, coasted through another, and came to a stop exactly halfway between two lights. She neutralized the cart, scrambled to her feet, pulled the cart off the tracks.

The door was just a few feet away, small but heavy. Sookie pushed it open, squeezed through with the luge cart, and closed it tightly behind her.

Total darkness now. Warm and fresh, comforting. She wanted to just sit, smoke a cigarette, go to sleep. She moved along the passage, cut left at the first opening she felt in the wall, then quickly right. Ten more steps and she dropped to hands and knees. She found the tracks by sound, listening for the quiet hum. Cart onto the tracks, hook in, cut the neutrality. Once again she shot forward.

No lights at all this time. Speed kicked up, the tracks dipped, banked left then right then left again. No brakes. Wild ride. The tracks straightened. More speed. A circle of light ahead. Sookie closed her eyes, kept them tight as explosions of light went off, nearly blinding her even through eyelids. Then a gentle dip and she was through the gauntlet, under the barriers, and tracking smoothly into the Tenderloin.

FIFTEEN

HUDDLED AGAINST THE rain, Tanner crossed the street and entered Li Peng's Imperial Imports. "Herb Heaven," Freeman had always called it: racks of dried seaweed; jars of roots and seeds; packets of dried flowers and leaves; a wall of wooden drawers; shelves stocked with boxes, tins, bottles; and a long glass display case filled with vessels of colored liquids in which swam bulbous, indefinable creatures. It was the kind of place where Lucy Chen would buy the ingredients for her horrible teas.

Li Peng, a small, wiry, gray-haired man, sat in a padded chair behind the counter, drinking tea and watching three silent, small-screen television sets. The televisions were propped on wooden crates at various heights; only one was in color, and all three were showing different broadcasts. He looked up at Tanner, but did not say anything.

Tanner approached the display case, and the swimming creatures appeared to orient themselves toward him, hovering in the colored liquids of their vessels, eyes staring. He pushed two fifties into a jar with a crude, handwritten label. The characters were all Chinese ideographs except for two words: HELP POOR.

Li Peng pushed something at the back of the case, and Tanner heard a loud click. He went to the door beside a rack of dried seaweed, opened it, and stepped through.

He stood at the foot of a long, steep staircase lit by strings of phosphor dangling from the ceiling. A steady thumping shook the right wall, punctuating a stream of muted shouts. Tanner started up.

There were no landings, no doorways at any of the floors, just numerals and geometric symbols painted in red on the concrete wall. Above the third floor the thumping and shouts faded away, and the rest of the climb was silent except for a single, loud crack somewhere between five and six.

On eight, the stairs ended at a metal door that opened into a bare corridor. Tanner walked the length of the corridor, then through another door and into a room. A tall, thin Chinese sat at a metal desk, surrounded by monitors, terminals, and keypads. He wore a bowling shirt with the name "Al" stitched onto the pocket.

"How much?" Al asked.

"Seventeen thousand, five hundred," Tanner said. He pulled the rolls of cash from his pockets and set them in front of the man. He was keeping several hundred for the street.

Al counted the money, put it away in a floor safe, then worked at one of the computers for a minute. He had Tanner look into a lighted tube for a retinal scan, then slid a keypad across the desk; Tanner keyed in an access code he had ready. Al finished things off, and another minute later reached under the desk to get Tanner's credit chip.

"Seventeen thousand five hundred," he said. "Two percent transaction fee for every withdrawal. You know where you can access it?"

Tanner nodded, took the chip, and secured it inside his shirt. Al nodded back, and Tanner crossed to the other door and went through. Another short passage, then Tanner stepped out onto a large balcony overlooking the swarming, brightly lit streets below. He was inside.

The Tenderloin was alive. A fine, warm mist fell, adding a lacy sheen to the lights and the snakelike movement of people, animals, and vehicles. Red, orange, and green streamers of light—the colors of the Asian Quarter—drifted through the mist, swimming in the air from one building to another, and the noise was louder even than the peak of the Chinese Corridor. Tanner could feel the energy of the Tenderloin rise from the streets, could smell the adrenaline rush of the crowds below.

He walked to the other end of the balcony and a second door leading back into the building. He opened the door, stepped through, and entered a world of shimmering lights and colored smoke, dizzying stairways and precarious balconies, steaming

tables and glass reflections, and an incessant babble of voices
that nearly washed out the underlying sounds of clacking cards
and tiles, rattling glasses, and strains of music.

Tanner walked between two sets of jinking tables to the
nearest interior balcony and looked over the railing. The swirling smoke was so thick he could not see more than two floors
down. A man approached Tanner and asked if he wanted
into any of the games or intimacy booths. Tanner shook his
head, and the man bowed and left. Tanner located the nearest
staircase—a constantly reversing double helix that shook with
each of his footsteps—and descended.

He descended through warm, billowing smoke and dancing
electric lights. The restaurant floor smelled thickly of curry
and peanut oil. The floor below that smelled of musk and
incense, and throbbed with a deep, steady bass line more felt
than heard. More gaming floors followed, wild and raucous
except the last, the second floor, which was quiet and hushed,
the sounds from above and below silenced by huge arrays of
acoustical baffles mounted on the balconies. Tanner paused,
watching the serious-looking players seated at the tables, most
of them wearing mirrorshades and subdued suits, most of them
smoking, most of them drinking. It was all show, Tanner knew.
The real players, the real games, with irrevocable stakes, were
deep in the Tenderloin buildings and out of public view—high
above ground level in the heart of interior mazes, or buried in
below-ground bunkers.

Tanner continued to the ground floor, an open concourse
ringed by trash arcades, electronics boutiques, video parlors,
bars, and tea shops. He worked his way through the crowd,
out open doors, and onto the streets.

The mist had ceased falling, but the warm night air was
still thick with moisture. The sidewalks teemed with people,
and the streets were filled with the chaotic motion of scooters,
mini delivery vans, pedal carts, and jitneys. The light streamers
danced in the air above him, periodically coalescing to form
advertisements: JUNEBUG MICROBIOTICS—JACK INTO LIFE!;
TESTOSTERONE DAYS, PREMIERING TONIGHT, CHANNEL 37B,
2:00 A.M.; CHUNG'S NIGHT SKY SECURITY—A NEW CAREER ON
THE EDGE.

Tanner walked down the street, feeling the energy rush
rise within him, the pump of excitement. He understood why

people lived here by choice—life played out at higher levels of intensity than anywhere else in the city, and that intensity never let up, night or day. He knew how addictive that could be. Almost anything could be addictive, and Tanner often thought that everybody alive was addicted to something.

He stopped at a sheltered sidewalk cafe and sat at a table with a view of the street, just under the awning. When the waiter came he ordered coffee, wishing he could handle an espresso, but his stomach was strung tight and sensitive. He sat back to watch the people on the street.

A young woman came up to Tanner, took his hand warmly in hers, and kissed him deeply on the mouth. She sat across from him, setting her handbag on the table. She was Southeast Asian, and wore a short black dress over skintight metallic black leggings. A band of pulsing energy beads circled her neck. Three glistening blue tears were tattooed to her left cheek. Tanner had never seen her before.

"I don't know you," he said.

The woman smiled, shaking her head. "No."

"Do you know me?"

"No," she said, still smiling. "Will you buy me coffee?"

Tanner hesitated, not wanting to get into anything unexpected. It had been too long since he had spent any real time in the Tenderloin, and it would take a while to get back into the rhythm of its ways, relearn the codes and patterns of its streets. "All right," he eventually said. "But I'm not interested in buying anything else."

The woman nodded once. "Fine with me. I just want to get off my feet for a few minutes."

The waiter brought Tanner's coffee, and when the woman ordered a double espresso, Tanner smiled to himself. She did not tell him her name, nor ask him his. In fact, she did not seem to be at all interested in talking to him. She sat facing the street, and Tanner watched her as she watched the people moving past. He did not think she was looking for anyone in particular, her gaze seemed too passive and relaxed. He drank his coffee slowly, his attention shifting back and forth from the woman to the street.

Rat packs in metal-strip rags sauntered past, each member with a pack color bead tied to the end of hair-loop earrings.

Head tuners strolled along the sidewalk, hawking their plugs and bands. Street musicians played their instruments, sale discs dangling from their clothes. Small-time drug dealers moved among the crowds, offering what Tanner and almost everyone else on the street knew was shit so stepped on there was nearly nothing left for a buzz; but they had customers anyway, those who couldn't afford anything else, or who no longer cared. The sidewalk was so thick with people Tanner only caught occasional glimpses of the various carts and vans moving along the roadway itself.

When her espresso came, the woman took a jimsonweed stick from her purse and chewed on it between sips of her espresso. Tanner guessed the stick was also laced with ameline. She was going to get one hell of a kick soon.

She finished off the espresso, popped the rest of the stick in her mouth, and chewed on it as if it were gum. Then she grabbed her purse, stood, leaned over, and kissed him again, this time on the cheek. "Thanks, honey."

"What are the tears for?" he asked on impulse.

She gave him a sad smile. "One for every month he's been away."

He had the feeling she was quoting something—a song, perhaps. The woman turned quickly and walked off, sliding easily into the crowd.

Tanner's coffee was nearly gone, and he signaled the waiter for a refill, then returned his attention to the street. Things happen, he thought, and most of them don't mean a damn thing. He wondered if the woman meant anything.

As he drank his coffee and watched the people move past him, Tanner thought about finding Rattan. He had no real plan yet, no step-by-step procedure to follow; there *was* no rigorous procedure he could follow in this case. He just had to work his way back into the flow of the Tenderloin, reestablish some contacts, send out a few feelers, and hope.

The one thing he did know was that he would start in the Euro Quarter. Despite being half-Mongolian, Rattan would go nowhere near the Asian Quarter, and would probably stay away from the Latin, Arab, and Afram Quarters as well. Once he had gone to ground, the cops would have looked in the Euro Quarter first, but Rattan would have expected that; and it was in the Euro Quarter that he would have the best protection, the most loyalty, the best sense of security. He had been *somewhere* the last year, and Tanner felt certain it was the Euro. He sure as hell hoped Rattan was not holed up in the Core.

Tanner looked at the card Alexandra had given him. Rachel, her sister, lived in the Euro Quarter, near the edge of the Latin. That's where he should be now. But he wasn't ready just yet. He remained at the table, drinking his coffee, watching, and letting the Tenderloin wash over him.

Tanner ended the night on the outer edges of the Euro Quarter. It was nearly dawn, the coolest part of the day, when he arrived at the building where Alexandra's sister lived. Not cool, exactly, but no longer hot, and that was something. The building was a twelve-story monstrosity of scarred brick, splintered wood, and dangling, disconnected sections of a metal fire escape—anyone above the second floor would have to jump if there was a fire.

A pack of teenagers blocked the building doors, ten or twelve boys and girls wearing pressed brown shirts and red arm bands emblazoned with black swastikas. That shit never dies, Tanner thought. It was one of the few things that still surprised him whenever he saw it, though he should have known better.

He pushed his way through the pack, and they grudgingly gave way to him. He guessed he was white enough for them. Tanner wondered if it was an all-white building; and what, if anything, that said about Alexandra's sister. Rachel. Some kind of biblical name, he thought.

The lobby was dark and smelled of mold. Rotting gold foil wallpaper peeled away from dark red walls, and large sections of the carpet were worn through to the flooring. Tanner walked past a huge bank of metal mailboxes and stopped in front of the elevators. One was closed, marked with an Out of Order sign. The other was open, and a dim light burned inside, illuminating a sign that had been taped to the back wall: USE THIS ELEVATOR AND YOU'RE DEAD, MOTHERFUCKER. Rachel lived on the eleventh floor, but Tanner decided he could use the exercise.

Fifteen minutes later, breathing heavily, Tanner reached the eleventh floor and leaned against the stairwell doorframe, gazing down the long hall. He had to smile at the possibility that Rachel would not even be here. He could not imagine why he had not thought to call first. Once again he looked at the card Alexandra had given him. Yes, there was a phone number.

He walked along the hall, glancing at the room numbers, metal figures tacked to the doors. He could hear faint music, barking voices, clattering, a yowl, running water. Rachel's apartment was at the far end of the hall, and he stopped in front of the door, reading the several handwritten quotations pinned to the dark wood. "Deep in the hearts of all men is a black core that needs purification." "White, white, everywhere it was white, and all was good." "Trust not in yourself, until you know you are pure." "And then the angels rose up and destroyed them all." Tanner did not have a good feeling about Rachel.

He knocked on the door and waited. A few moments later a voice called out from within. "Who is it?"

"Louis Tanner. Alexandra said she talked to you about me."

Rachel did not answer, but Tanner heard a bolt being thrown. He expected to hear several more locks being released, so he was surprised when the door opened after the first.

Alexandra was right. Rachel's face was just like hers, except for her hair, which was shorter; but the body was not even close. Rachel stood less than five feet tall, supporting herself with a cane in her right hand. She wore a pale brown dress that reached her calves, and heavy black shoes, the right built up six or seven inches.

Rachel stared at him a moment, her eyes with a hard glitter, then backed away, swinging the door wide. "Come on in," she said, her voice a harsh growl. "I just got back from work, getting ready for sleep." Tanner stepped inside and Rachel shut the door, locking it. The front room was sparsely furnished, but immaculate and well lighted.

"Nice bunch of kids at the street entrance," he said.

Rachel shrugged. "They help keep out the impure."

Was she serious? Christ, he thought, a Purist? Did Alexandra know? Why hadn't she told him?

"You look tired," Rachel said.

"I've been up all night."

"That's pretty standard around here," she responded. "But I guess I know what you mean. You've been up all day, too, right? Out there?"

Tanner nodded.

"Come on, then, I'll show you where you'll sleep. Like I said, I'm going to bed myself."

She limped across the room, digging at the floor with her cane, and Tanner followed her to the hallway, then into the first room on the right. She flipped on the light, revealing a small room with a desk and chair and a futon. On the futon was a neat stack of folded sheets and blankets, and a pillow. "Your bed. I'll show you the rest of the place."

In the hall, she pushed open a door on the left with her cane. "Bathroom." Then, farther down, she swung her cane and banged on a closed door. "My bedroom. You stay out of it."

Tanner didn't say a thing. Rachel led the way into the last room, the kitchen, which had large windows that looked out at more buildings across the way. The gray light of the coming dawn came in through the windows, casting soft shadows across the floor.

"You can help yourself to any of the food here," Rachel said. "But don't bother looking for booze, I don't have any." With that she turned away and limped back down the hall. She opened her bedroom door, went inside without turning on a light, then slammed the door shut. This time he did hear several locks and bolts—one, two, three, four.

Tanner walked back down the hall and into his room. He sat on the futon and leaned back against the wall. He had expected to like Rachel because she was Alexandra's sister, because Alexandra had arranged this for him. Now, finding that he did not like her at all made him uncomfortable. Alexandra had warned him, but still, this was worse than he had expected, especially if she was a Purist. He wondered if he could stay here very long while he looked for Rattan. For tonight, yes, or this morning, whatever it was, get a few hours' sleep. But how much longer? Maybe he could stay out of her way, not see her much.

Not a good start, he said to himself. But at least he could sleep; he was exhausted. He undressed, turned out the light, and lay out on the futon, not bothering to set up the sheets or blankets. Tanner closed his eyes and slept.

SIXTEEN

TANNER WOKE TO the strong aroma of coffee. He looked at his watch, saw that it was just after noon. Through the open door he could hear trickling water, footsteps creaking wood, and generalized city sounds filtering in through open windows. He had slept deeply, without any dreams that he could remember, and he felt rested.

Tanner showered, finishing off with cold water to cut through the heat of the day. He dressed, the sweat already dripping under his arms, then walked down to the end of the hall.

The kitchen was empty. It had a different feel now, light and open. All the windows were open wide, letting in the damp heat and the city sounds. The kitchen table was set for two, including a filter-pitcher of clear water. On the counter was a coffee maker, the pot full and steaming. Next to the coffee, laid out on a cutting board, were eggs, chopped onions and tomatoes, and a pile of grated cheese.

"Good morning." Rachel's head appeared outside the window above the sink. She was smiling. "Come on out," she said. She gestured to his left. "Around the corner's a door."

Tanner skirted the table, squeezed past the bulky fridge and around the corner to an open door leading out to a wooden platform built onto the walls of the building. An awning of clear plastic sheltered the platform, letting through light but, presumably, keeping off the rain. The platform was covered with potted plants, most blossoming with large, colorful flowers. Rachel, barefoot and dressed in a loose sarong, moved among the plants with a pink watering can, poking at the dirt with her fingers. Tanner was stunned by the bright, lush, unbroken green of the leaves—no brown streaks or spots, no holes eaten away by the rain.

Rachel set down the watering can and sat on a bench against the wall. Her arms and face glistened with sweat. "Have a seat," she said.

Tanner sat beside her. She bent forward to massage her right leg, moving from thigh to calf and back.

"You like eggs?" she asked. "Cheese, onions, tomatoes?" She turned to him and smiled. "A shot or two of Tabasco?"

"Sure. If you'll hold the Tabasco."

"Great, I'll make us an omelet. Coffee's already done, or I could find some tea if you prefer."

"No, coffee's fine, thanks."

She released her leg, stretched her back. "Come on, then."

They went back inside, Rachel's limp more pronounced without the built-up shoes. Now Tanner noticed the six-inch blocks fixed to the floor in front of the stove, counter, and sink. Rachel gathered up the food on the counter and carried it to the stove. With her right foot on the block, she started the omelet.

"Anything I can do?" Tanner asked.

"How about pouring us some coffee?"

There were two glass mugs next to the coffee maker, and Tanner filled them, brought one to Rachel at the stove, then sat at the table with his.

The coffee was hot and strong, and he drank it slowly as he watched her cook. Soon the smell of frying butter joined the coffee aroma, and then she was pouring eggs into the pan with a loud sizzle. Tanner felt relaxed and almost peaceful. It seemed like such a traditional domestic scene. He thought of mornings like this spent with Valerie and Connie, either in his place or at their apartment in San Jose; usually he had done the cooking. Sour cream french toast and bacon had been his specialty and Connie's favorite. The last time had been more than a year ago, but it seemed much longer—another century, another goddamn life. Most of the time he doubted he would ever experience anything like that again. This world stinks, Tanner thought.

Rachel turned off the gas, cut the omelet in half, then brought the pan to the table and slid a half onto each plate.

"Thanks," Tanner said.

She set the pan on the table and sat across from him with a shrug. "Least I could do." She poured two glasses of water from the pitcher. "Sorry about this morning. You showed up at a bad time."

He expected her to go on, explain further, but she didn't. Instead, she opened a plastic bottle next to the pitcher, shook out three white tablets. She popped all three into her mouth and swallowed them with half a glass of water.

Tanner looked at the bottle, then at Rachel, but did not ask the question. He knew they were not vitamins, and it was none of his business.

Rachel shrugged, then gave a short laugh. "Dilaudid," she said. "Only way I can keep the edge off the pain."

Dilaudid. It reminded Tanner of McMurphy, who had been Freeman's prime snitch. McMurphy used to take Dilaudid for "headaches." Last time Tanner had seen him, the crazy son of a bitch was getting headaches three or four times a day, popping those things and dry-swallowing them. McMurphy hated needles.

They did not talk while they ate, which was fine with Tanner. The omelet was good, and he was enjoying it. He was even, for some reason, enjoying the heat. The water, too, was good, tasted clean but not sterile. He pulled the pitcher close and looked at the filter. Braun.

"It was expensive," Rachel said. "But it's worth it. I've got a larger one for the plant water, too."

That explained the lush green color, the absence of dead brown streaks on the leaves. Some of the plants were visible in the windows, the deep green and bright reds, yellows, and blues taking some of the harshness out of the heat. Maybe that was why he was enjoying it.

When they were done eating, Rachel cleared off the table, poured fresh coffee, then took a set of keys from under the upper cabinets and handed it to Tanner. "How long will you be staying?" she asked.

Staying. Yes, he guessed he was. It seemed all right now. "I don't know," he said. "A few days at least. Maybe longer, if that's all right."

"However long, it doesn't matter." She paused. "You weren't too sure about it this morning, were you?"

"No." He still wasn't sure, but he felt better about it now. Again he thought she was going to explain, but again she said nothing. "That stuff taped onto your door," he said. "The quotes."

Rachel smiled, shaking her head. "I'm not a Purist, if that's what you're asking. But there are some in this building, the people who run the place. Putting that stuff on the door makes life a lot easier. And safer. They leave me alone." She shrugged. "And we all need to live somewhere, right?"

Tanner nodded. They took their coffee out onto the back platform and sat on the bench seat. Although the sun was high, the building gave them a narrow strip of shade so that only their legs and feet were exposed.

"Why are you here?" Rachel asked. "Alexandra didn't say."

"I'm looking for someone."

"Someone who's trying not to be found, I assume?" When Tanner shrugged she said, "Then you may be staying here a long time." After another pause, she asked, "You know the Tenderloin at all?"

"When I was a cop, I worked the Tenderloin."

Rachel snorted, a half laugh. "Cops don't work the Tenderloin. The Tenderloin works them."

Tanner nodded. "True enough. We did what we could."

"That's reassuring," she said, grinning. Then, "I'm sorry, I suppose that wasn't nice."

"That's all right. I understand."

"What part of the Tenderloin?"

"I started working the Asian Quarter." He could not keep the smile off his face, thinking of Nguyen Pham, his partner at the time. The guy was certifiable, the grandson of some old timer Vietcong hotshot who had been a hero during the war. Pham was big on practical jokes that often nearly got them killed, and the one time Pham did get shot up he laughed all the way to the hospital. But Pham's sister and her husband were killed in some gang power struggle, and Pham took his two nieces back to Vietnam. Tanner had never heard from him again. Which was how he ended up with Freeman as his partner. Tanner stopped smiling.

"Then I switched to the Afram and Euro Quarters."

"Black partner?" Rachel asked.

Tanner nodded, then shrugged. "Those days are over. I'm not a cop anymore." He did not want to talk about anything else, and Rachel seemed to sense that because she did not ask him another question, did not say a word. He shifted positions and leaned his head against the windowsill, a heavy yellow blossom brushing his cheek. Tanner closed his eyes and breathed in deeply the cool, clear scent. He was in no hurry to move from this spot. He was relaxed, and it was probably going to be a long time before he felt this way again.

The teenage Nazis were still crowded around the building entrance when he left. Once again they opened a path for him, though he thought it was a different group this time. Across the street, strung out on second-floor balconies and wearing their trademark khaki jumpsuits and black headbands, half a dozen Daughters of Zion kept vigil.

Tanner spent several hours wandering through the Euro Quarter, checking out old haunts, getting the feel of the streets. He did not really feel at home—he had never felt "at home" in the Tenderloin, even after working in it for several years—but he felt comfortable. The streets were that way, which was a funny thing. People who did not know the Tenderloin thought the streets were dangerous, wild and uncontrolled, where you would get mugged or killed or mauled because they were always so crowded, jammed with people, loud, bright with flashing lights and chaos. But the streets were the safest part of the Tenderloin. Inside was the real danger—in the warrenlike mazes of rooms and corridors that wormed through so many of the buildings; in the fortified below-ground basements and tunnels; in the vast, open attics run by the gangs and co-ops. Inside, things could get bad. People disappeared. Killed, certainly. You just didn't see the bodies most of the time; except for the occasional window fliers, they didn't show up in the streets or anywhere else. There were organ runners and crematoriums here in the Tenderloin to take care of that. For now, Tanner would stay in the streets, but he knew that eventually, if he was going to find Rattan, he would have to go inside.

He had a beer at Stinky's, but Stinky had died or moved, no one was sure, and Tanner did not know the new owner—a loud, obnoxious man called Rooter who smelled a lot worse than Stinky ever had. No one in the place looked familiar, and he left.

He stopped by the Turk Street Fascination Parlor and watched the old Russian women roll pale pink rubber balls up into the machines, numbers lighting silently on the vertical displays. But Lyuda was not in, and Tanner returned to the street.

A couple of bars, hotel lobbies, Tin Tin's Video Arcade, a transformer shop, two music clubs, and Mistress Wendy's House of Pain and Shame. Nothing, nobody he knew other than several people he wanted to avoid.

Just as the early-evening rain began, Tanner caught the last seat at a sheltered snack counter. He had a plate of curried bratwurst and french fries, and a tall glass of warm lemon soda that was too sweet. He sat sideways on the stool, watching the street as he ate, but still saw no one he recognized. When he was finished, he resumed walking the streets.

He bought a couple of changes of clothes, shaving gear, vitamins, and a few other things, and a small duffel bag to carry everything, then took it back to Rachel's. He had hoped to talk to her some more, but she was gone, so he went back out into the Quarter.

Darkness was falling when Tanner passed a window display that caught his eye outside a nightclub called The Open Gate. In large blue letters was:

RED GIANT AND WHITE DWARF
Beat Poets of the Twenty-First Century
TONIGHT 10:00

There was no picture of the beat poets. White Dwarf. Max? It seemed probable, if White Dwarf was an accurate physical description. Max was a poet of sorts. And if it *was* Max, Tanner had lucked out far sooner and closer to Rattan than he had hoped. He entered the club.

It was nearly full, the stage empty and dark. The floor consisted of table-covered platforms set at various heights. Spider lights hung from the ceiling in sheets, fluttering gently with the air currents. Cocktail jazz played softly from speakers mounted in the corners.

Tanner found an empty table near the back, on one of the higher platforms, five or six feet above the stage. A waiter dressed in a deep blue floor-length coat and wearing an eye patch over the center of his forehead approached the table.

"Here for the show?" the waiter asked.

Tanner nodded.

"Two-drink minimum before they start, two drinks at the break."

"How soon does the show start?"

The waiter grinned. "Five minutes."

Tanner ordered two scotches. Then, as the waiter turned to go, Tanner asked, "What's with the patch?"

The waiter swung around, still grinning. "My third eye went blind last week." He turned back, and left.

Tanner scanned the club, searching for familiar faces. It was a strange crowd, ranging from people in their twenties to some quite old, dressed in everything from SoCal casual to metallic Asteroid Gear. But he did notice that there were no metal add-ons, no fake prosthetics. No *Faux Prosthétique* here, and probably very little anywhere in the Tenderloin.

Just behind him, against the wall and only partially hidden by shadows, a woman was on her hands and knees under a table, her face buried in a man's lap. There was no pleasure on the man's face, only a grimace of pain.

The waiter brought Tanner's drinks and took his money without a word. A minute later all the lights went out, plunging the club into darkness. The jazz cut off; the audience went silent. Spots came up, lighting the stage and revealing Red Giant and White Dwarf. Red Giant was just that, a hulking man around seven feet tall with flaming red hair and beard. Rimless mirrorshades were grafted over his eyes, and he wore a black beret. White Dwarf was indeed Max—an albino dwarf also wearing grafted mirrorshades. He sat on a stool with a set of bongo drums in his lap.

A minute or two of silence followed, then Max tapped out a brief, loud intro on the bongos, followed by more silence. A smooth, woman's voice came over the speakers.

"Red Giant and White Dwarf," the woman's voice announced. "Stars at the end of their life cycles. Beat poets of the twenty-first century, of the future and the past."

More silence. Then Max resumed on the bongos, a slow syncopated rhythm, and Red Giant began to recite. His voice boomed, resonating throughout the club. The first piece was called "White Fountains and the Death of Angels." Tanner did not understand most of it—something about the arrogance of man's ventures into space, he thought, with a lot of vague references to relativity, the space-time continuum, and various astronomical objects like black holes and white fountains. When they finished, the applause was loud, but not extreme. Red Giant and White Dwarf followed with "Dancing With a Black Hole," "The Blue Light," "You Burn Me Up, Baby, I'm a Cigarette," and several others. Red Giant did all the speaking, and Max kept the beat. After they finished "Party in My Head," they announced a break, and the lights went out again. When the spider lights came back up, the stage was empty.

Tanner took out one of his business cards—LOUIS TANNER, IMPORTS AND EXPORTS—and wrote on the back: *Max. Let's talk. Tanner.* When the waiter came by, Tanner handed the card to him.

"Will you give this to Max? I'm a friend of his."

"Max? Max who?"

"White Dwarf."

The waiter hesitated, said, "You're a friend of Max's?"

"Sort of."

The waiter grinned. "That's the only kind of friend Max has. So what'll you have?"

"Two drinks?"

"That's right."

"Make it two coffees this time."

The waiter shook his head. "No courage." He pocketed the card and moved on to the table behind Tanner. The woman was no longer on her hands and knees; now she sat next to the man, apparently asleep with her head on the table.

Tanner searched out the men's room and joined the line for the urinals. He could hear moaning and grunting from one of the stalls, and the click of vein injectors from another. A graying man all in black leather stood at the mirror carefully applying mascara. Another man, in a powder blue leisure suit, stood in the corner with his huge cock drooping out of an open zipper, but he wasn't getting any takers.

Tanner had just stepped up to one of the urinals when he felt a hand on his shoulder. He turned and looked into Dobler's broken face. Most of the muscles in Dobler's face did not work anymore, so Tanner couldn't be sure, but he thought Dobler was grinning.

"Dobler," he said.

"It's been too long," Dobler said.

Not nearly long enough, Tanner thought.

"You just finish things here, Tanner. I'll be waiting for you outside." He released Tanner's shoulder and turned to the man in the leisure suit. "You goddamn faggot, you're lucky I don't go over there and bite that fucking monster off."

The man smiled, and Tanner realized the guy had no idea Dobler was capable of doing just that. Dobler growled, then turned and walked out.

When Tanner came out of the men's room, Dobler was waiting in the hall, his face worked into something resembling intense concentration.

"I heard you ain't a cop no more," Dobler said.

"That's right."

"Your partner gets it, and you gets out."

Tanner didn't reply. He considered just walking away, but he knew Dobler wouldn't let it go like that.

"I'm sorry Freeman got killed before I had a chance to do his face the way he done mine," Dobler said. He leaned forward, bringing his face to within an inch or two of Tanner's. His breath was warm and foul. "If I'd got to that damn nigger, it would've looked a lot worse than this." He pulled back a little. "Maybe I'll do *your* face since I can't do his." Something close to a smile worked its way onto his lips. "You think about that, Tanner. Think about this face when you go to sleep at night. Think about *your* face." The smile twisted, then Dobler marched down the hall and out the rear exit.

Tanner returned to his table. The waiter was sitting in the second chair, sipping one of the coffees.

"You on a break or what?" Tanner asked.

"Max says he'll meet you after the show. Wait for him at this table." The waiter finished off the coffee and stood. "You let me know if you need a refill." He held out his hand, palm up. Tanner paid him, and he left.

Tanner sat and looked at the remaining coffee, thinking about Dobler. Just what he needed, something else to worry about. Dobler probably wouldn't do anything, but you never knew

with that lunatic. Tanner drank from the coffee, grimacing
as it hit his stomach. He didn't need the coffee, either.
The lights went out, the spots came up, and the second set
began.

SEVENTEEN

MIXER WASN'T HOME. Sookie climbed into his place through the bathroom window, almost falling headfirst into the toilet. Her arm went in to the elbow, and she bumped her head on the rim of the bowl. After drying off, she wandered around the rooms for a while, checking for signs of new girlfriends, but she didn't see any. Looked like Mixer was alone again.

She left, out the way she came in, and caught a ride with a transplant man. She unhooked around the corner from The Open Gate, the nightclub Mixer ran. But he wasn't at the club, either.

Sookie sat in Mixer's office, face pressed against the one-way glass. She shivered, seeing the stage below her. Max and Uwe were performing. She didn't like either one of them, Max especially. She'd seen them do some things. Torch a pair of mating dogs. Torch each other. Do four-way foamers for a private audience of mondo pervs. And she'd heard a lot worse.

She looked around at the audience. Faces were hard to see except the ones close to the stage. Winnie and Rice were here, but it looked like they were mad at each other again—Rice was wearing ear cones focused on the stage so he could hear the show while blocking out Winnie's voice; and Winnie was wearing polarized blinders. So what's new, Sookie thought, smiling to herself.

Near the back, alone at a table—something familiar about that guy. Sookie shifted her position, cutting out some of the reflective glare. It looked like the man on the balcony that day, when the bodies were dragged out of the water. He'd been watching her. She'd waved goof signals at him. Was it the same guy? She couldn't be sure.

Sookie slid open the one-way glass and carefully crawled out onto the strings of dark spider lights. The webbed strings sagged under her weight, and she froze a moment. If she got any bigger she wasn't going to be able to do this.

The swaying stopped, she started forward. The sag and sway resumed immediately, but there was nothing she could do about it. Hope. Move slow and careful. She smiled, imagining the strings breaking, herself swinging down and crashing into the tables and people below. It wasn't that far, she wouldn't get hurt. Or not much. Scare the noodles out of some people. Get Max and Uwe mad at her. Oh, maybe not such a good idea.

It was slow going, but Sookie was having fun. The spider light strings were like a circus safety net, but with bigger holes. She could slip through if she wasn't careful. That was part of the fun.

She was two-thirds of the way across the club when she spotted Froggle directly beneath her. Sookie almost burst out laughing at the crazy head mask he was wearing. Then, looking more closely, she realized it wasn't a mask. A square patch of his hair and skull was gone, replaced by a metal panel with knobs and sockets, glowing lights. Over the sounds of Max and Uwe she could just hear an electronic buzz coming from the panel; Froggle's head twitched, tiny vibrations going through him. Feeling queasy, Sookie looked away and moved on.

A few minutes later she was almost directly above the man, in front enough to see his face. It *was* the man on the balcony. She wondered if he remembered her.

Sookie felt among the strings until she found the links, then unhooked several so a section of the lights swung down, dangling like a rope ladder. Halfway to the table. She clambered down. Legs dangling free, down a few more strings to the end of the section, hanging by her hands. Shoes only two or three feet above the table. Looking down between her arms, she could see the man looking up at her. Sookie let go the lights, and dropped.

EIGHTEEN

THE GIRL CRASHED to the table from above and the coffee cups went flying. Tanner put out his hands to keep her from sprawling to the floor. Red Giant and White Dwarf continued without pause. The girl smiled at him, and scrambled off the table. She picked up the two coffee cups, both amazingly unbroken, set them on the table, then sat in the other chair and stared at Tanner.

It was the girl from the junkyard across the slough. A pang went through him, that sense of painful familiarity again. This time it did not fade. Instead, the pain grew, and he felt close to recognizing the source, but it still eluded him. He felt flush, and a sweat broke out under his arms. What *was* this?

"Do you remember me?" the girl asked, voice barely above a whisper.

More than you know, Tanner thought. More than *I* know yet. He nodded.

"It wasn't a movie, was it?" the girl asked.

"What?"

"That day. They weren't making a movie, were they? Those bodies, they were real."

The brief images came back to him, the two dead white bodies being pulled from the slough. "The bodies were real," he said.

The girl nodded. She glanced at the stage, then turned back to Tanner, but did not say any more.

"What's your name?" Tanner asked.

She started to say something, stopped, then started again. "Sookie," she said. "What's yours?"

"Tanner."

She glanced at the stage again, then grimaced at Tanner. "You like this kind of stuff?"

"It's all right."

"They're sleazebugs."

"Red Giant and White Dwarf?"

"Max and Uwe, yeah."

"You know them?"

"I know who they are." She turned her chair so she could watch the show, and that did it.

Carla.

The pain blossomed again, expanding in his chest. It was Sookie's profile that made the final connection. She looked just like a thirteen- or fourteen-year-old Carla. Jesus.

He had not known Carla at that age, but she had given him pictures—photos of her as a baby, a young kid, a teenager. He still had them, along with dozens of pictures of her taken during their few years together. He had not looked at any of them in a long time. Christ, she had been dead almost fifteen years now.

Tanner turned away from Sookie; he just could not keep looking at her. Carla. Jesus. Twenty-six and dead. He picked up one of the empty coffee cups, wishing he had a double scotch right now. Twenty-six and . . .

He tried to concentrate on the stage. Max was frantically pounding at the bongos, and Red Giant was grunting explosively between unintelligible words. The pounding and grunting crescendoed, then ceased abruptly. Red Giant raised his arms, shouted, "Devolution of the species!" and the lights went out.

Applause filled the club. It faded gradually as the spider lights slowly came back up, revealing an empty stage. Cocktail jazz began playing once again over the speakers.

"That's their closer," Sookie said. "Show's over." She turned the chair around to face him. "So where you going now?"

It took Tanner a few moments to realize she had asked a question. "Nowhere," he said.

Sookie grinned. "*Everybody's* going nowhere. That's what Mixer says, and I think he's right."

Carla.

"Who's Mixer?" he asked.

"A friend. So where?"

Where the hell *was* he going? Staring at her, he had to force himself to concentrate on the reasons he was here. Rattan, the Chain Killer. Max. "I'm staying right here," he finally said. "Waiting to talk to Max."

"Max? He's coming here?" She sprang to her feet, looking around the club. Max wasn't in sight. "He's not a good person."

"I know that."

"He's the worst, you should stay away from him." She kept looking around the club. Max came out from the back of the stage and headed for Tanner's table. "Oh no, here he comes." Sookie grabbed her chair, lifted it onto the table, and clambered up beside it.

"What are you doing?" Tanner asked.

"I'm getting *out* of here." She climbed onto the chair and stood, crouching slightly, hands stretched upward.

"Wait, why don't you just . . . ?"

Sookie jumped, caught the hanging panel of lights. Tanner heard something tear, and thought the whole thing was going to come down. But the lights held, Sookie swinging back and forth. Tanner thought of Carla again, the ache rising in his chest. "Bye," Sookie called down. She hooked a leg onto the panel, pulled herself up, and climbed. When she reached the main web of lights, she started crawling along them. He soon lost sight of her behind the glare, but he could follow her progress by the sag and sway of the lights. She was halfway across the club when Max reached the table.

"Who the hell was that?" Max asked.

"I don't know."

Max watched the movement of the lights for another minute, then turned his gaze toward Tanner. Tanner could not see Max's eyes through the grafted mirrorshades; all he could see was his own reduced and distorted reflection duplicated, one in each lens. Max took the chair down from the table, brushed off the seat, and sat in it. Sookie was right, of course. Max was *not* a good person. One hell of an understatement. But he was the way to Rattan.

Neither of them said anything. The club slowly emptied, and a crew came out on stage, setting up electrical equipment:

microphones, floor lights, wrack boxes, and other things Tanner did not recognize. The waiter appeared with a large scotch for Tanner and a stein of beer for Max. The waiter's eye patch was gone, revealing a metal and glass eye embedded in his forehead. The glass was clouded, and *did* look blind.

"On the house," the waiter said, and immediately left.

Max drank half his beer, belched long and loud, then drained the other half and belched twice more. He sat back in the chair and stared at Tanner without a word, waiting.

"I need to talk to Rattan," Tanner finally said.

Another long silence followed. Tanner did not like being unable to see Max's eyes.

"I'm not a cop anymore," Tanner said.

Max snorted. "I know that."

"I don't expect you to take me to him. Just let him know I'm looking for him. It's an old matter, and all I want to do is talk. He *will* want to talk to me, Max." He paused. "Tell him it concerns angel wings."

Max did not respond. Tanner sipped at his scotch, resisting the urge to down it all at once. Max wasn't a hell of a lot more predictable or stable than Dobler. And he was far more dangerous.

Max turned away from him and watched the crew at work on the stage. "You're fucking crazy, Tanner, you know that?"

"Will you talk to him?"

Max turned back. "Got a pen?"

Tanner gave him his pen, and Max wrote on the back of the beer coaster. He slid the pen and coaster across the table.

"Tomorrow night, at exactly the time and place written there, you show up. Follow the damn instructions. You won't be talking to Rattan, but I'll be there to let you know if it's possible."

Tanner pocketed the pen and coaster. "Fair enough."

Max shook his head and stood. "Tomorrow, then." He walked down to the stage, around it, and through the back door.

Carla. He could not stop thinking about her now. Tanner finished his drink, then got up to leave. A bar, he thought, a real bar. That's what he needed now. He headed for the street.

Tanner was drunk, and it wasn't helping. Why am I doing this? he asked himself. It wasn't making him feel any better, and it wasn't making him forget. Hell, he wasn't really sure he *wanted* to forget.

He was in a drinker's bar—no glowing ferns, no doo-wop neon, no lounge show entertainment. The place was dark and quiet except for the occasional clink of glass and vague muttering. The television set above the counter was on without sound, showing an old black-and-white sports movie. Taped to the corner juke was a sign: PLAY THIS ON PENALTY OF DEATH. A recurring theme, he thought. And the place was full. Every seat at the bar was taken, and most of the tables and booths were occupied. Tanner was sitting at the bar between a bald old man who stank and a middle-aged woman wearing lederhosen. He had not spoken to either one.

The bartender came by and looked into Tanner's eyes. "Another," he said. Statement, not question. Tanner nodded, and the bartender refilled his glass.

Tanner looked down at the scotch, but wasn't sure if he could drink any more. Carla. Carla never drank, but she had no problem putting anything else into her body: pills, needles, smoke, inhalers, injectors. Whenever he was with her, Tanner had felt helpless, unable to do anything except watch her, try to keep her from lurching in front of cars, crashing through plate glass, or taking a header down a flight of stairs.

And then the day came when she pumped too much of the shit into herself and stopped her own heart. Dead. Twenty-six and dead. Accident or deliberate, he never knew. It was, he came to believe, an irrelevant distinction. She was fucked up, and she was dead.

That was why he had become a cop, and why he had gone into Narcotics. A personal crusade, save the world, save people like Carla from themselves. What a dumbfuck. It had not taken long for him to realize the absurdity and hopelessness of it. But it had taken years of swimming in the shit, and Freeman's death, to finally give it up.

But Carla. Late morning, early afternoon, that had been the best time. After she worked through her hangover but before she started in again. Her eyes clear and smile bright, her laughter clean and real. Her skin warm and firm, with color. Her tongue and lips delicious. Her body wrapped around him, her arms and hands and thighs and breasts . . .

Christ.

The bartender came by again, looked at Tanner, and said, "Another?" This time there was some question.

Tanner looked down, saw he'd emptied his glass without realizing it, then looked back at the bartender. "I'm not unconscious yet, am I?"

The bartender refilled his glass.

Tanner woke with cotton-mouth and a clouded head. He lay on the futon in Rachel's extra room, fully clothed, with no clear memory of getting here from the bar. He thought he remembered some kind of bouncing ride, sprawled out on the back of a cart, something like that. Surprisingly, he had no headache.

He got up and wandered through the apartment. It was one in the afternoon, and the place was empty. Rachel was either gone or locked in her bedroom.

Tanner shaved and showered and put on clean clothes. In the kitchen he ate two pieces of dry toast while making coffee. The heat was oppressive, the humidity so high there was a sheen of moisture on his arms and face. Breathing was like being in a sauna.

When the coffee was done he poured a cup and took it out onto the platform and sat on the bench. The narrow strip of shade wasn't any comfort. He drank the coffee steadily, not really thinking about anything. In the window across the way he could see two naked women dancing together, holding each other tightly. Street sounds, floating down from over the building, were muted.

He finished the coffee, went back inside for another cup, then returned to the bench. The women were still dancing. His head felt clearer now and he let himself think about the night before. Stupid, he told himself. Get completely drunk like that in the Tenderloin. And for what? It didn't change anything. All that was over, years ago. Fifteen years. She was dead. She was dead yesterday, and she would still be dead tomorrow. Nothing new.

Tanner set down the coffee, put his head in his hands, and quietly wept.

NINETEEN

TANNER DID NOT like the feel of the place. He stood at the end of a long, windowless corridor of concrete. Pale blue fluorescents hummed and flickered overhead. The door behind him, solid metal, had locked automatically when he closed it, so there was no way back.

Just after midnight, as instructed, Tanner had entered the Dutch East India Company, a store specializing in exotic electronic imports: head juicers, spastic vibrators, mind tuners, orgone generators, spitzers, spinal frequencers, bone boomers. The sales clerk, wearing electronic wrist and neck collars, led Tanner through the back rooms, then pointed him to the door, which was now locked behind him. Nothing else to do, he thought. He moved forward.

His footsteps echoed off the concrete walls. There were no doors, nothing to break the surface of the walls except an occasional featureless panel of shiny metal. No one appeared, and he could hear nothing but the hum of the lights and the echoes of his own footsteps.

At the end of the corridor was a narrow opening in the left wall. Tanner stepped through it into a tiny cubicle as featureless as the corridor. A metal panel slid across the opening, slamming tightly shut. He tried pushing and pulling at it, though he knew it would not open. Nothing. Tanner stood and waited.

Then he heard the quiet hiss of gas. He looked down and saw the faint signs of air movement—eddying dust—near tiny vents, though the gas itself was invisible. He did not move. His lungs quit working for a few moments, connections broken. He wanted to shout at Max that he was being absurd and melodramatic. He also wanted to bang and kick at the door. He fought down both urges. Breath came finally, halting, then regular, taking the odorless gas into his lungs. There was nothing he could do, except hope that the gas was meant to put him to sleep, not death.

A few more deep breaths, struggling for calm. Tanner sat on the floor and waited, wanting nothing more now than to awaken from sleep one more time.

And he did awaken. Tied to a chair. The glare and heat of the sun in his face. Max seated in another chair a few feet away, mirrorshades brightly reflecting the light.

"Good morning," Max said.

Tanner turned his head from the glare, blinking rapidly. They had him next to the window, directly in the sunlight. Eyes turned away from it, his vision adjusted and he could see the rest of his surroundings. The room was small and unfurnished; Red Giant stood in the middle of the room, head and upper body in shadow, mirrorshades directed at Tanner. He did not say a word. Tanner had the feeling the duo's roles were now reversed—here, Red Giant would remain silent, and Max would do all the talking.

Tanner looked back at Max. He had to keep his eyes partly closed against the glare. "Why are you doing this?" he asked. He tried to keep his voice calm and even.

"Questions," Max said. "And then I may kill you."

"Did you talk to Rattan? He'll want to talk to me, Max, he'll want to hear this."

Max nodded slowly. "I imagine he would."

"Did you *talk* to him, for Christ's sake?"

Max snorted. "If I ever do talk to him again, one of us will be dead by the end of the conversation."

Jesus Christ, Tanner thought, have I ever fucked up.

Max cocked his head. "You really didn't know, did you?"

Tanner shook his head. "I still don't."

Max grinned. "We had a parting of the ways. A difference of opinion. A contretemps." He paused, leaning forward. "I tried to kill the motherfucker, and I missed, and he knows." Max leaned back. "Now, what I want to know is what you, and the cops, and Rattan have going."

"Christ, Max. I told you I wasn't a cop anymore. You said you knew."

"And I still know, but that doesn't mean shit. You and Rattan and the cops are running something, and I want to know what it is."

"I don't know what you're talking about, Max, believe me." He *didn't*, but he began to wonder about it. "What I need to talk to Rattan about, it's old business. It's personal, it's got nothing to do with cops."

Max slowly shook his head. "You don't get it, do you, Tanner?" Max leaned forward again. "I *will* kill you. I got no problem with that."

Tanner breathed in deeply, and slowly let it out. "I get it, Max. But I don't know a thing about it. Christ, Rattan killed two cops, they aren't going to have anything to do with him."

Max erupted from the chair and lunged forward, but stopped with his face just a few inches from Tanner's. "I don't want to hear that kind of shit, motherfucker!" He straightened and turned to Red Giant. "Bring her in."

Red Giant left the room. Christ, now what? Tanner thought. He was having trouble breathing again, and it wasn't because of the ropes. He wished he *did* have something to tell Max. "Not a good person," Sookie had said. No shit. How the hell was he going to convince Max he didn't know anything?

Max paced the room, not talking. Tanner wanted to say something, try to get Max to understand, but he could not think of a thing to say that wasn't just as likely to make things worse. Try telling him about the Chain Killer, Rattan's three-year-old message? Shit. He closed his eyes and waited.

The door opened and closed. Tanner opened his eyes and turned to see Red Giant leading a woman across the room. Tanner did not know who she was. She was gagged, her hands bound behind her back. Strands of her blond hair were plastered to the sweat on her face. She looked strong, but she hung limply in Red Giant's grip, and her eyes were dead with despair. She had given up, and seeing Tanner did not, apparently, give her renewed hope.

Red Giant pushed her into the chair Max had been using and tied her to it. Max turned his gaze to Tanner.

"*She's* looking for Rattan, too," Max said. "And not for the killings. She's a cop, the two of you are both looking for Rattan, and you tell me there's nothing going on."

There probably *was* something going on, Tanner thought, but he had no idea what it was.

"For Christ's sake," Tanner said, "I don't even know her."

Max went crazy again, stomping across the floor, shoving his face into Tanner's. "What *is* this shit from you?" He dug a wad of paper from his back pocket. "And what is *this*?" He unwadded the paper and held it in front of Tanner's face. It was the note Lucy Chen had given him with Francie Miller's name and address. "You don't fucking know her?"

Jesus, this was Francie Miller? Man, they were both in deep, deep shit. He looked at the woman, who gazed emptily back at him. "No," Tanner said. "I don't know her. I've never seen her before. It was just a name someone gave me, said she could help out if I got into trouble."

Max slowly shook his head, crumpling the paper and dropping it to the floor. "Well, Tanner, you're in trouble, but I don't think she's going to be much help." He backed away and looked at Red Giant. "Hand it."

Red Giant withdrew a knife from a sheath strapped to his belt and handed it to Max. Max took the knife, approached Francie Miller, and put the tip of the blade against her throat. She blinked once, and her eyes widened, coming back to life. But with fear. Max looked back at Tanner. "I am not fucking around here, Tanner. And I want some answers."

Before Tanner could say a thing, Max jammed the knife deep into Francie Miller's throat. Blood gushed, Francie lurched violently backward as Max let go and retreated, leaving the knife in her throat. She hit the ground, her legs kicked, her body jerked spasmodically for several moments, and Tanner could see the blood running and spattering across the floor, the knife flipping free.

Jesus.

He was a dead man.

He didn't have much time. A minute, maybe two. He opened up and shut down, letting pictures and thoughts click through his mind. Knife on the floor. No. Legs and feet. Blood. The window. How high above the street? Didn't matter. Max standing over the woman, watching the final spasms. Lower legs free enough?

Only a foot from the window, it was low, wouldn't take much. Try not to land headfirst on the street. Now or die, man. Go.

Tanner leaned forward, lifting the chair from the floor. He dropped slightly, then lunged sideways at the window, closing his eyes. Glass shattered, hip hit the sill, he fell outward, through the glass, glass slicing skin, then out the window. He hit metal immediately, twisted, bumped, started down, then jolted to a stop. He opened his eyes.

Tanner was three floors above the street, upside down. A leg of the chair was caught in the tangled remnants of a fire escape. He glanced at the shattered window just a few feet above him, waiting to see Max's face. Jesus.

He shook himself, rocked and jolted, side to side, up and down. Harder. The chair leg cracked, then finally broke, and he dropped.

Tanner tried to twist himself as he fell, legs kicking. He hit the street hard on his side, a wall of pain jolting through him. A burst of silver glitter, then he couldn't see anything at all for a few moments. The darkness cleared away, and he saw people standing over him. He wanted to pass out, but he was afraid to. If he passed out now, he would probably die; Max would find him and he would die. He didn't know if he could even free himself from the rope and chair. The pain was a pounding vibration jamming through him, like bone boomers strapped all over his body. He wanted Rachel's Dilaudid.

Then Sookie's face appeared above him, and she dropped to her knees. There was a man with her, a gaunt spikehead with clear, bright wide eyes. The spikes of twisted skin seemed to move across his forehead.

"I told you to stay away from him," Sookie said.

Tanner tried to speak, but couldn't get anything out.

"We've got to get him the hell out of here *now*," the spikehead said.

"We'll take care of you," Sookie told him. "Don't worry."

For some reason Tanner found her voice completely reassuring. When he felt their hands on him, he closed his eyes and let himself slip away.

TWENTY

SOOKIE LOOKED UP, saw Max's face in the shattered window. Mirrorshades. Who knew what he was seeing?

"Come on!" Mixer said.

Sookie and Mixer grabbed Tanner's arms and shoulders and lifted.

"Don't move him," someone in the crowd said. "You know, in case of spinal—"

"Shut the fuck up!" Mixer said. Then, to Sookie, "Let's move it."

They half carried, half dragged Tanner, pieces of rope and broken chair still hanging from him. Sookie watched his face, his closed eyes. It had to hurt.

They pushed through the crowd, around a corner. Mixer let go, and Sookie fell with all the weight. Mixer jumped a pedal cart going by, jamming it to a stop, almost knocking the driver off.

Sookie was back on her feet by the time Mixer got the cart backed up, and they loaded Tanner into the storage well. Sookie stayed with him while Mixer hung on behind the driver. "Go!" he yelled.

The driver swore and pumped, and the cart moved slowly forward. Too slow, Sookie thought, looking back. She didn't see Max or Uwe, but she was sure they were coming. Anyone else following? Hard to tell.

The cart picked up speed. Mixer yelled in the driver's ear, and the driver whacked Mixer on the side of the head. The driver was a stocky woman with short hair and a necklace tattooed around her neck. She kept calling Mixer names, and he kept shouting directions at her. Sookie couldn't keep up with it all, but it seemed that the driver was following Mixer's instructions, zigzagging from one street to another.

They turned a corner, and Mixer had the driver stop. Mixer and Sookie pulled Tanner off the cart, dragging him against the wall. Mixer glared at the driver and pointed down the street. "Keep going, bitch!"

The woman nodded. "You owe me for this, you goddamn spikehead. I know your face." She pushed off, gaining speed more quickly now.

Mixer unlocked a metal door, pushed it open, and they dragged Tanner through. Mixer jammed the door shut, cutting off all light.

"All right," Mixer said. "We're safe for now. No way they'll find us here."

"Where we going to take him?" Sookie asked. She couldn't see Mixer in the dark, but she could smell him—something like sweat and sawdust. Tanner smelled like pain. She held on to one of his hands. "It's a good thing we followed him," she said.

"I know a place." Mixer laughed. "I know a lot of places." He lit a cigarette, and the match light showed a small passage empty except for the three of them. Mixer blew out the match; his cigarette glowed. "Let me think a minute." The glow moved back and forth in the darkness, as if he were shaking his head. "Every time you show up, Sookie, something like this happens."

"My life is too weird," she said.

Mixer laughed again. "Yeah, no shit. But wait'll you grow up. It's only going to get weirder."

"Great." She sat on the floor beside Tanner and waited for Mixer to make a decision.

TWENTY-ONE

TANNER CAME TO in a narrow, windowless room. He lay on a cot, surrounded by concrete walls, a lamp at his head, a tiny fan whirring in the far corner. The door was closed, the air stifling despite the fan.

He remembered waking several times, disoriented from dull pain and drugs. He remembered fluids trickled into his mouth; he remembered being walked down a hall to a toilet. Someone had been keeping him sedated. He didn't know if that was good or bad.

Tanner sat up slowly, a little woozy but otherwise feeling all right. He was wearing a pair of light cotton pants, but nothing else. His left wrist was heavily taped and in the dim light from the lamp he could see dark, yellowing bruises on his arms and chest, particularly on his left side; also a number of cuts that seemed to be healing. Overall, though, he did not appear to be too badly hurt. Everything except his wrist moved freely and without much pain.

There was a plastic pitcher of water next to the lamp, and Tanner, looking at it, realized how thirsty he was; his mouth was dry, yet gummy. He drank deeply from the pitcher, and the water went to his head, almost like alcohol. He had to lean back against the wall to keep from losing his balance. He drank some more, then set down the pitcher.

He rose to his feet, took the five steps to the door, and tried the handle. Locked. Had Max got hold of him? Tanner did not think so. He thought he remembered seeing Sookie during his brief conscious periods, and the spikehead who had been with

96

her. Also some other guy, a thin unshaven man, gaunt face bent over him. Who the hell was that?

Tanner looked around the tiny room. Nothing but the cot, the lamp, the water, the fan. No clothes. No money, no credit chip. And no way out. He banged on the door a few times, but got no response. He would have to just sit and wait. That was all right. Waiting was bearable, it was something he had learned to do—wait without going crazy. He could do it again.

He spent some time pacing the room, then did some stretching, working through the pain in his muscles. He sat on the cot, breathing heavily. The pacing had tired him, but the muscle pain felt good. He sat with his back against the cool concrete wall, waiting and thinking. He thought a lot about Francie Miller. He tried not to, but the images kept returning—Max driving the knife into her throat; blood; Francie arching violently, chair driven back and over; Francie jerking spasmodically on the floor; blood again; the knife flipping free; Max's shaded eyes.

When no one appeared after an hour or so, Tanner lay out on the cot and slept.

He dreamed of Freeman again: the hot, dark hallway; the fat man with the smell of tuna; the gun at Freeman's face, the explosion of blood and flesh and bone. This time, though, as Tanner ran down the hall, before the second gunshot, he tripped over Francie Miller's body. He tumbled to the floor, somehow twisting around so his face was looking into hers, staring at the knife still embedded in her throat. Her eyes stared back at him.

Then he awakened.

A junkie stood over him, staring into Tanner's face. Tanner could see needle marks in the guy's neck. A gaunt, unshaven face, glittering eyes. The face he had seen before.

"I'm your doctor," the junkie said. He grinned, retreating a couple of steps.

Tanner lay without moving for a minute, watching the junkie, who continued to grin. Tanner slowly sat up, saw a medical kit on the floor beside the cot, and realized the junkie was serious.

"I'm a hell of a doctor when I'm not strung out or just shot," the junkie said. He shrugged. "I fixed you up, and you're going to be fine." Another shrug, then he put out his hand. "My name's Leo."

Tanner did not shake Leo's hand. "Why have you been sedating me?" he asked.

Leo dropped his hand. "To keep you quiet. This room's safe enough, but . . ." He shrugged again. "Didn't want you crying out."

"Why would I cry out?"

"Pain." Still another shrug. "Nightmares."

Tanner did not respond. He didn't remember any nightmares other than the one he'd just had, but then he didn't really remember much of anything after hitting the street.

"You have a small fracture in your left wrist," Leo said. "It doesn't need to be casted, just taped like that to keep down excess movement. Couple weeks should do it. Other than that, nothing serious. Bruises and abrasions, minor lacerations."

"I want my clothes," Tanner said.

"Mixer has them," Leo said.

"Get them."

"He's not here." Another shrug. The shrugging, Tanner thought, was like a facial tic with this guy. "He'll be back soon, half hour, something."

Tanner nodded, more to himself than to the junkie. He stood. "I've got to piss."

Leo looked at the door, then back at Tanner, but didn't say anything.

"You holding me prisoner?" Tanner asked.

"Of course not. It's just . . . I think Mixer wants to talk to you."

"The spikehead?"

Leo nodded.

"I'm coming back. Where the hell am I going to go without clothes?"

Leo laughed. "In this part of town, you could go far." He shrugged once more, then gestured at the door. "Take a right, second door on the left."

Tanner crossed the room, opened the door, and stepped out into the corridor. Sputtering fluorescent lights, spaced irregularly along the ceiling, cast a shifting, fragmented illumination. The corridor stretched into darkness in both directions as the

lights gave out. Tanner was fairly certain he was underground.
He went right, following the junkie's directions. The cement
floor was warm under his bare feet, but the flickering lights
hurt his eyes. Second door on the left. Tanner stopped, pulled
open the door.

A woman sat on the toilet inside the small bathroom, trou-
sers bunched on the floor. She looked up at him, her expression
even and unalarmed.

"Sorry," Tanner said. He backed out and closed the door.
She had not seemed at all embarrassed. Tanner stood against
the opposite wall and waited, listening to the sounds of the
corridor. A nearly inaudible hum emanated from the walls,
and now that he wasn't moving he could feel a slight vibration
in the floor. The hum and vibration ceased for a moment, then
resumed. Tanner noticed now that there was graffiti on the
walls—the lettering was tiny, and not inked but etched into
the concrete with acid pens. ABOVE GROUND RADIO. LOVE
IS NOTHING MORE THAN BIO-HYDRAULICS. BE RIGHT BACK—
GODOT.

The bathroom door opened and the woman came out. Her
blouse was transparent, and Tanner found himself staring at
her breasts—one was only half the size of the other, but they
seemed, somehow, to match. A design job, he figured. He
looked up at her face.

The woman was staring at his crotch. Only fair, he decided.
She stared at it, he thought, as if she could see through the
pants. Then she tipped her head up to meet his gaze.

"It's not augmented, is it?" she asked.

"No."

She shook her head slowly. "You're missing out. And so is
she, whoever she is." Then she smiled, said, "Bye, Slick," and
headed down the hall. Soon she was no more than a shadow
moving in and out of the sputtering lights, footsteps growing
faint. Then she was beyond the lights and gone.

Tanner opened the bathroom door and stepped inside. The
room was brightly lit with silver-gray fluorescents, and was
far cleaner than he had expected. The porcelain was white and
almost shiny, the metal fixtures polished and bright. A large
mirror above the sink reflected his image from the waist up. In
the fluorescent light the bruises around his ribs looked worse,
and he could see more of them now. A cut on his neck had

opened, and a thread of dark red blood oozed slowly from it. His face didn't look too bad, though he needed a shave. Three days, he guessed.

Tanner moved to the toilet, raised the seat, and stood there, waiting. Nothing happened. He could feel the pressure of his bladder, but nothing came. Then there was a brief, sharp pain, and the stream burst forth. After the initial jolt, the pain eased, until it was nearly gone. When he was finished he felt empty, and a little dizzy. He flushed the toilet, then went to the sink and splashed cool water across his face. He stared at his reflection for a few moments, watching the water drip from his skin, then left and walked back.

Sookie and the spikehead were in the room with Leo when Tanner walked in. Sookie sat on the cot next to Tanner's clothes, his shoes on the floor at her feet. Tanner gazed at her, pain and memories of Carla surfacing once again.

He turned away and looked at the spikehead. Over his eyes, the spikehead was wearing a contraption of bamboo, something like glasses. A weave of bamboo formed eye shutters that slid back and forth on tracks across his eyes like moving cages. His forehead was studded with twenty-five or thirty crust-tipped spikes of twisted skin.

Leo approached Tanner, looked him over. "That cut'll be all right," he said, pointing at Tanner's neck. "Any blood in the urine?"

"Not that I noticed."

Leo nodded. "Good. There was a little at first. Fall like that's hard on the kidneys."

"I'm going to get dressed and leave," Tanner said.

Leo shrugged, glanced at the spikehead.

"We risked a lot saving your ass," the spikehead said. "I want to know why."

"Your name Mixer?" Tanner asked. The spikehead nodded, then Tanner said, "You risked it because you're a nice guy."

Mixer tipped his head forward, looking at Tanner through flicking shutters of bamboo. "No, I'm not. So what are you doing that's got Max after you? Got a right to know why I'm taking chances."

Tanner shook his head. "No, you don't. I didn't ask for your help."

The shutters flicked sideways; a twist formed on Mixer's lips. A smile? "You'd be dead if we hadn't."

"Maybe so. I appreciate what you did. But it's my business, and it's going to stay that way."

Sookie stood, stepped to Mixer's side. "Maybe we can help," she said. "Mixer knows the Tenderloin. He knows the runners and the grounders, and he knows . . ."

Mixer reached out and put his hand gently but firmly over Sookie's mouth. She tried to bite him and he pulled his hand away, but she did not say any more.

Tanner walked to the cot and dressed. His clothes, though torn or frayed in spots, were clean. His I.D. packet was, surprisingly, intact, but there was no money, and the credit chip was gone.

"There wasn't any money when we found you," Sookie said. "Really. We wouldn't take anything."

Tanner glanced at Leo, then turned to Mixer. "And no credit chip?"

Mixer shook his head, and they both looked at Leo. The junkie shrugged once more. "What the hell am I going to do with your credit chip? I don't have your eyes, do I?"

Mixer's bamboo shutters clicked several times. "Sell it back to the originating streetbank for two cents on the dollar."

No shrugging this time, just a set expression on the junkie's face. "I wouldn't do that."

Mixer turned to Tanner. "I believe him."

Tanner nodded. "I'm leaving."

"All right," Mixer said. "We'll show you a way out."

"I'll find my own way."

"I know a way'll bring you up outside the Tenderloin."

"What if I want to stay inside?"

"Do you?"

Tanner shook his head. "Not right now. But just get me up to the street, I can get out just fine."

"Not a good idea," Mixer responded. "You've got Max after you. Remember?"

"I have to face that sooner or later."

"Why? You coming back in?"

Now it was Tanner's turn to shrug. "I don't know. Probably."

"Fine. Then face it later. For now let's do it my way."

Tanner hesitated. There was something to be said for Mixer's thinking, and he was getting tired of arguing with the guy. "All right," he said.

Mixer started toward the door, then stopped, looking at Tanner. "Maybe Sookie's right. Maybe we *can* help you."

Tanner was going to shake his head, but stopped himself, thinking about the offer. Mixer did seem to know his way around the Tenderloin, and he and Sookie had pulled Tanner out of some deep shit. Tanner did not have to reveal much, nothing about the Chain Killer, nothing about *why* he was looking for Rattan. And, Tanner had to admit to himself, he didn't have much else at this point. In fact, he didn't have shit. But he hesitated, looking at Leo.

Leo shook his head. "I don't want anything to do with it. I'm gone." He retrieved his medical kit and left.

"I'm looking for Rattan," Tanner said.

Mixer rolled his head to the left, gaze swinging toward the ceiling. "Je*sus*, I don't even want to *know* you." He looked back at Tanner, the bamboo shutters clicking rapidly. How the *hell* did he do that? Tanner wondered. "Forget I asked you anything," Mixer said.

Tanner nodded. "Forgotten."

Mixer shook his head, dug his hands into his pocket, and pulled out several bills, then handed them to Tanner. "You'll need a few bucks to get you wherever."

Tanner took the money, pocketed it.

Mixer led the way, with Tanner next and Sookie following. The corridor was empty, and they headed left, gradually moving into a gray darkness as they moved beyond the lights. The corridor curved sharply, grew still darker. Tanner could barely make out Mixer in front of him.

Mixer stopped, slipped a plastic card into a slot, then punched a sequence of numbers into a glowing, recessed keypad. Metal slid aside, revealing a narrow, brightly lit passage, one wall metal, the other concrete. Tanner and Sookie went through, then Mixer followed, sealing the doorway behind them. Mixer took the lead again.

As they moved along the passage, Tanner thought about Mixer's question—"You coming back in?" He had to, didn't he? There was no other way to find Rattan, he knew that. But it wouldn't do anyone any good if he got killed while looking.

And he thought about Carla. Whenever they stopped or changed from one passage to another, he would turn around and look at Sookie. Every time he did, the pain twisted in his chest, building steadily. One time, as he silently stared at her, Sookie held her hands out in exasperation and blurted, "What?" He did not have an answer for her.

They shifted to a metal-walled passage with dim, sputtering lights and a ceiling so low they were forced to proceed on all fours. Tanner was wearing down, and finally he called out to Mixer and stopped. He felt dizzy, queasy, short of breath. He sat with his back against the warm metal wall and breathed deeply. Mixer squatted a few feet ahead while Sookie sat in a lotus position at Tanner's side. Mixer lit a cigarette.

"Don't," Tanner said. "Unless you want me puking all over you."

"*Jeez!*" Sookie waved at Mixer. "Put it out, *I'm* the one closest to him."

Mixer crushed the cigarette against the floor. He rocked on his haunches, the bamboo shutters gliding slowly, smoothly from side to side. "It's not much farther," he said.

They sat awhile in silence, and with each minute's rest Tanner felt stronger, though he knew it would not last long once they resumed.

"Something I want to ask," Mixer said.

Tanner looked at him.

"You're looking for Rattan, and you go to Max?"

Tanner nodded. "I didn't know. I haven't been here in a while." He paused. "It was a mistake."

Mixer snorted. "No shit. Mistakes like that find you dead."

Tanner did not reply. There was nothing to say to that.

They resumed moving, still on all fours. The sputtering lights gave the passage a surreal cast, tiny but silent explosions of light and shadow. Several minutes later the passage began to rise, angled off to one side, then ended in a wide, circular chamber. Metal rungs were bolted into the wall leading up to the ceiling a few feet above their heads.

Mixer put his plastic card into another slot, and the metal ceiling slid back, revealing more rungs leading upward. "This'll take you right up to street level," Mixer said. "There's a grille, and to the right on the wall will be a switch that'll open it."

Tanner was breathing heavily again, and sharp pain jabbed his ribs, but he figured he could make it the rest of the way. "Where do I come out?" he asked.

"Tornado Alley."

"Terrific. What time of day is it?"

"About two in the morning. Want to wait for daylight?"

Tanner shook his head. "Night's not much worse than day, really. Better, maybe. Most of them are asleep."

Mixer smiled. "The smell's worse."

Tanner nodded. The pain in his ribs had eased a bit, and he put a hand on one of the rungs. "Thanks for the help."

"Sure thing," Mixer said. "But I'd forget about looking for Rattan if I were you."

Tanner sighed, then looked at Sookie. The ache swelled in his chest again, worse in some ways than the physical pain of his bruised ribs. "Good-bye, Sookie. Thanks."

She remained silent a few moments, then looked away and said, "Bye."

Tanner turned back to the rungs and started climbing.

By the time he was a few feet above the chamber, the smell reached him. Unwashed bodies, mainly, mixed with the ammonia odor of piss and traces of alcohol and Sterno. People who hadn't bathed in weeks, or months, even years. Tornado Alley.

The stench increased as he climbed, making him queasy in the close confines of the vertical shaft. The shaft opened in front of him, elbowing horizontally for a few feet to the metal grille. Tanner crawled forward and looked out through the bars.

Tornado Alley wasn't really an alley. It was a block-long strip of empty lots on both sides of a barricaded street, lit at night by half a dozen cords of phosphor strung between surrounding buildings, and now occupied by several thousand sleeping forms. It had acquired its name a few years before when a city politician, vowing to clean it out along with other street-people havens, had said it looked as though a tornado had swept through the city, sucked up all the derelicts and homeless, then dumped them all in one place—Tornado Alley. The politician hadn't cleaned up anything, of course, and the city pretty much left Tornado Alley alone. There was no other place to put these people anyway. The city certainly was not going to find housing for them.

Tanner felt for the grille switch, pressed it, and the grille clicked ajar. He pushed it open, crawled through, and stepped down onto a tiny space of cement between two sleeping, stinking bodies, one of them snoring heavily. Tanner pushed back the grille, pressing until it clicked shut.

The stench was almost overwhelming in the heat, and he stood motionless for a minute, trying to get his bearings. During the winter Tornado Alley would be ablaze with trash-can fires, but at the peak of summer only a few small flames flickered—Sterno cooking fires. There was nothing else but body after body, most keeping a little space between themselves and the bodies around them.

Tanner worked his way through the Alley, carving out a wandering path among the sleeping bodies. The Alley was fairly quiet, silence broken only by snores, mutterings, and occasional stifled cries. Once someone clutched at his ankle, but he freed it easily—the person's grip was weak, sickly— and resumed his progress.

When he reached the boundary of the Alley, Tanner looked up and down the street, trying to decide where to go next. Finding a cab in this part of the city, this time of night, would be impossible. Walking back to his apartment was too far and too dangerous. Besides, he wasn't so sure going back to his place was a good idea—Max almost certainly could learn where he lived.

A transient hotel? Not a great idea, either. Who lived around here? The only people he could think of were Hannah and Rossi. Tanner sighed heavily. He knew they would take him in, no matter what time of night it was. But the idea depressed him. Still. It was his best option; he did not want to stay out on the streets any longer than was necessary, and it was better than sleeping in Tornado Alley.

It was a short walk, a total of three blocks to a five-story building on Larkin. Tanner pushed Hannah and Rossi's doorbell, waited a minute, then pressed again. He pressed it a third time, and Hannah's sleepy, gravelly voice came over the intercom.

"Who is it?"

"It's Tanner."

"Tanner who?"

"Hannah, it's Louis."

A pause, then, "It's three in the fucking morning."

"I need a place to drop for the night."

Another pause, then the door buzzed several times, locks and bolts thunking back. Tanner pushed the door open and stepped into the building. He climbed the stairs to the third floor, walked down the hall, and knocked on Hannah and Rossi's door.

The door opened and Hannah, wearing only a long T-shirt, stepped back to let him in. She was in her early forties, but looked older, worn out and worn down. Living with Rossi had done that to her.

"So nice to fucking see you," she said, closing the door. "You look like shit."

The front room was lit by a floor lamp. Rossi was passed out on the sofa, one leg drooped over the edge, surrounded by piles of cracker crumbs. He reeked of gin. Rossi had been a cop once, too. He hadn't quit, though. He'd been shit-canned. The force put up with a lot of drinking these days, but Rossi had gone above and beyond the call too many times. He had fucked up too many times. Tanner knew he still did.

"You can sleep with me," Hannah said. "You'll never move him off the couch."

They went into the bedroom, and Hannah immediately got into bed, her back to Tanner. In the light from the front room, Tanner undressed, then climbed into bed with his own back to Hannah's. They both shifted positions until their backs were firmly pressed together. Neither said a word. Tanner closed his eyes and fell immediately asleep.

TWENTY-TWO

TANNER WOKE TO the sounds of vomiting. Bright orange light slashed through the window blinds, ragged strips across the bed. He was alone in the room, the bed rumpled but empty beside him. He felt better than the night before, but not really rested. He lay in the late-morning heat without moving, listening to Rossi.

The vomiting sounds ceased; they were followed by the toilet flushing, then water running in the sink. A minute later Rossi stumbled out of the bathroom, came around the corner, and stopped in the bedroom doorway, grinning sickly at Tanner. He was barefoot, wearing jeans and no shirt, belly drooping over his belt, holding cigarettes and matches in his left hand. He looked even older than Hannah.

"Hey, Tanner. You haven't been screwing my wife, have you?"

Tanner did not answer. He was fairly sure Rossi wasn't serious. He sat up, wincing at the stab of pain in his ribs. "Good morning, Rossi."

Rossi coughed several times, then lit a cigarette. "You haven't been by in a while," he said.

"No."

"Maybe you should be," Rossi said.

"What?"

"Screwing my wife." He shrugged, looked out the window. "You might as well. I mean, *somebody* should be."

Jesus, Tanner thought, I don't need this now. "Is Hannah still here?"

Rossi shook his head, still looking out the window. "She went to work." He turned back to Tanner. "I'm going to take a shower."

"Can I use your phone?"

"Sure. I think Hannah's paid the bill." He turned, staggered back into the bathroom. Tanner heard a spluttering hiss of water, then a steady spray.

Tanner got up and dressed, then went out to the front room. Gin smell still hung in the air along with stale cigarette smoke. He stepped into the kitchen, hoping to see some coffee already made, but all he saw were stacks of dishes in the sink, glasses all over the counter, and half a dozen open cracker boxes. Tanner returned to the front room, sat in the stuffed chair next to the phone, and picked up the receiver.

His first call was to Carlucci. The dispatcher patched him through to Carlucci's comm unit, and he keyed in his old priority code and Rossi's phone number. He hung up and waited. Two minutes later, Carlucci called.

"Tanner?"

"Yeah."

"Figured it was you. The priority code came up blank. I'll set up a new one for you."

"We need to meet," Tanner said.

"We sure as hell do. I was hoping to hear from you sooner. Some shit's gone down in the Tenderloin you should know about."

"I probably already do, but yeah. I've been off-line for a couple of days."

"Where are you now? Inside or out?"

"Out. Rossi's place."

There was a pause, then, "How's Hannah doing?"

"All right, I guess. Surviving." Tanner looked toward the bathroom, listening to the shower sounds. Carlucci wouldn't ask about Rossi. Carlucci had no tolerance for drunks, especially if they were cops. Especially when it was Rossi.

"You know where Widgie's is?" Carlucci asked. "It's not far from you."

"Yeah, just a few blocks. Meet there?"

"Yes. An hour okay?"

"Make it two. I've got a few things to do, and I've got to get something to eat."

"Two hours, then. I'll see you."

"Right."

Tanner hung up. The shower was still going. He should call Rachel, make sure she was okay. Max must have the card with her name and address. Tanner called information, but there was no listing for Rachel, so he called Alexandra.

"This is Tanner," he said when she answered.

"About time you called."

"Why?"

"Rachel called me. Said she hadn't seen you for three days, and that an albino dwarf and a redheaded giant had come to see her, asking about you."

"Jesus. She all right?"

"Oh yeah, what were they going to do, beat up a cripple? She told them the truth, that you'd stayed a couple of days, then disappeared without a word. They took your stuff and left her alone. But I don't think it'd be a good idea to go back to her place."

"No." Images of Francie Miller surfaced, then sputtered away. At least Rachel was all right. "I'm not even going back to my own place for a while."

"You've got another problem," Alexandra said.

"What's that?"

"Connie."

"Connie?"

"Yes. She showed up in the building courtyard two days ago, waiting for you. I told her you weren't around, but she wouldn't leave. I've put her up in my place, but she won't go home until she's had a chance to talk to you."

"Christ." Tanner rubbed at his face, at the rough stubble on his cheeks.

"She's a good kid, Louis. I've spent a lot of time with her the last two days, and I really like her."

Tanner sighed. "Yeah, she is, but right now she's being a goddamn pain in the ass."

"Louis . . ."

"I know, I know." He paused, closing his eyes. "Is she there now?"

"Yes. Will you talk to her?"

"Sure."

Tanner sank back in the overstuffed chair, gazing up at the

ceiling. The plaster was heavily cracked, the paint peeling away; someone had painted the cracks blue so they looked like rivers on a map.

"Hi, Louis."

"Hello, Connie." He wanted to ask her what the hell she thought she was doing, but he didn't think that would be very constructive. Instead, he waited for her to take the initiative.

"I need to talk to you, Louis." Her tone was even and self-assured, without a hint of pleading.

"Now is not a good time," Tanner said. Jesus, he thought, what an idiotic thing to say. "What I mean is, I'm in the middle of some things, I've got too much going on. Give me a couple of weeks, until I can finish things here, then I'll come down to San Jose and talk to you. Take a day, spend all the time we need together."

"Don't patronize me, Louis."

"I'm *not,* Connie. I'm in the middle of some complicated shit, and I just can't pull away from it. It's important."

"So is this. And I'm not going back until I see you. I just won't."

Tanner did not say anything, unsure of how to respond.

"Do you understand me, Louis?"

"Yes." He understood how damn stubborn she could be.

"Do you believe me?"

"Yes, Connie. I know you, *testa dura.*" Hard head. What his Italian grandmother had called him when he was a kid. He heard her laugh; it was a term of affection he'd had for Connie for years. "All right. But listen, it's not a good idea for me to go back to my apartment right now, so how about we meet for dinner? Alexandra can bring you."

"Okay."

"And will you go home after we talk?"

"Yes."

"Have you talked to your mom, let her know you haven't been kidnapped or anything?"

"Of course, Louis. She doesn't know where I am, but she knows I'm okay."

"All right, why don't you put Alexandra back on, and I'll see you tonight for dinner."

"Okay. Bye."

A moment later Alexandra came back on.

"So what is it?"

"Dinner at Joyce Wah's tonight. Make it seven o'clock. I'd like you to come with her, then bring her back. It's not a good idea for her to be . . ."

"I know, Louis. We'll be there."

"All right, see you then."

"*Ciao.*"

He hung up the phone and looked back up at the ceiling. Rivers in the plaster. The shower was still going. What the hell was Rossi doing?

Tanner got up and hurried into the bathroom, afraid something had happened to Rossi. The shower curtains were wrapped completely around the big old clawfoot bathtub, and the water hissed steadily behind them. Tanner pulled open the curtain. Rossi was curled up in the bottom of the tub, fast asleep and snoring under the steady shower of lukewarm water.

Tanner reached in, turned off the water. He thought about waking Rossi, but decided it wasn't worth it. Let the bastard sleep. He folded a towel, put it under Rossi's head for a pillow, then walked out.

Widgie's was something like an open-air cafe, a vast network of interconnected fire-escapes between two red brick buildings; swaying catwalks linked the fire-escape platforms across the alley, along with a seemingly random system of dumbwaiters that moved up and down among the dozen or so levels. Another network of pneumatic tubes for orders ran among the ladders and catwalks. A clear plastic dome covered the entire alley, shelter from the daily rains.

Tanner entered the alley, searched the platforms, and spotted Carlucci at one of the most isolated tables, up on the sixth or seventh level. Shit. It was going to be a climb.

A host approached Tanner to seat him, but Tanner said he was meeting someone. The host frowned, bowed, then retreated, and Tanner started up the nearest ladder.

After leaving Rossi's place, Tanner had gone to a cafe down the street for breakfast, a tiny run-down place called Maria's Kitchen, where he had an enormous, and delicious, plate of black beans, rice, eggs, and salsa. He had eaten every bit of it, including two warm tortillas, surprised at his appetite. He decided it had something to do with being alive. It was only now sinking in just how lucky he was.

Tanner stopped twice to rest on the way up, and felt exhausted by the time he reached Carlucci's table, sweating heavily in the damp heat. But the exertion and sweat felt good, almost cleansing. He dropped into the seat across from Carlucci. There was a thermal pot of coffee on the table, along with two cups. Carlucci poured a cup for Tanner, pushed it to him. Tanner was ready for coffee, something to help get his head going again.

"You look like shit," Carlucci said.

"Thanks. That's what Hannah said, too." He drank from the coffee, which was hot, but not too strong. It would help, and his stomach would survive it.

"Well, she was right. What the hell happened to you?"

"Long, painful story," Tanner said. "You won't like it."

Carlucci grimaced. "I don't guess I will." He shook his head. "You know that name I gave you? For help in the Tenderloin. Francie Miller." He breathed deeply once. "She's dead."

Tanner drank from his coffee, sipping slowly, not looking at Carlucci. "I know," he finally said, turning to face him. "I watched her die."

Carlucci didn't say anything for a long time, staring back at Tanner. When he finally spoke, his voice was quiet, almost without inflection. "Jesus . . . Christ." Another long pause, a shake of his head, then, "So tell me about it."

Tanner did. Everything from the time he entered the Tenderloin until he emerged into Tornado Alley. Carlucci listened without interruption, occasionally grimacing or shaking his head or pressing his temples, but not saying anything. When Tanner was finished, neither one of them said anything for a long time. Tanner looked around Widgie's, listening to the mix of voices, clattering dishes, dumbwaiter squeals, muffled thumps of pneumatic tubes, echoing footsteps.

"Well, shit," Carlucci eventually said. "This is real fucking progress." He leaned back and patted at his shirt pocket. "God damn it, times like this I wish I hadn't quit smoking." He set both hands on the table, stared at them for several moments, then looked up at Tanner again. "And we've got more bodies."

"How many?"

"Four. One triple, and a single."

"A single?"

"Yeah, that's a new one. Kind of strange, guy chained to himself. We pulled him out of a cistern back of a condemned warehouse." He rubbed his face with his hands. "Not typical, but it's definitely our old friend, the same mother fucker. Maybe he's just 'expanding his horizons.'" Carlucci made a harsh growling sound in his throat. "Wonderful thought."

"Are they coming faster than last time?"

"So far, looks that way. Making up for lost time, that's what Rollo says. He may have something."

Carlucci poured another cup of coffee for himself. Tanner held his own cup with both hands, tipping it from side to side, watching the dark brown liquid swirl. High above them, rain started on the plastic dome, a high, echoing clatter; at the far end of the alley, Tanner could see it coming down in sheets, a real downpour. He did not like the way any of this was going.

"What about what Max said?" Tanner asked. "Rattan and some cops working something together."

Carlucci breathed in deeply, slowly let it out. "May be true. I've heard some things the last few months. Didn't pay much attention, really, none of it seemed too likely." He paused. "No idea what it's all about, but I guess I'll have to check it out now."

"Yeah, do that. I don't like feeling like I don't know shit about what's going on. It's my ass out there, and I've already come damn close to losing it."

Carlucci nodded once. "Maybe it's not a good idea to go back in there looking for him."

Tanner gave him a brief, chopped laugh. "It's a *terrible* idea. But have you got a better one?"

Carlucci shook his head. "I tried. I even set up a private session with one of the slugs, fed him the info about you and Freeman and Rattan, anything I had."

"So what did he come up with?"

"A lot of useless bullshit, and one concrete course of action."

"Which was?"

"Find Rattan."

Tanner tried laughing. "That's fucking great. The slug boosted all that brain juice to come up with that?"

Carlucci shrugged. "You want to reconsider?"

"I'm constantly reconsidering," Tanner said. "But I'll go back in. I'll find the son of a bitch." Tanner wished he actually felt that confident.

"Where you going to stay now?" Carlucci asked.

"Probably not inside. I'll be better off now going in and out. And with Max running loose, I'll have to stay away from my apartment."

"I know it probably won't do much good, but we'll put out a warrant for Max's arrest, try to pick up the little fucker. Another goddamn cop killing." He paused, looking steadily at Tanner. "I wonder what the hell Francie was up to, trying to find Rattan."

Tanner nodded. He had asked himself the same question. One more thing he didn't know. "Trying to nail him for the cop killings?" Tanner suggested. "A boost for her career?"

Carlucci shook his head. "No, not the way it played out, something not right about the whole thing. So, where *are* you going to stay?" Carlucci asked again. "I want to be able to reach you."

"With Hannah and Rossi, probably. I'm sure they'll put me up."

Carlucci nodded. He sipped at his coffee, made a face, then poured it back into the thermal pot. He swirled the pot, poured himself a fresh cup, then poured some for Tanner. "You don't carry a gun, do you?"

Tanner shook his head.

"You should. Now, anyway."

Tanner shook his head again. "A gun wouldn't have done me a damn bit of good with Max. What I could use, though, is some cash. I'll be able to get most of the money back from the streetbank, but I'm broke until then."

Carlucci took several bills from his wallet, handed them to Tanner, who stuck them into his pocket. "I'm also trying to work up a few more grand," Carlucci said. "In case you need it."

"I hope I get the chance."

They drank their coffee in silence. Tanner listened closely to the sounds of the rain, letting it wash out all the other sounds in Widgie's. He was tired and depressed, yet somehow invigorated as well. A part of him wanted to just collapse and sleep for a few days. But another was anxious to get back into the

Tenderloin, anxious to resume his search for Rattan, anxious to *talk* to Rattan. Tanner wanted to know what the hell was going on, and what, if anything, it had to do with the Chain Killer.

"I want to meet every two or three days," Carlucci said. "We've got to stay in touch. We have *got* to keep together on this, or we'll both end up in deep shit, and you deeper than me."

Tanner nodded. "I'll call you," he said.

"You going to rest up a couple days?" Carlucci asked.

"No, I'm okay. I want to get back at it. I'm tired of hearing about more and more dead bodies."

"Yeah, well just make sure yours isn't one of them."

Tanner smiled. "Good thinking. I'll keep it in mind."

TWENTY-THREE

SOOKIE FOLLOWED HIM all night and day. Behind him up the rungs and out into Tornado Alley. Creeping along a few feet back, silent and on all fours, crabbing among the bodies. What a stink!

Worse, though, was waiting all night across from the apartment building. He went in and didn't come out, so she had to wait. She wedged herself onto a second-floor ledge directly across the street, jammed between a window frame and a sewage pipe. It rained once. Noises from the pipe all night; wood jammed into her side. She didn't sleep much.

Morning, and nothing. Lots of other people came out of the apartment, but not Tanner. Maybe she'd missed him? She crawled down from the ledge, her ribs and knees aching, walked around, working it out. She had to keep moving to stay away from the pervs who kept after her.

Then, close to noon, he came out, and she followed him to Maria's Kitchen. Hung out while he sat inside and ate. Crouched behind a trash bin, she could see him in the window. Her stomach twisted in on itself, a few sharp pains. A long time since she'd eaten, but she was afraid of losing him.

On to Widgie's, more than an hour in there, then back to the apartment for a couple more hours. What was he doing in there, taking a sleep? Maybe. And what was *she* doing out here, waiting for him? Goofball.

Finally, early evening, he came back out again. She followed him over to Chinatown and a restaurant on the edge of the Tenderloin. Joyce Wah's. He met two people in front. A very

116

tall, long-haired woman, beautiful in a dark shimmer coat. And a girl wearing white jeans, brown jacket, and blinking sneakers. Fifteen or sixteen years old, Sookie thought. Tanner hugged the girl, and that made Sookie feel funny. Then they all went inside.

She waited a few minutes, then went in and ordered some food to go. Three small cartons and a pair of chopsticks. She liked eating with chopsticks, they were like funny long fingers. Sookie took the food and crossed the street. When she looked back, first at the ground floor, then up, and up again, she saw Tanner and the woman and the girl in one of the third-floor windows. The girl was sitting across from him, and they were talking to each other. Arguing, maybe. The woman didn't seem to be talking at all, sitting back a little.

Sookie squatted down against the brick wall, opened one of the cartons, and dug in with her chopsticks. Ate and watched. She didn't really know why she was following him. She wanted to talk to him again. The way he had kept looking at her. What was that? She wanted to ask him.

But there was something else, too. Something she wanted. She just couldn't figure out what it was.

Sookie sat and ate and watched . . . and waited.

TWENTY-FOUR

"WHY DID YOU stop seeing Mom?" Connie asked.

There it was, Tanner thought, the point of all this. He drank from his tea without taking his eyes off Connie, trying to decide how to answer her. Alexandra was silent, sitting back and away from them. She had offered to go somewhere else, or eat at a different table, whatever, but Connie had insisted she stay. Moral support?

Dinner itself had been relatively quiet, no one talking much. No one ate much, either. A lot of picking at the food, picking at conversation, both Connie and Tanner biding time. Then the meal was finished, the plates taken away, fresh tea brought to the table. And Connie asked the question.

There was not, of course, a simple answer to it. He had learned that a little over a year ago when he had tried to explain things to Valerie. Tanner wondered why Connie had waited so long to come to him with the question.

"I was afraid of hurting her," he finally said. The statement was so broad and general that it was true to a certain extent. Tanner felt almost embarrassed at giving it as an answer.

"What do you mean?" Connie asked.

"You remember the time I broke your mother's nose?" He felt a little sick now just thinking about it.

"You said it was an accident."

"It was. I'd had a nightmare, and I'd come out of it swinging my fists. It wasn't the first time I'd hurt her like that, but it was the worst." He paused. "I didn't want to risk doing that again to her."

118

"Nightmares that bad?" Connie said.

Tanner nodded, glancing at Alexandra. She was not looking at him.

"Do you have them a lot?" Connie asked.

Tanner breathed in slowly, deeply, then gradually let it out as he shook his head. He did not like talking about this. "Not really," he said. "Now and then. More than I'd like, though."

Connie didn't say anything for a minute or two. She sipped at her tea, and Tanner could see she was thinking about what he had said. She frowned, shaking her head, and set her teacup carefully on the table.

"You know, Louis," she said, "that's just bullshit. If that was the real problem, it's so easy to take care of." She stopped; hesitating, Tanner thought, to actually mention sleeping arrangements. She finally went on. "If you really loved each other, you could live with that. And you did love her, didn't you? I know she loved you." She paused, looked down at the table, then back up at him, defiant. "She still does. Do you?"

Jesus, Tanner thought, how was he supposed to answer that? He looked at Alexandra, who was holding her teacup without drinking from it, gazing out the window. She glanced at him, then looked away without expression. Alexandra had asked him the same questions a year ago, trying to pull answers out of him with patience and persistence. He resisted now, as he had then, and said nothing.

"Why did you stop seeing Mom?" Connie asked again. "Did you stop loving her?"

"No," Tanner answered. He tried to leave it at that.

"Then *why*?"

Stalling—he *knew* she would not be satisfied with anything less than a full explanation—he asked, "Why did you wait so long to ask me?"

Connie sighed. "I was afraid. But I'm older now, and I'm not afraid anymore, and I think I have a right to know."

Tanner nodded. He guessed she did have that right. Except he did not know if he could explain it to her. He did not think he had been very successful at explaining it to either Valerie or Alexandra. Or to himself.

"Things were always real hard between your mom and me," he began. "It wasn't that we didn't get along. We didn't fight, it wasn't that kind of thing, but it was hard, it took a lot of work. Which is all right, to a point. But it just got harder and harder, kind of wore us down. Wore *me* down." He paused, still struggling to put things into words after all this time.

"It had a lot to do with being a cop," he continued. "The people I saw, the things I watched people do, the things *I* had to do, it all depressed the hell out of me. The bad thing was, I brought a lot of it home. I tried to keep it from you and your mom, but I really wasn't able to." He smiled. "You remember, when you were younger, you used to come up to me and scream 'Lighten up!' right in my face?"

Connie smiled and nodded. "Yeah, I remember. It worked, too."

Tanner shrugged. "Yes, but never for very long. I thought that when I quit the force things would be easier for me, for us. I thought I'd 'lighten up.' " He paused. "But I didn't. I don't know, in some ways things just got worse, I felt like I was bringing clouds into the room every time I walked in. I just . . ." He shook his head. "I don't know, I tried real hard, Connie, I tried a long time, but I just couldn't do it anymore, I . . ." But that was it, he couldn't get out another word.

Connie did not say anything at first. She was not making a sound, but he thought she was shaking slightly. Her hands were out of sight beneath the table.

"Do you still love her?" she finally asked.

Jesus, Tanner thought, why won't she let me be? He rubbed at his face with his hand, but did not answer.

"*Do* you? Do you still love *me*?"

Tanner looked down at the table for a moment, then back at Connie, a terrible ache in his chest. "Yes," he finally said. "I still love you both."

"Isn't that enough?"

How could he answer that? He slowly shook his head. "No. It's just not that simple."

"Why not?"

Tanner did not know what to say. He *wanted* to give her an answer, he wanted to be able to say something that would make things all right with her.

"I don't know, Connie," he finally said. "I just don't know."

Connie was shaking her head slowly from side to side as if she could not believe what he was saying. She was crying now, quietly, steadily, and she put her head in her hands.

Tanner reached across the table, put his hand on her arm, and said, "I'm sorry, Connie."

She pulled her arm away from him, not quickly, but sadly, he thought. She raised her head and looked at him, dark makeup streaking her face. He thought of the woman with the tattooed tears.

"You're such an idiot sometimes, Louis. You probably think I'm crying for myself, don't you? Well I'm not, I'm crying for you." Connie breathed in deeply, held it for a minute, then let it out. She stopped crying, and wiped her face, smearing the streaked makeup. She slowly shook her head, looking at him, then stood up and said, "Excuse me, I'll be back in a minute." She turned and walked to the back of the restaurant and into the hall leading to the rest rooms.

Tanner looked at Alexandra, who gazed steadily back at him. He could not read her expression.

"Don't look at me like that, for Christ's sake," he said. "I'm doing my best."

Alexandra blinked twice, but otherwise did not change her expression. "And it's not good enough, is it?" she said. "She's young, Louis. But she's probably right about a lot of it."

He turned away and looked out the window. Night had fallen, and he wished a rain would start, fall long and hard, wash things away. Across the street a small figure huddled against the building, partially hidden by shadows, eating with chopsticks from a white carton. He could not be sure, but he thought it was Sookie. Was she following him? Why else would she be here?

Connie returned to the table, but did not sit. Her face was clean, but her eyes were puffy. She looked at Alexandra.

"I'm ready to go now," Connie said. "I asked my questions, and I'm ready to go home." She turned to Tanner. "Good-bye, Louis."

"Connie . . ." But that was as far as he got. He still had no idea what to say. "Good-bye, Connie. Take care of yourself."

Connie nodded. "Sure, Louis."

Alexandra stood. "I'll make sure she gets off okay tomorrow," she said to Tanner. "Keep in touch, will you? And if you have a problem, go ahead and get to Rachel, she'll find a way to help."

"Thanks for everything," Tanner said.

Alexandra nodded, then she and Connie walked away. He watched them cross the room and start down the stairs. Then he was alone.

Tanner stood on the sidewalk and gazed across the street at Sookie, who was standing now, her back against the building, watching him. Though it was not raining, the air was heavy and tense with the damp heat. At a break in the traffic, he hurried across the street and joined her.

"You've been following me," he said. When she did not deny it, he asked, "Why?"

"Why did you keep looking at me that way?" Sookie asked.

Tanner did not immediately reply, the pain returning once more. Her voice was nothing like Carla's, but her face was just too damn similar. "You remind me of someone," he finally said. "A woman I knew. You look a lot like she did when she was your age."

Sookie's eyes widened, and she gnawed at her lower lip. "Who is she?" Sookie asked, her voice hushed and tentative. "Maybe . . . maybe she's my mother." A brief pause, then, "I never knew her."

Tanner shook his head. "She died before you were born." He had wondered briefly about that himself when he had first made the connection; but if Carla had had a child before he had known her, the child would be close to twenty years old now.

Sookie kicked at the empty Chinese food cartons at her feet.

"So why were you following me?" Tanner asked again.

Sookie shrugged. "I don't know." She looked up at him. "To ask you that, I guess." She gestured with her head at the building. "You going back into the Tenderloin?"

"Yes."

"Even with Max after you?"

Tanner nodded. "Which is why you shouldn't be following me. You should stay away."

"You *need* someone following you," Sookie said.

Tanner shook his head. "Don't, Sookie. I'll be fine, and I don't want to be worrying about you. I mean it."

"I know a safe way in," she said.

"Don't you understand?" Tanner wanted to grab her by the shoulders and shake her. "You *know* what Max is like."

Sookie nodded. "I understand." She looked down at the food cartons, crushed one slowly with her foot. Then she looked back at him. "Was she your daughter?" she asked.

Tanner did not reply at first, confused. Was she talking about Carla? "Who do you mean?"

Sookie glanced across the street, pointed at the windows of Joyce Wah's. "The girl. You met her there."

"No," Tanner said. "She's the daughter of a friend."

Sookie nodded once, still gazing across the street. "You don't want me to show you a way in."

"I have my own ways."

"And you want me to stay away from you."

Tanner hesitated. He had the feeling something more was going on with her questions than he understood. "Because of Max, yes."

Sookie kicked at the food cartons again, smiled softly, and looked at Tanner. "Good-bye, then." She turned and walked quickly down the street.

"Sookie . . . wait."

She kept on without slowing, without looking back.

"Sookie . . ."

Tanner started forward, then stopped, letting it go, and wondering why he felt as if he had screwed up. What could he have said different? What *should* he have said? Christ. He watched her until, a block away, she slipped out of sight—into the crowd or into a building, he couldn't tell. Tanner turned around and headed the other way.

TWENTY-FIVE

TANNER RETURNED TO the Euro Quarter, walking the hot night streets. He wore nightshades, which looked like mirrored sunglasses from the outside but did not actually cut down on the light that reached his eyes. And he had decided not to shave. He did not really expect the nightshades and a few days' growth of beard to be much disguise, but he hoped it would at least make things more difficult for Max.

He had most of the money back on a new credit chip—replacing the chip had cost him five percent—and several hundred in cash. Having less money did not bother him, though; he suspected it would be more than enough. Tanner had the feeling that money was no longer a key issue in any of this.

But he felt a greater sense of urgency now. Part of that was Max—Tanner had to find Rattan before Max found *him*. But he also had the feeling that other things were coming to a head, all this stuff with Rattan and the cops. If they did, he might lose Rattan, one way or another, and he would be back where he had begun—nowhere. He had to find Rattan, and he had to find him soon.

It was just after midnight, street life peaking, when Tanner stopped by the Turk Street Fascination Parlor. The place was jammed, every single Fascination machine being played, almost all of them worked by old Russian women in their sixties or seventies, a few even older. They rolled the pink rubber balls into their machines, hoping to eventually win enough game tickets to cash in for a Tenderloin Flight Coupon,

124

good for a month in a Life-Sim Spa.

This time Lyuda, who owned and ran the parlor, was in. Tanner spotted her behind the bar in back, pouring comp Stolis for the old women. Two waiters, skinny old guys older than the Russian women, carted the tiny glasses of vodka from the bar to the machines. Tanner slowly worked his way to the bar, careful not to bump any of the players.

Lyuda, a small blond woman in her forties, was the only junkie Tanner had ever known who had managed to quit the stuff by slowly tapering off. She hadn't any other choice. She had started shooting up in her teens and, defying the odds, had survived into her mid-thirties, when she decided she had to quit—or die. Twice she tried it cold, and both attempts nearly killed her—twenty years of doing junk had changed her body too much; she needed heroin to live.

But she was still determined. So she began slowly, patiently, cutting back. She set up a strict regimen, tapering off minutely and infrequently, sticking to it for more than three years until she thought she had cut back enough. Then she quit completely . . . and lived. Now she ran the Fascination Parlor, and generously kept the old Russian women tanked on imported Stolichnaya vodka.

As Tanner approached the bar, he watched Lyuda's expression change from puzzlement to a smile and then to a tight frown. Tanner leaned against the counter, the two waiters left with full loads, and Lyuda shook her head.

"Didn't recognize you at first," she said. "Is that supposed to be some kind of disguise?" When Tanner shrugged, she said, "I gotta say I'm surprised to see you here, with that lunatic after you."

Max? It was difficult for Tanner to believe that Max would go that route, taking it public. He thought Max would want to come after him as privately as possible. "What lunatic?" he asked.

"Dobler."

"Dobler?"

"Yeah, Dobler, *that* lunatic, that amateur. You didn't know?"

Tanner shook his head.

"Sure, he's put the word out on the street. Wants you alive, if that's any consolation."

"What's the price on my head?"

"Negotiable upon delivery."

"What kind of nonsense is that?"

"I told you he was an amateur. Want a Stoli?" She held up a bottle, and when Tanner shook his head she poured one for herself and went on. "Anybody with any brains'll just ignore the whole thing, but he'll have other lunatics and amateurs shooting for you. And because they're amateurs they won't have too much control over the keeping-you-alive part of the deal."

"Terrific." Tanner scanned the Fascination Parlor, half expecting some psychotic moron to leap out from under one of the machines and take a potshot at him.

"So why you here?" Lyuda asked.

Tanner turned back to her. "I'm hoping you can help me out with something. I need to talk to you."

Lyuda pressed a button, and a buzzer sounded faintly through the walls. "We'll go to my office. Beyat can watch things."

"How clear is your office?"

Lyuda raised one eyebrow. "Like that, is it?"

Tanner nodded.

"All right."

A tall black woman in a shiny silver aviator jumpsuit appeared from the back hall, and Lyuda came around the bar.

"I'll be gone, I don't know how long," Lyuda said to Beyat. "Watch things, all right?"

Beyat nodded, adjusting the Stolichnaya bottles. "Keep the old dames juiced."

"Just keep them happy," Lyuda said.

Beyat grinned. "That means keeping them juiced."

Lyuda finally smiled and nodded. "All right." She glanced at Tanner, then led the way to a bolted door between the two rest rooms. She unlocked it, and they walked down a narrow passage, then into a small room filled with cases of Stolichnaya. They went through another door at the back, then up a flight of stairs to a covered porch looking out over an alley filled with garbage cans, packing crates, loading docks. In the mist-filled cones of light, people moved about the alley, either on foot or narrow transport carts. There were three chairs in the room and Lyuda sat in one, gesturing at the other two.

Tanner chose the one farther from the window. He wondered if he was becoming paranoid.

"So what is it?" Lyuda asked.

"I should tell you, someone else is looking for me. Other than Dobler." He waited for her to ask him who, but she didn't. She sat silently, waiting for him to continue. "Max," he said.

She did not respond immediately. Her gaze was steady, penetrating. Almost accusing. "You've got no business being in the Tenderloin," she said. "You get out right now, quickest way you can."

"I can't," Tanner said. "I'm looking for someone. Here. I have to find him."

Lyuda shook her head. "Everybody's looking for somebody. What the hell is all this?" She breathed in, expelled it slowly. "All right, who you looking for?"

"Rattan."

Again there was a silence before she replied. He could not read her expression.

"You are not a good insurance risk," Lyuda finally said.

"Can you help me find him?"

Lyuda slowly shook her head from side to side. "Shit, Tanner. I shouldn't even try."

"Will you?"

Lyuda did not answer.

Tanner and Lyuda walked the crowded streets, headed deeper into the Tenderloin. Two Red Dragons had flown in from the Asian Quarter and now hovered thirty or forty feet above the street, engaged in mock combat while video ads for Red Dragon sake shimmered along the length of their bodies. Green sparks flashed from their eyes while smoke poured from the dragons' nostrils and drifted down to street level. Tanner breathed in the smoke, which smelled faintly of incense and opium.

Lyuda had spent nearly three hours making phone calls and going out to talk to people, while Tanner waited on the porch. He had sat on the floor with his back against the wall, dozing, slipping in and out of a dreamlike state. At one point he thought he was involved in an intense, incomprehensible conversation with Carla, who was quite young, and who gradually transformed into Sookie. He only halfheartedly fought the exhaustion and the fragmented dream images, and several times nearly slipped into a deep sleep. Finally, close to four in the morning, Lyuda had returned and told him they would go meet someone who *might* know something. Now they were on their way as night came to a close, though there were not yet any traces of light in the sky.

By the time Lyuda turned into a busy alley lined with street-level shops, cafes, and taverns, they were very close to the Core. Tanner wondered again if that was where Rattan had gone to ground. But he could not believe it, could not believe that Rattan was that desperate.

They entered a crowded espresso bar and Lyuda led the way through it to the opposite entrance, which opened into a large lobby. Three people stood in the lobby, talking and sipping from paper cups. All the lobby windows were boarded over, but the lobby itself was brightly lit. This was, or had once been, an office building.

Lyuda nodded at the boarded windows. "Faces the Core," she said. "Every window on the first seven floors of that side is boarded over, steel plating on the outside."

"We're that close?" Tanner said.

"Just across the street."

One of the elevators was open and waiting. Inside, Lyuda pushed the ninth-floor button, the doors closed, and the elevator rose with a jolt. Tanner had been up and down a lot of floors in the last few days, but this was his first elevator ride since he had seen Teshigahara.

The elevator stopped at five, and three short, fat men got on. They wore business suits, but they smelled bad. Milky green fluid oozed from an open sore on one man's forehead. They did not push any of the floor buttons.

At nine, Tanner and Lyuda got off. The elevator doors remained open for a minute, the three men standing silent and motionless. Then the doors closed, and the lighted arrow showed the elevator descending. Odd, Tanner thought.

The hall floor was beige linoleum, edged with ragged strips of rotten carpet that had once covered the floor. Offices on the Core side of the building were dark and silent. On the other side were lighted door windows of frosted glass, muffled voices, the clatter of machinery, music, and the whine of a dentist's drill. At the end of the hall was a staircase, which

they climbed to the tenth floor. Here, all the offices were dark
and silent.

Lyuda unlocked a door on the Core side of the building, and
they entered a dark room. She took Tanner's hand and led him
through the darkness, along a corridor, then into another room
with two large windows. They stepped up to the windows, and
looked out onto the Core.

The Core was four square blocks of hell. Some people
thought the hell was literal, and believed supernatural demons
and ghosts haunted the place. Most of the buildings were in
ruins, and those that were not looked as if they soon would
be. Unlike the rest of the Tenderloin, the streets and buildings
of the Core were not brightly lit, though a few dim lights
were visible in the ruins—wavering lights of candles or fires,
pulsing blue glows, drifting clouds of pale phosphorescence.
The streets were deserted except for the shadowy movement
of animals.

Tanner had heard the stories, though no one really knew for
sure what went on inside. The Core was populated by those
who could not, or would not, cut it in either the city or the Tenderloin. For all that the Tenderloin functioned outside the laws
of the city, state, and country, it *did* function quite well with a
structure and order of its own. The Core, so the stories went,
had no order, no structure, no laws or rules or morals. Nothing.
Tanner suspected it was not quite the chaos-driven place it was
said to be, but certainly the rules were different. The Core itself
existed, but that was all that could be said of it.

Lyuda raised the window, and Tanner half expected to hear
wild screams and wailing, but there was relative quiet. Several
floors up in the building across the way, something resembling
a large cat stuck its head out a window and growled. A huge,
furred hand grabbed it and pulled it back inside.

"You don't think Rattan's in there, do you?" Tanner asked.

Lyuda shook her head. "He's not insane." She looked at her
watch. "Quiet, now. Listen. It's almost time." She gestured at
the Core.

For what? But Tanner kept quiet, and listened.

The Core, already quiet, grew quieter still, almost completely silent. Even the surrounding areas of the Tenderloin
became quiet. An acoustic guitar began playing somewhere
inside one of the buildings across the street. The sound, loud

and clearly defined, echoed among the ruins, and Tanner could not pinpoint its origin. The music was classical and delicate, with a Latin feel. Then a woman's voice joined it.

Her voice was strong and beautiful, a clean, high soprano. She sang something from an opera, Tanner thought, though he did not recognize it. The words were Spanish or Italian, he couldn't be sure. Clearly, she'd had professional training. There was no way anyone could sing like that without years of training and practice. And here she was, singing from within the Core.

Tanner stood and listened, amazed at what he was hearing, amazed at where it came from. Spanish, he finally decided. A love song of some kind, filled with yearning, tempered with anxiety. He searched the ruins, looking for a light or something that would tell him where she was. He saw nothing.

The song ended. There was a brief silence, then the guitar started in on another song, playing a few measures before the woman joined it again. This song was sadder than the first, melancholy and quite moving, though again Tanner had no idea what any of the words meant. Her voice had great power, and Tanner felt a dull ache develop in his chest. During the most intense section of the piece, the woman hit a series of incredibly high notes with such painful perfection that a shiver ran through Tanner from his neck to the base of his spine, leaving a strange chill in its wake.

By the time the second song was finished, the sky had noticeably brightened, and morning was fully upon them. There was another extended silence, then the natural city sounds gradually resumed, filling the morning air. There was no more guitar, no more singing. Lyuda closed the window.

"She sings every Saturday at dawn," Lyuda said. "Started about three and a half months ago."

"Who is she?"

"No one really knows. I've heard of people who say they recognize her voice, who say it's Elisabetta Machiotti."

"Name sounds familiar," Tanner said. "But . . ." He shrugged.

"A highly acclaimed soprano with the Berlin Opera who disappeared a year ago. But like I said, no one really knows. Whoever she is, though, she's really quite good." She looked at her watch again. "Arkady should be here any minute now."

They waited without speaking for several minutes, watching the morning sky brighten. Tanner could see the first reflections of the rising sun glint off glass and metal on building roofs in the Core.

The office door opened, closed, and a moment later a tall, young blond man walked into the room. Lyuda shook the man's hand.

"Arkady . . . Tanner," she said. "Tanner . . . Arkady."

Tanner nodded at Arkady and they shook hands. Arkady nodded back, then turned to Lyuda and began speaking in Russian. She replied, also in Russian, and Tanner realized their entire conversation was going to proceed in a language he did not understand. At first he watched them, watched their faces and listened to their voices, hoping to get some sense of the conversation. But their expressions told him nothing, nor did their voices, and soon he stopped even trying to understand.

Tanner turned back to the window and looked out onto the Core. Although he could not see anyone in or around any of the buildings, did not directly detect any motion, he was struck by a vague sense of movement from within the ruins, a shifting of atmospheric patterns. Something. An alien place. Though the heat of the day was growing, the sweat already filming across his skin, he could somehow imagine a light dusting of snow laid over the Core, cold and silent.

Elisabetta Machiotti. In a way it did not matter *who* the woman was. What mattered was that she was in the Core, and that she sang. Tanner was certain that most people would be dumbfounded at the idea of a world-famous opera singer living in the Core; but, amazed and awed as he was by the woman's performance in that hellhole, Tanner was not any more surprised at her presence in the Core than he was at the presence of *anyone* in that place. Given that the Core existed, why *not* a world-famous opera singer?

The conversation stopped, and Tanner turned away from the window. Arkady nodded once at him, shook hands with Lyuda again, then walked out of the room. A few moments later Tanner heard the outer door open and close. He looked at Lyuda, who shook her head.

"I don't have a damn thing for you," she said.

"Nothing?"

"Nothing. No one has any idea where he is, and no one *wants* to know. Something's in the air with Rattan, but nobody knows what. Something more than Max, though Max doesn't make the situation any easier. People don't want to deal with Max, and people don't even want to talk about Rattan." She shook her head. "You're going up against thick walls, Tanner. You want, I can keep asking around, put out a few sensors, but Arkady was my best shot, and to be honest I'm not wild about the idea of pushing it any further. I've got myself to watch for."

"No," Tanner said. "It's not worth the risk. I have some other lines to try. I appreciate what you did, and let's leave it there." He turned to the window once more, looking out at the Core as if it somehow had the answers he was searching for. He knew it did not have the answers to *anything*, but he gazed at it all the same.

Lyuda joined him at the window. "You know what she is?" Lyuda asked.

"The woman who sang?"

Lyuda nodded. "You'll think I'm crazy, but . . ." There was a long pause, and Tanner waited silently for her to continue. "Hope," Lyuda said. "That's what I think of when I hear her sing."

Tanner stared at the Core. Hope. Not even close to what he now felt. Standing at the edge of the Core, with no leads to Rattan, no leads to a psycho who was going to keep on killing again and again and again, all Tanner felt was despair.

TWENTY-SIX

SOOKIE KNEW THAT voice. Hearing those songs made her want to cry. She didn't understand any of the words, but the tears came anyway. It was the third time she'd heard the woman sing. Who was she? Sookie thought the woman must be trapped in the Core, chained to a wall, unable to do anything but sing.

Two songs, then the woman stopped. Sookie closed her eyes, still crying a little, listening, hoping for another song. But there wasn't any more.

She wiped away the tears, looked into the Core. It was filled with long shadows from the rising sun. Sookie sat on top of one of the street barricades at the edge of the Core. Mixer would think she was crazy, but she wasn't afraid, as long as she was outside.

She'd been inside the Core once, by accident. Not far inside. A couple of years ago, when she'd been younger and kind of stupid. She'd been running away from someone, middle of the night, she didn't remember who or why. She'd climbed one of the barricades to get away, dropped down to the other side, then run across the street and into the closest wrecked building. She hadn't really known what the Core was, not then. She didn't really know what it was now, either, but now she knew enough to stay out.

No one had followed her over the barrier or across the street. Sookie had figured she was safe. She was inside a dark and dusty room, with a couple windows looking out on the street. Silver light from across the road came in through the windows, lighting up the dust. Something brushed her foot and she jumped away. A huge rat as big as a small dog scampered through one of the light beams and Sookie squealed. Rats didn't bother her too much, but she'd never seen one that big.

Then she heard a moaning laugh from the corner of the room. A click, then a pale light came on overhead. Sookie saw a young woman dressed in a white body suit crouched at the edge of a pit in the floor. The woman, head shaved, held a metal pipe in one hand and a hammer in the other. Her mouth was open, making the moaning laugh. Then the laugh stopped.

The woman leaped across the pit and ran at Sookie, pipe and hammer held high. Sookie turned and ran, stumbled, fell. The woman couldn't stop, tripped over Sookie, yowling. Sookie scrambled to her feet, headed for the door. Something hit her arm—the hammer. She made it to the door, out, onto the street, and dashed for the barricade. The woman did not follow her out of the building. Her arm hurt, but she clambered up the barricade. Someone grabbed her, helped her up and over and back into the Tenderloin. It was a spikehead who had helped her up. That was how she had met Mixer, escaping from the Core.

Sookie shivered, remembering. Sometimes she dreamed about that woman. In her dreams, the woman sometimes shouted "Dinner!" just before leaping across the pit at Sookie. In her dreams, the woman always caught her.

Clouds started to fill the sky. It was going to rain soon. Sookie climbed down from the barricade and returned to the head of the alley. She stood and watched the store entrances, waiting for Tanner to reappear.

TWENTY-SEVEN

TANNER WAS SOAKED by the time he reached Hannah and Rossi's, drenched by a second and unexpected cloudburst. He dripped water on the carpets as he climbed the stairs, walked down the hall, then entered the apartment. The place was quiet. There was no sign of Hannah, and Rossi was asleep in the bedroom, lying faceup on the bed. In the bathroom, Tanner undressed, hung everything on hooks and racks. He took a short, cool shower, then put on clean, dry clothes.

He stretched out on the couch and tried to sleep. He was hot, exhausted, and depressed, and sleep would not come. A clock ticked weakly in the bedroom. Someone in the building was playing loud music, and Tanner could feel the beat gently thumping up from the floor and through the sofa. He looked up at the blue-painted cracks in the ceiling and imagined water dripping from them, splashing across his face, cooling him. Sweat trickled under his arms, down his neck.

He was nowhere. Things were slipping away from him. He and Carlucci knew no more now than they had several days before, which meant they were losing ground. And tonight he would head back into the Tenderloin and go through it all again. Flying blind, that's what it felt like. How long could he keep it going without making a mistake? It did not matter how careful he was, eventually there would come a night when he would ask the wrong person the wrong question, like he had with Max, or simply be in the wrong place. Tanner wondered again if he would survive the summer.

Unable to sleep, he got up from the couch and walked into the kitchen. It was still a mess of food and filthy plates and stained glasses. Hannah, too, had given up on a lot. Well, it gave him something to do.

Tanner spent the next hour washing dishes and glasses and silverware, cleaning counters, putting some of the food away while dumping most of it into the garbage. He swept the floors and washed the table. Then he dug through the cupboards, looking for something to drink. There was plenty of gin, but he couldn't stand the stuff. In the back of a cupboard, behind some jars of Hungarian preserves, he found a dusty pint of cheap scotch.

He fixed himself a drink, drank it slowly, then fixed another. It had been a long time since he had needed alcohol to sleep. His thoughts were scattered, but they kept moving through his head at wild speeds, and he needed something to slow them down, ease them back, put them away for a little while. So he sat at the table and drank.

When he finished his third drink he returned to the front room. A pleasant warmth had settled in his limbs, and his thoughts had slowed and fuzzed over. He lay out on the couch, staring at the blue cracks once more, then closed his eyes. Heat of the day, warmth of the scotch. It was enough. Tanner slid slowly and softly into sleep.

Tanner woke to the sensation of being watched. He lay facing the back of the sofa, and he slowly turned over to see Hannah in the overstuffed chair, gazing at him. The room was stuffy and hot, late-afternoon sun slashing in through the window. Hannah's face was in shadow from her nose up, her mouth and chin brightly lit.

"How long have you been there?" he asked.

"About a half hour," Hannah said. "Couldn't think of anything better to do." She looked beat, as usual.

Tanner sat up, stretched cramped muscles, popping neck and shoulder bones. He felt as tired as Hannah looked.

"Where's Rossi?"

"Down at the Lucky Nines having a few beers with the guys. It's a daily ritual." She ran her hand slowly through her hair, watching him. "Make love to me, Louis."

Tanner stared at her a few moments without answering, then said quietly, "No, Hannah."

"Louis . . ."

"No, Hannah."

She looked away from him. The sun was dropping quickly now, and the stream of light had worked up to the bridge of her nose, just below her eyes.

"You did a hell of a job in the kitchen," she said. "You'd make someone a good wife." She turned back to him. "I just don't care about much anymore."

Tanner did not know what to say. He did not want to be sucked down into the pit of Hannah and Rossi's life; he had enough problems of his own. But he had known them both a long time, Hannah for more than twenty years. Hannah had known Carla, had been there to help him through all the shit when Carla had died.

"I know," Hannah said. "You want to know why I don't leave him."

"I'm not going to ask that anymore," Tanner said. "I know it's not that simple."

Hannah sank back slowly into the chair. Now her entire face was bathed in the deep red glow of the setting sun, and she squinted against the glare.

"Look at us," Hannah said. "I should leave Rossi, and you should never have left Valerie. You and Valerie are both still paying for Carla's death."

"She died fifteen years ago," Tanner said. "They don't have anything to do with each other."

"You don't think so?"

Tanner shook his head. "No."

Hannah slowly shook her head in return, a sad smile working its way onto her face, but she did not say anything. She closed her eyes for a few moments, then opened them slightly, still squinting in the sun. Tanner waited for her to speak, but she remained silent.

"I'll buy you dinner," he finally said.

Hannah sighed and nodded. "All right." She stood up from the chair and went to the front door. Tanner got to his feet, joined her, and they left.

● ● ●

When they got back from dinner, Tanner called Carlucci. He suggested meeting at the apartment, but Carlucci refused; he did not want to take the chance of seeing Rossi. Instead, they agreed to meet at a coffee shop down the street.

Tanner arrived first and sat at a booth by the front window. He ordered coffee from the sour-looking waitress, and while he waited for it he looked around the restaurant. The place was dirty and run down, which matched most of the customers at the tables and counter. A pall of despair hung over the place, cut through with the smells of charred toast and frying fat. A thin layer of grease on the window blurred his view of the street.

When the coffee arrived, Tanner looked at it with concern. It was too dark, and a burnt smell drifted up from the cup. He sipped it tentatively and burned the tip of his tongue; the coffee was so hot he could not really taste it, which was probably just as well.

He could not stop thinking about what Hannah had said about Valerie and Carla. Carla had died fifteen years ago, he *must* have let that go by now. Right? But Hannah's words stuck hard somewhere inside him, almost painful, and he could not shake them loose. Which made him think there was something to them. He did not want to think about it, though, he could not afford to right now. There were too many other, more immediate, concerns. Like the Chain Killer. So why *couldn't* he stop thinking about it?

He pushed the coffee cup from him in disgust. The coffee was just too much; he had managed less than half a cup. He signaled the waitress, told her to take the coffee away, and asked for tea. She glared sullenly at him, but took away the cup.

Carlucci slid into the booth, across from him, just as the waitress brought Tanner's tea.

"Stay away from the coffee," Tanner said.

Carlucci grunted, ordered coffee anyway, and the waitress smirked at Tanner. It was the closest thing to a smile he had seen from her. She was probably in her thirties, and in a few more years, Tanner thought, she was going to look like Hannah. Or worse.

"I hope you're not going to tell me more bodies have been found," he said to Carlucci.

Carlucci shook his head. "No new bodies, not a damn thing new on this son of a bitch. What about you, any luck?"

"No," Tanner said. "Nobody wants to even talk about Rattan. Lot of people seem to think something's on the move with him, but no one knows what. And they don't *want* to know. The more people I ask, the greater the chance that someone's going to end up dead. I don't like it at all." Tanner sighed. "But what the hell else are we going to do?" He gave Carlucci a half smile. "Tell you, though, I'm going to be real pissed if I find Rattan and it turns out he doesn't know shit. A three-year-old message. Christ."

"I've been looking into things, digging around trying to find out if something's going down between Rattan and some of our 'fellow officers.' "

"*Your* fellow officers."

"Fine, whatever. I haven't got a whole lot, and I doubt I'm ever going to get much more. Any cop actually dealing with Rattan in *any* way is going to keep it real tight, or find himself either out of a job or dumped dead in an alley somewhere. Hardly anyone liked the two cops he killed, they were bad cops, but they were still *cops*. Hell, it's the same thing you're running into. A lot of cops have heard about something shaking out with Rattan, but they don't know what it is, and they don't *want* to know."

Tanner nodded. "We're both hitting walls." He shook his head. "I've been on this for a week, but it feels like a fucking month."

" 'Fucking'? I don't usually hear you use that word," Carlucci said, smiling.

"Yeah, well, this is the fucking time for it."

Someone on the street banged at the window. It was Rossi. He pointed at Tanner and Carlucci, then at himself, then hurried away. A few moments later he came through the front door and walked up to the booth. He did not sit down, and neither Tanner nor Carlucci asked him to.

"Hey, Carlucci," Rossi said. He stuck out his hand. "It's been a long time, yeah?"

Carlucci would not shake Rossi's hand. Tanner could smell the alcohol on Rossi, mixed with the heavy odor of sweat. Rossi continued to hold out his hand, which shook slightly. Tanner watched Rossi's smile fade, his expression tighten.

Carlucci stared back at Rossi, his face blank. Finally, Rossi pulled his hand back, made a fist, and pounded the table.

"What's the matter with you?" Rossi said. "Can't you ever forget? Can't you ever forgive?"

"Not you," Carlucci said. His face remained expressionless, his voice quiet.

The two men stared at each other for a minute, and Rossi finally pushed back from the table. He turned to Tanner, arms shaking, lips quivering. Tanner felt he could actually see Rossi breaking apart inside.

"I'll see you later," he said, voice cracked and hoarse. He turned and walked out, crashing loudly through the front entrance. Tanner watched him run awkwardly across the street and into the apartment building.

"You're awfully hard on him," he said to Carlucci.

"Shouldn't I be? He cost my best friend an arm."

"That was six years ago."

"Six years, ten years, what difference? Brendan still doesn't have an arm. When it grows back, I'll ease up on Rossi."

Which meant never, of course. Tanner had heard about experimental work on full limb regeneration being done up in New Hong Kong, yet as far as he knew there had been no successes. But he nodded to Carlucci. He *did* understand. Brendan had never adjusted to the loss of his arm; he would not even consider a prosthesis. His marriage had disintegrated, and he had lost most of his friends. Carlucci blamed Rossi for more than the loss of Brendan's arm; he blamed him for the loss of Brendan's life.

The waitress stopped by, refilled Carlucci's cup, and poured more hot water for Tanner's tea. Tanner bobbed the tea bag in the water, swirled it, watched the water grow slowly, slowly darker.

"The coffee's not that bad," Carlucci said.

Tanner looked at Carlucci's cup; the coffee did not look any better than what he had tried, and he just shook his head.

"You going back in tonight?" Carlucci asked.

"Sure. What else?" He lifted the tea bag, watched it drip. "There are some other people I might be able to talk to, if I can find them." He dropped the tea bag back into the water. "I don't expect too much, to be honest. In fact, if you want to know the truth, I'm hoping to stumble onto something by accident more than anything else."

"I wish I had something better to offer."

"What about Koto?" Tanner asked.

"What about him?"

"Can't we go to him, see if he can't find a way to get to Rattan? He's been in the Tenderloin all these years. I mean, now that I'm thinking about it, what the hell is he being saved for? Isn't this important enough to use him?"

Carlucci did not answer. He leaned back in the booth and looked out the window. A light mist was falling, swirled by gusting winds. Tanner waited patiently, watching Carlucci, drinking his tea. Carlucci turned away from the window, finished his coffee, carefully set the cup in the saucer, and finally looked at Tanner.

"It's not that simple," he said.

Phrase of the day, Tanner thought. "I don't doubt that," he said, "but you want to explain why?"

"No. I can't. But it is something worth considering. Let's give it a few more days, and if we still aren't getting anywhere we can talk about it again."

Tanner nodded, looking outside at the swirling mist. "All right. Who knows? Maybe I'll get lucky tonight and we won't need him."

Tanner did not get lucky. In fact, the night was a complete washout. An hour after he entered the Tenderloin, a freak monsoonlike storm struck, with heavy rains and gale-force winds, effectively clearing the streets. Tanner spent a couple of hours in a video parlor watching a program of five-minute riot videos intercut with a series of one-minute animations about a scrawny, ugly dog named Fifi.

When the program ended, the storm still raged. Water ran in streams down the sidewalks and gutters, flooding at the intersections. Tanner left the video parlor, pushed through the wind and rain, down half a block and into a building, then up two flights of stairs to a music lounge. He took a seat at the window counter and ordered a beer. A slash-and-burn band was playing somewhere inside the building, the music blaring from speakers scattered throughout the lounge. The music was harsh and loud, frenetic, with only a hint of melody. It suited him, providing a wall of sound that gave him a sense of privacy as he sat at the window, watching the rain sweep through the streets. He nursed a couple of beers through the next two hours, enclosed by walls of music, glass, and driving rain.

Around two in the morning, the storm ceased almost as abruptly as it had begun. Tanner left the lounge and joined the throngs of people returning to the streets. The air smelled fresher, clear and crisp even in the heat. Windows, vehicles, pavement, lights, buildings, *everything* seemed sharper and cleaner, as if purified by the storm. Tanner wandered the streets, moving back and forth between the Euro and Asian Quarters, not really looking for anyone, just taking in the refreshed and invigorating feel of the streets.

But then, around four, he got caught in a ground skirmish. Within seconds, barriers went up at either end of the block he was on, and there was no way out. Everyone in the street knew what the barriers meant, and they all got off the street as best they could.

Tanner managed to get inside a noodle shop just before the doors were locked. The shop was jammed, and most people crowded around the front window to get a view of the action on the street. Tanner had no desire to watch people mauling each other. He moved to the back of the shop and sat on a stool at the bar.

He spent the next hour drinking tea, eating a bowl of noodles, and talking occasionally with the cook, who had no more interest in the fighting than he did. The window spectators made noises throughout the skirmish, but Tanner paid no attention to them, paid no attention to the other sounds of the street that penetrated the glass and walls. Instead, he concentrated on the bubbling hiss when the cook dropped fresh noodles into a pot of boiling stock; on the fragrant sizzle of frying pork; on the tick-tick-tick of cooling metal when the cook turned off the flame under the teakettle.

At dawn, the skirmish ended, and people returned to the streets. Tanner stayed in the noodle shop for a few minutes, finishing his tea. Then he got up, thanked the cook, and left.

When he stepped outside the shop, the air had a different feel. It no longer smelled clean and fresh; now it carried the faint stench of blood, smoke, and charged sweat.

Tanner stood on the sidewalk, watching the sky slowly brighten with the morning. He could see, in the gutter across the street, a splash of thick, darkening blood, flies already gathering above it. He did not want to move. It was time to go back to Hannah and Rossi's, try to get some sleep before coming back here tonight for another run. Time. What did it matter where he went? Tanner remained motionless, hands at his side, waiting for the first appearance of the sun.

TWENTY-EIGHT

THE NEXT NIGHT did not start out any better. He walked the streets almost in a stupor, without direction or purpose. He was hoping to see someone or something that would give him an idea; hoping for a flash of inspiration, a bit of luck.

He spent half an hour wandering through the maze of The Bomb Shelter, glancing into the rooms and cubicles, turning down a wide variety of propositions. He did not know who or what he was looking for in the place, and he felt like an apathetic voyeur, observing people engaged in intimate acts but with no real interest in what they were doing.

After The Bomb Shelter, Tanner checked half a dozen fang fights, thinking he might find the Barber at one of them, betting on his favorite wolverine or leopard. He saw lots of blood and flying fur and feathers, but no Barber.

At the edge of the Asian Quarter he stood gazing at the building that housed the Gang of Four tong. It was very likely that they knew where Rattan was, or at least how to reach him, but there was no asking them. He would not be able to get an audience, let alone ask any of them a question. And of course even if by some fluke he *could*, no one would answer him.

Tanner felt a tugging at his shirt and turned to see a young girl looking up at him. She was a Screamer, her lips smoothly, surgically fused together, with two trache tubes in her throat—one for eating, one for breathing. She was about ten or eleven years old. He wondered if, when she was old enough, she would want to undo what her parents had done to her. Probably not; most of them didn't.

The girl held up a clenched fist, rotated it, then uncurled her fingers, revealing a folded sheet of paper in her palm. Tanner took the message and the girl ran off, disappearing into the crowd. Tanner unfolded the message and read it—an address, followed by the words "Watch the sky."

He looked up and down the street, searching for a familiar face, for someone who might be watching him. He didn't see anything unusual, no one he recognized. Who had sent the message? The answer to that was pretty damn important. Max? Dobler? Either one was bad news. Sookie or the spikehead? Probably not; they would have signed it. Someone who knew he was looking for Rattan? Someone after Dobler's bounty? Most of the possibilities were trouble, but Tanner knew— he *knew,* damn it all—that he could not afford to ignore the message. For a moment he wished he had followed Carlucci's advice and carried a gun.

Tanner stood motionless, rereading the message as a new, hard-edged energy worked through him. Here it was, he tried telling himself, the break he was waiting for. But he knew that probably wasn't true, this was more likely to get him worked over or killed.

The address was three blocks away. Once again he scanned the street around him, but still did not see anyone he knew. He refolded the note, stuffed it into his shirt pocket, and started off down the street.

His stupor was long gone now, replaced by heightened sensations and blazing nerves. Everything around him had an extra shot of clarity around the edges, a shimmer of light. It was like being on speed. He even felt a little jumpy. Adrenaline rush. Tanner wished he could tone it down a bit. He felt just slightly out of control.

When Tanner reached the address, he stood in front of a tattoo parlor that was locked shut, bars over the windows and door. He checked the note to make sure he had the correct address and street; he did. He banged on the bars, rapped at the glass, but got no response. He searched the window and bars for another message, some sign, and found nothing. There was a donut shop on one side of the tattoo parlor, and a juicer studio on the other, but nothing seemed out of place. The crowds and traffic around him were normal for the Tenderloin.

Maybe it made sense. "Watch the sky," the note said. Perhaps the address was just an observation point, a place for Tanner to be when something happened in the skies above. As long as it wasn't death falling on him. He looked up, saw a sick green haze blocking out the stars, but again nothing unusual.

A sound blasted the air, like an air-raid siren. Tanner's chest tightened. He knew what was coming. Someone would soon be flying out a window. People in the street looked up, searching the upper reaches of the buildings on both sides of the street. Most of them, too, knew what was coming.

The signal finally appeared—a black flag telescoped out from the roof of the building directly across the street from Tanner; it flapped gently in the breeze. People quickly cleared the sidewalk below the flag; even the street traffic adjusted, halting and clearing out that part of the road. People took up positions in doorways, on ledges, in windows, watching and waiting; a few people dragged cafe tables and chairs out onto the sidewalk and settled in for the show.

This time, though he would have preferred not to, Tanner watched and waited as well. Whatever was coming, he knew, was meant for him to see.

A window on the tenth floor opened. The street noise swelled for just a moment, then dropped quickly to near silence. Nothing happened for a minute or two. The air grew heavy and tense, as if the heat had jacked up a bit, almost pulsing through the night.

A muffled roar emerged from the window, growing louder, then a large figure shot out headfirst. As the figure plummeted, still roaring, hands bound behind its back, Tanner saw that it was Red Giant. The roar continued all the way down, then ceased with a sickening crunch as Red Giant hit the edge of the street. His body shuddered once, then was still. Tanner could see blood already pooling around the man's head, trickling into the gutter.

No one in the street moved; the tension did not break. Tanner looked back up at the window. It remained open, and the flag continued to fly, which meant someone else would be coming. Tanner had a pretty good idea who was next.

No cry, no roar this time. Max hurtled out the window, hands bound, back arched. There was no sound at all as he fell until, at the last second, his mouth opened and an explosive scream burst forth, only to be abruptly cut off by impact as he struck the ground next to Red Giant.

No shudder, just a motionless, crumpled and broken form. Tanner felt sick as he stared at the two bodies just twenty feet away. Max's face was crushed, his grafted mirrorshades shattered. He still could not see Max's eyes, only a mess of flesh, blood, plastic, and bone.

Tanner glanced up at the top of the building, saw the window close and the flag pulled in. He returned his gaze to the two crushed figures, but his view was soon blocked by crowds as people returned to their business and the street traffic resumed.

Tanner felt a hand on his shoulder. He turned to see the Asian woman with the tattooed tears. A new tear had been added to her cheek.

"That's taken care of," the woman said. She took his hand in hers. "Rattan is ready to see you now."

TWENTY-NINE

SOOKIE FLINCHED AND shuddered when Uwe hit the ground. A couple of minutes later she jerked again when Max hit, and she had to turn away. She thought maybe she was going to be sick. She hated them both, and she wasn't sorry they were dead, but . . . She breathed deeply, leaned her head against the brick.

When she looked up again, she saw a woman talking to Tanner. The woman took hold of Tanner's hand. Sookie was too far away to hear the woman, but Tanner didn't look happy to see her. He didn't give her a kiss or hug or anything. But he didn't pull his hand away. Maybe she wouldn't let him.

The woman pulled Tanner back a few feet, then let go of his hand. She unlocked the door of the tattoo parlor and waved Tanner inside. The woman followed him and pulled the door shut. Sookie hurried down the street, stopped in front of the tattoo parlor, looked inside. She didn't see anyone in the tiny front room. She tried the door, but it was locked. Sookie wrenched at the door handle, kicked at the door, but it just wouldn't budge.

Rats. She had the feeling he was going to be inside a long time. She also was pretty sure that when he *did* come back out, it wouldn't be here. Somewhere else, who knew? Maybe not even the same building.

If he came back out. That scared her, thinking about it. He needed someone watching out for him. Well, maybe not so much anymore, with Max and Uwe dead. But maybe still, looking for Rattan. She didn't know who Rattan was, but

148

Mixer said he was pretty bad. She just didn't know about Tanner. She hoped he would be okay.

A young Screamer grabbed hold of Sookie's arm, pulled at her. Sookie resisted, and the girl yanked harder, dragging Sookie away from the tattoo parlor.

"What?" Sookie said.

The Screamer just shook her head. She let go Sookie's hand, pointed at the tattoo parlor, and shook her head again.

"All right," Sookie said. She backed away from the tattoo parlor, then turned and worked her way through traffic across the street. A transplant crew was already set up, loading the bodies into their van. Lots of money was changing hands, and she didn't see a single cop anywhere. Cold smoke rolled out of the van. The crew got the bodies lashed down inside and slammed the doors shut. They climbed into the cab, and the van pulled away.

Sookie stared at the street and gutter, watching the blood. Some of the deeper pools rippled from traffic vibrations. Pieces of Max's mirrorshades were scattered across the pavement, and she could almost see herself in one of them.

"You still following him?"

Sookie looked up, saw Mixer crouched against the building, watching her. She shrugged, walked over to him.

"Who?"

"Hah." Like a dog bark. "You know, Sookie. You're still following him."

"I guess." She sat down next to Mixer. He took out a couple of cigarettes and gave one to her. Flicked open a lighter, lit them. "I'm worried about him," she said.

"You should be," Mixer said. "He's going to get himself killed. Which is why you shouldn't be following him. You can't help him, Sookie, but you're liable to get yourself offed along with him."

"I can take care of myself."

Mixer sighed heavily. "I know," he said. "But I know you, Sookie. Weird shit happens around you, you know that. And anyone can get into it around here. Just leave it alone, Sookie. Leave *him* alone."

Sookie nodded, looking at the tattoo parlor. She wondered how long it would take her to pick up Tanner again. She sucked in on her cigarette and settled in to wait.

THIRTY

TANNER STOOD ALONE in the corridor, waiting to be admitted to Rattan's "sanctum." That was what the woman had called it, though she *had* been smiling. He felt as if he were waiting for an audience with a king. Maybe that was how Rattan thought of himself.

The corridor was short but wide, the walls dark gray cinder block. There were only two ways out—the door at the far end of the corridor, through which the woman had brought him, and the door he now faced, which led to Rattan. The woman, whose name was Britta, had ordered him to wait in the corridor, then had gone through the door. He had been waiting fifteen or twenty minutes now.

He could not be sure, but he thought he was underground again. The way in had been relatively simple, though extremely secure: multicoded door seals, body searches, radiation scans, and two elevator rides so smooth he had not been able to gauge distance or direction for either one. He and Britta had encountered only two other people; both were silent and thorough guards.

The door opened and Britta appeared. "You can come in now," she said.

Tanner entered a large room filled with a cool, swirling fog of odorless smoke. The ceiling was high, close to twenty feet above the floor, and there was too much smoke to see how far back the room went. Through the mist, Tanner made out stretches of bamboo along the windowless walls, and the flickering light of torches. This was Rattan, all right. Theatrics.

Absurd, Tanner thought. A machine was probably producing the smoke, swirling it about the room.

Rattan was nowhere to be seen. Hidden in the mists? Tanner walked farther into the room and nearly stepped into a narrow stream of water that flowed silently through a curved channel in the floor. The channel was no more than a foot and a half across, maybe two feet deep.

"Wait," Britta said.

Tanner stood at the edge of the channel and gazed about the room, searching through the mist for Rattan. On the right wall, set against a stand of bamboo, was a wooden bench flanked by two flaming torches. Toward the left, along the channel where it entered another stand of bamboo, was a second bench. He still could not make out the rear wall because of the smoke.

"All right now," Britta said. "Cross the water, go to the right, and sit on the bench."

Tanner stepped across the channel and walked to the right, listening for Britta's footsteps. She did not follow him. He reached the bench, glanced at the two flaming torches, then looked into the dense stand of bamboo, wondering if it hid anyone or anything. He could see nothing inside the bamboo, could only hear a slight hiss and creak of the plants rubbing against one another.

"Sit," Britta said.

He turned around and looked at her. Partially hidden by the shifting mists, she remained at the door. Tanner sat.

There was silence for several minutes. No, not complete silence. The torches, burning atop wooden poles, made an occasional light whipping sound, and there was the irregular hiss and creak of the bamboo, as if its own height and weight were too much to maintain without great effort.

Then new sounds, almost inaudible—a faint whir, a sliding sound, a tiny squeal. Tanner looked at the rear wall. The smoke had parted enough to reveal an opening like the mouth of a tunnel. A large, complex wheeled contraption appeared at the opening, then moved into the room. Rattan.

The contraption was a fantastic wheelchair mounted with a framework of scaffolding and hooks from which hung clear plastic sacks filled with variously colored fluids and a complex network of tubes and modular units, all feeding into Rattan's limbs. Or what remained of his limbs. Rattan sat in the midst of it all, manipulating the controls with his right hand—the only whole limb remaining. His left arm was cut off at the elbow, his left leg halfway up his thigh, his right leg at the knee. Strange sacks and webs enveloped the cut-off limbs, with several fluid tubes emerging from each. Rattan's face was still recognizable, intact except for a long, ragged scar on his left cheek.

Rattan manuevered himself to a spot a few feet in front of Tanner, then locked the chair into place.

"Hello, Tanner." He gestured at the various fluid bags dangling above him. "Can I offer you something to drink?" He laughed, closing his eyes, then shook his head as the laughter faded. He opened his eyes. "Seriously, Tanner. Britta can get you whatever I haven't got."

"Nothing," Tanner said. He did not want to be affected in any way during the coming encounter with Rattan—not by alcohol, not even caffeine. And he did not want to be affected by pity. Much of Rattan's presence and power appeared to be gone now. Entrapped in the fantastic wheelchair, Rattan seemed very much a different person. But Tanner knew that could also be deceptive.

Rattan reached back and opened a small cabinet mounted on the right side of the wheelchair, withdrew a glass, then a bottle. He poured himself a drink—scotch or bourbon, Tanner thought—then set the bottle in one of the holders on the chair arm. He held out the glass toward Tanner, nodded, then drank from it.

"I hear you're looking for me," Rattan said.

"Yes."

Rattan nodded, smiling slightly. "You wouldn't have found me."

Tanner did not doubt that. He had no illusions about that now, nor did he have any illusions about this meeting. Rattan had not set this up out of generosity. Rattan wanted something from Tanner. The biggest question, though, was whether or not Tanner had any chance of getting what *he* wanted from Rattan.

Rattan adjusted himself in the wheelchair, then took another drink. Tanner glanced toward the door, but Britta was gone. He searched through the mists, but did not see her anywhere. He had not noticed her go out the door, nor had he noticed her leave through the tunnel. He wondered if she was still in the room somewhere, hidden.

"You sure you don't want something to drink?" Rattan asked.

Tanner returned his attention to Rattan. "I'm sure."

Rattan nodded, finished off his drink, then poured himself another. "I drink a lot these days," Rattan said. "Takes the edge off the pain." He shook his head. "Never liked pharmaceuticals. They're a great business, but I've never trusted them for myself." He frowned, set down his drink, then manipulated the controls, unlocking the wheels and moving the chair slightly before relocking them.

"You know who did this to me, don't you?" Rattan asked.

"Max."

"Yeah, Max. And he almost killed *you*. I screwed up on that one. But Max is taken care of now, permanently, and you're here." He paused. "Three weeks ago, I didn't give a rat's ass where you were or what you were doing. I want something, I'm sure you realize that, but three weeks ago I had no way to get to you. I've been pushing some other lines, without much luck. But something changed."

"The Chain Killer."

"Yeah, the Chain Killer. You all thought he was dead, didn't you? Well. You were wrong."

Rattan lapsed into silence, gazing into his half-empty drink. Tanner needed patience now. He wanted to press Rattan, ask him questions, but he knew that would only work against him. Rattan was in control of the situation, and they both knew it. He would get around to things in his own way, at his own speed. Tanner just had to be patient and wait; everything would come out.

"I knew you'd come looking for me," Rattan said. "I know you, Tanner. I knew you'd remember my message, and I knew, I know you're not a cop anymore, but I knew you'd come looking for me. I knew you wouldn't be able to let it go." He swirled his drink, but did not bring it to his mouth. "I was waiting for you. With Britta. I wasn't in any hurry, I mean, I had some other things playing out, I wanted to kind of check in on you, let you flop around a couple of days. Pump up the pressure a little." He shook his head. "But I screwed up, and I didn't count on Max, that bastard's been more fucking trouble.

Well, not anymore, not where he is. I let you go, and I didn't know you'd made contact with him. I would never have let it go any further, I'd have brought you in, but by the time I picked you up again, you were on your way to meet him, which I didn't even know, and I lost you. Nearly lost you for good."

He stopped and took a few sips from his drink. He punched several buttons on the chair console, studied some figures flashing across the display, flickering green lights reflecting from his eyes.

"It's what I get for being an honorable man," he resumed. "Max and I had an arrangement. After he tried to kill me. We were both out to kill the other, someone was going to get it sometime, but it might take months, or longer, for one of us to pull it off. Max, he's an artist. *Was* an artist. I didn't care much for his crap poetry or his performances with the Red Giant, but that was beside the point. I understood and appreciated his . . . what? Dedication. So we worked out an arrangement. We had a way, he'd notify me in advance when and where he would be performing. I'd stay away, pull all my people back during his performance, an hour before and after, too, so he could come and go without giving away where he was bunkered in. We could trust each other. He knew I'd honor the agreement and stay away, and I knew he wouldn't pull any shit, like maybe set up a phony performance to put me off guard so he could come at me again. With this, we *could* trust each other. Might seem kind of weird, but there it was." Rattan sighed heavily, melodramatically. "Which was how I missed you meeting him."

Patience, Tanner reminded himself. Rattan was liable to ramble on for hours, but Tanner had to go with it. Patience. He'll get there eventually. *We'll* get there.

"How's the smuggling business?" Rattan asked.

Tanner hesitated a moment, surprised by the change in direction. "It's all right."

Rattan nodded slowly. "Think you could smuggle a body up to New Hong Kong? A *live* body?"

Again Tanner hesitated. A live body. Who? Rattan? Yes, he thought—Rattan. He was starting to put it together. "I don't know," he said. "Never thought about it before. Not as a passenger, you mean."

"Not as a passenger."

"I suppose it would be possible. It would be expensive as hell, but I imagine it could be done. Who do you want smuggled up?"

Rattan shook his head and waved his glass in dismissal. He put the glass in another of the holders, then grasped the wheelchair armrest, fingers tightening over it.

"I *do* know who the Chain Killer is," Rattan said. "And I know *where* he is."

Tanner watched Rattan and waited.

Rattan smiled. "You know what he calls himself?" Rattan said.

"What?"

"Destroying Angel." He nodded. "I may be the only person alive who knows that. And now you know it."

Destroying Angel. Christ. It fit with everything the bastard did. Destroying Angel, angel of death. Jesus Christ, Tanner thought, the hard bite of certainty digging at his chest. Rattan *does* know who it is.

Tanner breathed deeply and slowly, trying to calm himself. *Who is it?* he wanted to ask, but he knew he couldn't. He had to wait.

"I want my legs back," Rattan said. "I want my arm back." He tossed off the rest of his drink, poured another. He stared hard at Tanner. "I want them back."

So did Brendan, Tanner thought. So did Spade. Well, maybe not Spade, he probably *liked* having a leg that converted into a scattergun. And Rattan wanted his legs and arm back. Here it comes, he thought.

Rattan looked at his left arm, what was left of it, and moved it slowly, raising arms and sacks and tubes. What *was* all that stuff? Tanner wondered. He had never seen anything like it.

"I don't like being confined to this damn thing," Rattan said. "I want to walk again. I *will* walk again."

There was something going on here that Tanner did not understand. The kind of money Rattan had, he could buy the best cyborged prosthetics available, be walking around as well as he ever had with his real legs.

"I know what you're thinking," Rattan said. "And if you knew . . . well, if you knew some things, maybe you wouldn't be wondering. Prosthetics, right? That's what you're thinking.

State-of-the-art cyborged prosthetics. Look and move like the real thing, if you want. Better." Rattan finished off his drink, shook his head, then leaned forward, staring at Tanner. "Never. Never. I want to remain human."

Rattan glared at Tanner for another minute, silent and tight. Then the intensity left his eyes and he sank back in the wheelchair, apparently exhausted. He closed his eyes. The only movement Tanner could detect was the labored rise and fall of his chest with each breath. Rattan opened his eyes.

"You don't know what all this is for, do you?" Rattan gestured with his hand and head at the sacks and tubes.

"No," Tanner said.

"To keep the stumps from healing over," Rattan said. "An artificial circulatory system to keep the wounds open but alive." He paused. "I've been like this for three months, ever since that motherfucking dwarf got at me." Another pause. "It gives me the best shot at full regeneration."

There, finally, confirmation; he had been right about what Rattan wanted. With the realization came a rush of elation, which he tried to control, because he knew he probably *could* give Rattan what he wanted, and get in return what *he* wanted.

"It was a mistake to kill those two cops," Rattan said. "I didn't think I had any choice at the time, but I guess I should have found, I don't know, another way. It's been causing me grief for two years. They were scumbags, Tanner. The worst, most corrupt cops I've ever known. They wanted a percentage of the profits, which was bad enough. But when I refused, they threatened the lives of my sister and her family. Not *my* life, my sister's. So I killed the fuckers. No choice, I thought. But it's been nothing but trouble ever since."

Rattan stopped, picked up the bottle, started to pour another drink, then changed his mind. He recapped the bottle, then put it and the glass back inside the cabinet.

"I've had too much," he said. "It's not enough, but it's too much." He looked up at Tanner. "You see where we're going?" he asked.

"I think so."

"From the beginning I figured you could help me, but I knew you wouldn't. You might be doing a bit of smuggling, but it's too well intentioned, and you're basically too damn honest, and what the hell did I have to offer you? Money. You wouldn't have done it for money, would you?"

Tanner shook his head. "No."

"You know what I want, don't you?"

"You want to get up to New Hong Kong."

"Yes." He was leaning forward again, straining the limits of the tubes running from his left arm.

"Have they been having successes I haven't heard about?"

Rattan sagged back into the chair, slowly shook his head. "No. Some partial successes, with a very few. I know my chances aren't good. But they get better with each one, and they're the best damn chances I've got." He smiled. "But I can't get up there. The doctors doing the regen work are expecting me. We've made arrangements, I've even done the funds transfers. One hell of a lot of money. But I can't get up there, and they can't get me up there, either."

Tanner understood. You couldn't just book a flight on a shuttle as if it were an airplane or a train. Trying to use a false name would be completely useless because the security checks on every passenger involved fingerprint and retinal scan confirmations. No matter what name Rattan used, or how he made arrangements, there was no way to bribe his way through the security clearances. A few crates of cargo was one thing, if the loaders knew who you were. But passengers? Not a chance. And Rattan would be arrested on the spot when his name came up on the monitors.

"I've been trying to buy a way into police records," Rattan said. "Get everything in the fucking computers changed. Prints, retinals, everything, so my prints and scans will match a nice, clean profile with a different name. But I'm not getting shit. That's where killing those two cops has fucked things up for me. The only cops I've been able to buy into are scumbags so low they can't do shit for me. Security on records is too damn tight."

So *that's* what's been going on between Rattan and some of the cops. Things were starting to make sense.

"You're another way up," Rattan continued. "But like I said, I had nothing but money, and I knew that wouldn't buy you. Then a stroke of luck. A few weeks ago I start hearing things about . . . well, some things, and then *three* weeks ago, it starts up again. A stroke of luck for me, not for the poor bastards being killed by this guy. And suddenly, I have something to offer you."

"Who is it?" Tanner finally asked. He just could not keep it back any longer. Rattan was capable of stretching this out for hours.

"Will you find me a way up to New Hong Kong?"

Tanner did not have to think about it, not after everything he had gone through to get here. "If I can, yes. And you tell me who the Chain Killer is, this Destroying Angel."

"When it's set," Rattan said. "When I'm about to get loaded up onto a shuttle headed for New Hong Kong." He paused, as if waiting for Tanner to object, but Tanner remained silent. "I told you," Rattan went on, "I'm an honorable man. I *will* tell you who it is, and where to find him. You can trust me. Just as I'll have to trust *you*, trust you won't fuck me over, have things set up to haul me off as soon as I've told you. We both have to trust each other. And we can, can't we?" Rattan paused, his expression serious and intent. "Do we have a deal?"

Again there was no hesitation, no need to consider. Rattan was right, they had to trust each other. He nodded. "Yes, Rattan, we have a deal."

THIRTY-ONE

THE FIRST CALL he made was to Alexandra. It was early morning, and he was back at Hannah and Rossi's. He was exhausted from his encounter with Rattan, which had continued until dawn—working out details, putting up with Rattan's rambling. Tanner wanted to sleep, but he needed to talk to people first, get things going.

There were two real options for getting Rattan up to New Hong Kong. The first, which was what Rattan expected from Tanner, was to actually crate up Rattan like cargo and smuggle him aboard the cargo holds. A doctor would have to be crated with him; he was going to need medical attention just to survive the trip, and going this way would be riskier from that perspective than going as a passenger. Which was the second option. As a passenger. Rattan was convinced that going as a passenger was impossible, but Tanner was not. It was by far the better way to go, so it was worth exploring fully. Which was why he called Alexandra.

When he got her on the phone, he explained what he needed, and asked her if she could do it. "You're the hotshot computer demon, right?" he said.

"Right," Alexandra said. "First time you ever ask me to do something, and you ask the near impossible."

"But you did just say *near* impossible."

"Yes. Very little in this business is truly impossible, but that doesn't mean I can do it. I *do* know that I can't do it on my own. I'll need to talk to one or two other people,

159

maybe even bring somebody in to actually make the run. That a problem?"

"Yeah, but acceptable, if you can trust the person."

"I won't use anybody I can't."

"All right. How long will it take you to find out if it can be done?"

"I should know by tonight. You at the same number?"

"I am now, but I may go home today, so you could try me there."

"I'll call you, then, one place or another. Or drop by."

"Thanks, Alexandra. I appreciate it."

"Sure. *Ciao*."

"Bye."

He broke the connection, then punched up Paul's number. There was no answer—Paul refused to get an answering machine—so Tanner tried the hospital. The receptionist told him that Paul was with a patient, so Tanner left his name and both phone numbers.

He hung up the phone and sank back in the overstuffed chair, thinking. He was not sure what to do about Carlucci. He did not know how far Carlucci would be willing to go. Carlucci would do almost anything to find the Chain Killer, Tanner knew that, but would he let a cop killer escape to New Hong Kong where he would be free and untouchable? Tanner could imagine Carlucci promising Rattan anything, and then, as soon as Rattan told them what he knew, coming down on him and hauling him in.

Tanner could not allow that to happen. He understood Carlucci, but he had given his word to Rattan. He could not take the chance. No, he could not tell Carlucci what he was going to do.

Hannah appeared at the doorway in her T-shirt, hair mussed, eyes half-closed.

"Good morning," she said. Her voice was harsh and gravelly.

"Morning, Hannah."

She remained in the doorway without saying any more, looking at him. Tanner did not know what to say, either, so they stared at each other in silence until Hannah finally turned away and went into the bathroom. He listened to her morning noises—toilet seat dropping, streaming liquid, the toilet flushing, then the spitting of the shower.

There was no reason to stay here any longer. With Max and Red Giant dead, there should be no problem going back home. He missed his apartment, the quiet warm comfort of familiarity. He missed his own bed. It struck him as absurd, but it was true.

The phone rang and Tanner picked it up. It was Paul. Again Tanner explained the situation, as briefly as he could. He emphasized Rattan's physical condition, why he was going to New Hong Kong.

"He's going to need a doctor with him either way," Paul said. "Even as a passenger. He'll be lucky to survive liftoff."

"*Can* he survive it?"

"Oh, yeah. If he's got a good doctor with him who knows what he's doing and watches him every second."

"You willing to be that doctor?" Tanner asked.

"Figured you were getting to that," Paul said. He did not say anything else for a while, and Tanner listened to his regular breathing over the phone. In the background he could hear the faint sound of someone screaming, then a crash, and then laughter.

"Yes or no," Tanner said. What were his options if Paul said no? Leo, the junkie doctor?

"Let me think about it. How soon you need an answer?"

"Soon. Today."

"Give me an hour or so. You be there?"

"I hope I'll be home."

"Okay. I'll let you know. Talk to you then."

"Good-bye."

He set the phone down but did not move. He remained motionless, listening to the shower until it stopped. A couple of minutes later Hannah emerged from the bathroom wearing a thin robe, her hair half-wrapped in a towel. She sat on the sofa, facing him.

"Can I fix you some breakfast?"

Tanner shook his head. "I'm leaving. I'm going back to my apartment."

"I thought it wasn't safe."

"It should be all right now."

"You get what you were looking for?"

"I think so."

Hannah nodded. She rubbed at her hair with the towel, then pulled it away from her head and let it drop into her lap. "We're a lot better at figuring out other people's lives than we are at figuring out our own." When Tanner did not say anything in response, Hannah said, "I hope you think about it, Louis, what I said about Valerie." Tanner still did not respond, and Hannah shook her head. "Fine." She got up, wrapping the towel around her shoulders. "Good-bye, Louis." She walked into the bedroom and closed the door.

Tanner got up from the chair and began packing.

Tanner splurged and took a cab. He still had most of the money from Carlucci, and he figured he had earned it. Inside the cab, he punched up the intercom, gave the driver his address, then told her to take a longer route, up and through the Marina along Marina Drive. The driver, an Arab woman wearing a black flash suit, confirmed, and turned up the radio. Ether jazz rolled smoothly through the cab.

Tanner could hardly stay awake during the trip. It was not just exhaustion. Tense situations and nervous anticipation tended to make him sleepy. When he had been a cop he had often fallen asleep during the tensest moments of waiting before some action was to begin. Once things started, the adrenaline kicked in and he was fine, but until then he could hardly keep his eyes open. Freeman had spent a lot of energy kicking Tanner in the shins trying to keep him awake.

The cab came over the top of a hill and dropped down toward the Marina and the bay. The water was steel gray, overlaid with bits of color: streaks of dark orange, splotches of yellow foam, patches of red, all bobbing in the waves whipped up by a stiff breeze. Two Bay Security cutters were anchored close to shore, almost touching each other, and the Bay Soldiers, jumping back and forth between the boats, seemed to be having a party.

At the bottom of the hill, the driver swung the cab along Marina Drive, between the abandoned art colony at Fort Mason and the cyclone fence surrounding the twenty-four-hour Safeway. Tanner punched up the intercom again, said, "Stop here a minute." The driver pulled over and parked, engine and meter still running.

Tanner gazed at the Safeway parking lot, which was filled with cars, carriages, shopping carts, and people moving between the vehicles and the store, many of them with armed escorts. It was here his father had been killed, seven years ago. Two in the morning, decided he had to have some ice cream, drove to the Safeway. He had gotten the ice cream. When Tanner had arrived, called in by someone he knew in Homicide, the melted ice cream had formed a puddle beside his father's body, leaking out of the carton, mixing with the blood from a torch wound in his father's belly. Häagen-Dazs. Vanilla fudge ripple. His father should have known better.

"Go on," he told the driver. The driver pulled back out into traffic; Tanner laid his head back against the seat and closed his eyes, listening to the ether jazz, drifting again toward sleep.

The cab stopped abruptly, jolting him awake. The driver's voice rattled through the intercom. "We're here."

Tanner put money in the metal box, told the driver to keep the change. The driver slotted the money through, counted it, then released the door locks, tapping at the partition with her knuckles. Tanner got out, closed the door, and the cab pulled away.

A woman who lived on the second floor was in the front courtyard cutting back the overgrown foliage. She and Tanner nodded their greetings as he walked along the path and entered the building. His mailbox was full, jammed with crushed and mangled envelopes—the carrier had managed to cram a week's worth of mail into the narrow box. Tanner sorted through it, but there wasn't anything of interest. He climbed the stairs to the fourth floor.

His apartment was quiet and stuffy. There was a strange, abandoned feel to the place, and he felt as if he had been away for several weeks. He walked through the apartment and opened all the windows. It was hot outside, but a slight breath of wind came in, which helped a little.

Tanner went into the kitchen and opened the refrigerator. There wasn't much inside, and half of it had gone bad since he had left. He knew he should clean it out, but he was too tired. He opened a half-empty bottle of apple juice, smelled it, then drank deeply from the bottle. The cold, sweet liquid hit him hard; it made him a little dizzy, and the cold sent a shot of pain through his sinuses, right behind his left eye. But the pain and dizziness passed, and he felt much better, even refreshed.

The phone rang. He put the juice away and went into the hall to answer it. It was Paul.

"I'll do it," Paul said. "But I'd like to see if you can set something up for me."

"What's that?"

"I'd like to stay up in New Hong Kong for a few months and work with the regeneration teams up there. I told you I've been getting burned out, and this sounds like the kind of thing I need. Something positive, for a change. Beat the hell out of the ER night after night."

Tanner could actually hear the renewed interest in Paul's voice. He had not felt that from Paul in years.

"I'll see what I can do. My guess is I'll be able to work something out."

"Thanks. I appreciate it."

"No problem. You're helping me a lot with this. I'll let you know."

When he hung up, he dialed the number Rattan had given him. Britta answered the phone. Tanner told her he needed to talk to Rattan, and Britta said she would pass on the message. Rattan would return the call sometime later in the day.

Tanner could not decide whether or not to go to sleep. He was tired, but it was only noon, and now that he was out of the Tenderloin he wanted to go back to something like a normal schedule. He was afraid that if he slept now he would be unable to get to sleep tonight. But he did not know if he could stay awake.

He went into the front room and turned on the television. He could not remember the last time he had watched it. Three, four weeks, maybe longer. He flipped through the channels until he came to a video call-in show; only callers with videophones and willing to appear on-screen were allowed. The host was the only participant *not* on camera. The topic was universal health insurance, which was up in Congress again this session. A man on the screen was ranting about the poor getting better health care than they deserved, punctuating each statement with a thrust of his fist. He had just launched into an incomprehensible analysis of the connection between economic status and the desire to be diseased, when Tanner fell asleep.

Tanner woke to the ringing of the telephone. The TV was still on, now showing a soaper. Still half-asleep, he staggered into the hall and picked up the receiver, expecting either Alexandra or Rattan. It was Carlucci.

"You're back home," Carlucci said.

"Yes."

"You sound awful."

"I was asleep."

"I talked to Hannah. She said you told her you thought it was safe now."

"Yes."

"Why?"

Tanner hesitated, trying to decide what to tell Carlucci. Lying was no good. "Max is dead."

There was a slight pause, then, "Did you kill him?"

"No."

"Who did?"

"I don't know," Tanner said. Technically that was true. He did not know who had thrown Max and Red Giant out the window. He did know that Rattan himself could not have done it.

"How do you know? You see this one happen, too?"

"Yes. A kind of show was arranged for me."

"Yeah?"

"I was told to go to a place, and then Max was thrown out of a tenth-floor window." He paused. "I think Rattan is responsible."

"What, did you find him?"

"No." He found *me,* Tanner thought. "But I'll be talking to him soon. I'm close, Carlucci. He knows I've been looking for him."

"Then he's contacted you."

"Yes. And I'll be talking to him."

"When?"

"I don't know. Soon."

There was another silence, longer this time. "What aren't you telling me?" Carlucci finally asked.

"Nothing."

"Bull*shit*, Tanner. What is it?"

Tanner started to say "nothing" again, but held back. There was no point saying it when Carlucci knew it wasn't true. But he didn't know what to say instead of that, so he did not answer Carlucci's question at all. "Don't worry about it," he eventually said. "There's no problem. When I get anything, I'll let you know."

"We'd better meet somewhere and talk. Now."

"No," Tanner said. "I've got too much to do, and I've got to get some sleep. There just isn't time."

"God damn you, Tanner, don't go solo on me now. I don't want to be calling in the coroner for you."

"It's okay, Carlucci, it's nothing like that."

"Shit, Tanner." But he did not say anything else.

"I'll call you when I've got something," Tanner said again.

After a short silence, Carlucci said, "Yeah, all right." Resigned and pissed. "Shit, just don't do anything stupid."

"I won't." Tanner smiled to himself. "I'll talk to you." He hung up the phone before Carlucci could start in again.

He walked back into the front room. On the soaper, a man with a cyborged leg, an eye patch, and several days' growth of beard, held a gun and was threatening a woman with it. They were on the balcony of a resort hotel, a swimming pool visible far below them.

Tanner turned off the TV. He felt more tired now than before he had fallen asleep. Maybe he should just give in, crawl into bed, and sleep. Maybe he would sleep all the way through to morning.

Except he had two calls coming in. Rattan and Alexandra. He had to stay awake. Tanner walked into the kitchen and put the teakettle on to boil. Coffee might help. Probably not. He had noticed that, as he got older, drinking coffee when he was tired often would just about put him under. So why was he making coffee now? Something to do. And maybe it *would* help.

He was halfway through his second cup, his stomach souring, when the phone rang again. He answered it, and a harsh voice said, "Tanner, it's me." Rattan.

"I've got a doctor to go with you," Tanner said. "But there's a condition."

"What is it?"

"He wants to stay in New Hong Kong for a while and work with the regen teams up there. Can you set that up?"

"Fuck, I'm paying those bastards enough, I sure as hell hope so. Anything else?"

"Yes. Don't know for sure yet, but I think you'll be going as a passenger. It'll be a lot less dangerous for you, a lot easier for the doctor."

"And the security checks?"

"I'm working on that right now. Tonight or tomorrow I should know if we can pull it off."

"There's a shuttle leaving in two days," Rattan said. "I want to be on it."

"We'll see," Tanner replied.

"I want to be on it," Rattan said again.

"I'll talk to you." Tanner hung up. He stood by the phone, half expecting it to ring again, Rattan calling him back. But the telephone remained silent.

Tanner was half-asleep, listening to Taj Larsen, a wild trumpet player from the late nineties, when he realized someone was pounding on his front door. Not buzzing from the street, but banging at the door. He got up from his easy chair, turned down the stereo, and went to the door. "Who is it?" he called.

"Me."

Alexandra. He opened the door and let her in.

"I think we've got a way to do it," she said. Then she cocked her head at him. "You growing a beard?"

"Only until I find the energy to shave it off."

They went into the kitchen. Alexandra took a couple of beers from the refrigerator, opened them, handed one to Tanner, then they walked into the front room. Alexandra sat on the small sofa, Tanner in the easy chair.

"So there's a way," Tanner said.

Alexandra nodded. "Getting into those kinds of records is a bitch," she said. "So many walls, so many alarms, and traps ready to suck you right in and bury you." She shook her head, smiling. "But we got in."

"Who's 'we'?"

"Me and Kaufman. You wouldn't believe this guy, looks nothing like a computer demon, but man is he good. Mid-forties, bit of a potbelly, wears nice tailored suits, runs a very conservative business distributing toilet-seat liners to office buildings downtown. But sit him down at a keyboard and he just goes nuts. Sometimes I think maybe he's a little schizoid. A functional schizoid."

"So you and Kaufman got in."

"We got in, but getting in's not the same as doing anything. And there's no way to change anything in there without blowing off a dozen alarms and leaving traces. But . . ." She shrugged, drank from her beer. "Kaufman thinks there's a way to take care of your problem. It's only good for one shot, but it should cover you. You only need one clearance and confirmation, right?"

"Far as I know. Just the boarding."

"Well, here it is. What Kaufman does is create a mimic. Kind of a program overlay right at the access point of Rattan's ID data. It'll only work once, and it'll only work with Rattan once he sets it up. Rattan will have to make arrangements for the shuttle trip, and get basic document ID for someone else who's already in the data base. It's got to be someone clean, of course, who will get approval for all the initial arrangements. But it's also got to be someone no one at Hunter's Point will know. You don't want some freak coincidence of pulling a name at random and it turns out to be the upstairs neighbor of the guy running the confirmation check. Rattan's got to choose the name, he's going to be in the best position to know what's safe.

"So what happens is this, without getting too damn technical. Actually, I can't *be* too technical, because I don't really understand it all myself, but Kaufman says it'll go, and I trust him. So. Rattan goes through security at the launch field, they check the documents, then hook him up. All his fingerprint and retinal data go into the system and search for the matchup, right? Finds the match, and Rattan's name and status come off and head back out. This is where the mimic kicks in. It rides piggyback on the confirmation all the way out to the Hunter's Point field terminals. Just after it enters the system, before it comes up on the screens, it does a dump of Rattan's name and status and substitutes this other guy's info, which then comes up on their screens. Identity and status confirmed. Then it all does a self-destruct, program and data, and there's not a trace anywhere. No traps, no alarms go off, Kaufman says, because nothing in the data base or programming is changed, nothing even touched, really. All basically passive until the final step." She paused, drank the rest of the beer, and breathed deeply. "Anyway, Kaufman says it'll work."

"Can it be set up in two days?"

"Probably. Kaufman's working on the mimic right now. He'll just need a name from Rattan to complete it."

Tanner slowly nodded, more to himself than to Alexandra. That's what *he* needed from Rattan as well. A name.

"Why are you doing this for him?" Alexandra asked. "You must be getting something from Rattan."

"Yes, I am."

"What, then?"

Tell her or not? He knew she would do it without an answer, but that was not really the point. Tell her. "The name and whereabouts of the Chain Killer."

"Jesus. Rattan knows?"

"If he doesn't, I'm going to follow him up to New Hong Kong myself and cut off the one intact limb he's still got."

It was well after dark, nearly ten o'clock, by the time Tanner was finally done for the day, but he felt good. Things were falling into place, and in two days he should have what he wanted from Rattan.

Rattan had called back just a few minutes earlier. He had been in touch with the New Hong Kong doctors, and arrangements were set for Paul. Tanner had told him what he needed for Alexandra, and Rattan had said he would have it for Tanner by the next day. It was all moving forward. Tanner had done everything he could, and now he just had to wait.

He went into the bedroom and stood at the window, looking down at the street. Oscar, the blind cat, sat on the sidewalk, licking himself. The night was quiet. Tanner was back home, and things were done, and he could sleep now. He would need the sleep. Once he got the name from Rattan, he and Carlucci would probably get very little sleep until they had tracked the Chain Killer down and taken him in. *If* they could find him. There was no guarantee, no matter how good Rattan's info was.

Then what? Once they had the guy, then what? What would it mean, anything?

Don't think about it now, he told himself. He undressed, got into bed, and closed his eyes. He slept.

THIRTY-TWO

SOOKIE WAS FEELING pretty proud of herself. She'd been the one who spotted the ambulance. She could hardly sit still, she was so excited. Mixer sat beside her, and they were both smoking. Mixer seemed a lot more relaxed than she was. They were sitting outside a crasher shop, watching the ambulance.

She had lost Tanner for two or three days. Mixer had stuck with her a lot of the time. Worried about her, she guessed. She tried to tell him not to bother, she was fine, but he just grumbled a lot and stuck with her anyway. Sookie really liked Mixer. He was a good person.

They had wandered around the Tenderloin, but they'd hung out a lot near the tattoo parlor, since that was the last place they'd seen him. And it paid off.

Tanner had shown up with another man. Sookie thought maybe it was the man Tanner had been sitting with that day by the water, when she'd seen the bodies. They had met the woman again, in front of the tattoo parlor. Then they'd all gone inside. The tattoo parlor was still closed and locked.

Sookie and Mixer had waited around awhile, and then they'd decided to check out the other streets, the back of the buildings, the alleys. That's when she'd spotted the ambulance and pointed it out to Mixer. Mixer had grinned and said, "Good girl, Sookie. Good eyes." And they'd set up outside the crasher shop to watch.

A real city ambulance was a rare sight inside the Tenderloin, and it meant money. Money to get in, money to get out. It might have nothing to do with Tanner, but Sookie had a good feeling about it. So did Mixer.

Hah! Sookie said to herself. She'd been right. Tanner came out of the building nearest the ambulance, waved at the attendants and guards. Ambulance doors were opened. Then the other man and the woman came out of the building, pushing a crazy-looking wheelchair with a chopped-up man in it. There was all kinds of stuff hanging all over the wheelchair.

"Man," Mixer said, "will you scope out that thing. That guy's a fuckin mess."

Sookie was holding on to her legs to keep them from wiggling too much. "Who is he?"

Mixer shook his head. "No idea."

The woman and the attendants were working with the wheelchair, loading it into the back of the ambulance. The man swore at them once. Tanner and his friend and the woman all got in the back with the wheelchair, along with an attendant. Guards closed up the doors, then got into the front with the driver.

"Let's go," Mixer said. He jumped up and pulled Sookie to her feet. "Follow me."

They hurried along the streets, running hard whenever there was room. Sookie didn't know where they were going, but she was sure Mixer knew what he was doing. They hitched a ride with an organ runner for a few blocks, to the edge of the Tenderloin, then hopped off and hurried through a bunch of shops to an exit leading out of the Tenderloin. Once outside, they ran a couple of blocks to the end of an alley leading back into the Tenderloin.

"There's only two places you can get in and out with something as big as an ambulance," Mixer said. "This is the closest one, so I figure this is where they'll show up. Man, it must have cost a lot to buy passage in and out."

Mixer started moving around the street, looking into cars and trucks and carts, trying doors.

"What are you looking for?" Sookie asked.

"A free ride. How else we going to follow them when they come out?"

Sookie tried to keep an eye on the alley and stay with Mixer while he bounced around. All the doors were locked, he couldn't get into anything. Somebody yelled at Mixer, told him to get the hell away from his cart. Mixer ran across the street, Sookie right behind him.

Suddenly Mixer stopped, and Sookie almost ran into him. "Hey," he said.

"Hey what?"

Mixer was staring across the street at a parked brown car with a man sitting behind the wheel, drinking something out of a paper cup. The man in the car looked familiar. Sookie *knew* she'd seen him before. But where?

"That's the same guy," Mixer said.

"What same guy?" She still couldn't remember where she'd seen him.

"That guy Tanner kept meeting outside the Tenderloin. I told you I'd check him out, see who he is." He turned to Sookie and grinned. "He's a cop."

"A cop?"

"Yeah. His name's Carlucci. Tanner *used* to be a cop. I checked him out, too. He quit a couple years ago after his partner got killed. He got shot pretty bad himself."

Sookie was about to ask him more when the ambulance appeared, creeping out of the alley. There wasn't more than a couple of inches of space on either side, and it couldn't even turn, it had to come straight all the way out.

"Damn," Mixer said, hitting the roof of the locked car beside him. "We're going to lose them."

The ambulance cleared the alley, turned south, and picked up speed. The brown car with Carlucci started up and pulled out into the street, following the ambulance.

"I'll be damned," Mixer said. "Wonder what the hell is going on here?" Within a minute both the ambulance and the brown car were out of sight. Mixer sat on the hood of the car, and Sookie hopped up beside him. "Carlucci's Homicide."

"What's that mean?" Sookie asked.

"He investigates murders. He's the top guy on the Chain Killer case."

"Chain Killer?"

"Yeah, that guy who kills people and chains them together and dumps them in the water."

Sookie got a funny feeling in her stomach, like something bouncing around inside.

"I've seen him," she said.

"Who?"

"The Chain Killer."

Mixer turned and stared at her, grabbed her shoulder. "You serious, Sookie? You're not screwing around?"

"I saw him," she repeated.

"Where?"

"In the Tundra."

She told him about trying to get away from the thrasher pack, going down into the basement. How the hatch was locked. Seeing the door, going down the passage, into the room. All the machines, and the chains hanging on the wall, then the man with the metal skull and machine voice and something like wings coming after her.

"Shit," Mixer said. "Sookie, you gotta show me where this is. You remember it? You can find it again?"

Sookie nodded, the funny feeling changing to fear inside her.

Mixer jumped off the hood. "Let's find a car and go," he said.

THIRTY-THREE

THEY ARRIVED AT the Hunter's Point launch field more than two hours before liftoff. Night was falling quickly, the sky a strange deep purple headed toward black. Paul, Britta, and Tanner helped unload Rattan from the ambulance, and wheeled him into the processing station. Through the station's huge view windows Tanner could see the shuttle, its form outlined by lights, cradled in the brightly lit gantry.

The processing teams were prepared for Rattan, though they thought he was someone else, of course. They informed him that he would be boarded first, a half hour early, so all the special physical arrangements could be made; formal processing and security checks would start in about forty minutes.

Rattan had dyed his hair, shaved his mustache, patched one eye and shimmered the other, and added a few ritual strips to his cheeks. Tanner would never have recognized him.

"It's time to talk now," Tanner said. "Or you don't go any further."

Rattan nodded. "We'll go back outside. Britta, stay here with Dr. Robertson. Mr. Tanner and I have some things to discuss."

Tanner and Rattan went back out the front entrance, Rattan expertly guiding the wheelchair out the doors and down the concrete ramp to the tarmac. Tanner followed as Rattan turned the corner of the building and wheeled to within a foot of the charged fencing. He positioned himself for a direct view of the lighted shuttle, and locked the wheels. Tanner stood beside him.

"Am I really going?" Rattan asked. He turned and looked at Tanner.

Tanner nodded. "You'll get through. You'll get aboard, and you'll still be aboard at liftoff." He paused. "I gave you my word."

"I wonder if I'd be able to tell if you were lying."

"I'm not."

Rattan stared at him, then grunted. "What about Carlucci? You're working with him on this."

Tanner was not surprised that Rattan knew. "Carlucci doesn't know. He knows I'm looking for you, he knows about your old message, but he doesn't know I've talked to you. He doesn't know we're here."

Rattan slowly nodded, but did not say anything.

"So who is it?" Tanner asked.

"The name won't mean a damn thing. You won't find him with it. But it's Cromwell. Albert Cromwell. What a name. Least his parents didn't name him Oliver." Rattan emitted something like a chuckle. But it quickly faded, and he wiped sweat from his forehead with his hand.

"If I get my arm and legs back," Rattan said, "I'm going to give up this business." He sighed. "Hell, even if I don't. I'm getting too old for it. I *feel* too old." He shook his head. "You know how old I am?"

"No."

"Thirty-nine. Forty next month. I know, it's not really that old, but . . . I've been doing this a long time. What is that, younger than you, right?"

"A little," Tanner said.

"Do you feel old?"

"Not really. I don't think about it much."

"*I* do. Getting your legs blown off'll make you feel old, tell you that. I don't know, I've been dealing drugs too many years now, and I like the odds less and less. *My* odds. I keep thinking they're going to catch up with me, I've had it my way too long." He wiggled his left arm stump, jiggling the overhead sacks. "I guess they did. And I don't want to push it any further."

He remained silent a long time, staring at the shuttle, and Tanner had the feeling Rattan was not going to say any more unless he prodded him. But, just as he was preparing to ask him for more about Albert Cromwell, Rattan began talking again.

"It cost me a fucking fortune to get onto this flight," he said. "Damn thing was full, and I had to buy four people off of it, and they didn't come cheap. Not much is cheap anymore. Shit, not much of any value ever *was*." He shook his head, gazing out at the shuttle. "You ever been in love, Tanner? You must have been, sometime in your life."

Tanner could not figure where Rattan was headed, but he could not think of anything to do except answer.

"Yes."

Rattan nodded. "I never was, up until a year ago. Always thought it was too much a pain in the ass, too much trouble. I *still* feel the same, but I fell in love anyway. Another sign of getting old, maybe. But of course I can't do it right, I've gotta fuck it up, I've gotta fall in love with guess who?"

"Not me, I hope."

Rattan laughed, so hard the chair shook. "Very good, Tanner. Don't want to be getting too . . . what's the word? Not *morbid*."

"Maudlin?"

"Yeah, maudlin." He shook his head, sighing heavily. "No, not you. Britta. Fucking crazy, yeah?"

"Why crazy?" Tanner asked.

"Because she's young and she's in love with a carnival stud who's got an augmented cock and, according to Britta, the strongest, longest tongue in the city. Me, I say who gives a shit, you can get a fucking machine to do all of that, if you want. But see, that's just it. We've got different priorities. Different interests. Different everything."

"She's going with you to New Hong Kong," Tanner said.

"Purely business. Purely temporary." He shrugged, then violently shook his head. "Why the *fuck* am I telling you all this, I must be going fucking senile." He turned and grimaced at Tanner. "You don't really care, either, do you? All you really want to hear about is Mr. Albert Cromwell, yes?"

Tanner shrugged. "That's what all this is about."

Rattan nodded, but did not resume speaking immediately. He spent a minute with the chair's controls, making minute adjustments to his position. When he was finished, nothing looked any different to Tanner.

"He was a customer," Rattan said. "A damn good customer. I mean, I didn't know he was the Chain Killer. He was just some guy who bought a lot of expensive shit. Well, not just some guy. See, he's fucking half machine. Maybe more than half." He turned to look at Tanner. "Yeah, he's the closest thing to a real cyborg *I've* ever seen. I mean, I don't know what the technical definition of a cyborg is, but I got a feeling this guy is it. *One* human arm and hand is all the guy had. The other arm's metal, and both legs. No flesh look-alikes. Fuckin' high-tech state-of-the-art cyborged. For all I know, the guy's got a metal dick, too. Metal plating up one side of his neck, and about half his skull's been removed and replaced with all kinds of hot-shit micro-circuitry. And who knows what else? And here's the fuckin' kicker. This guy *chose* to have all this stuff done to him. He *volunteered* to have them cut off his arm and legs and turn him into a fucking machine."

"Volunteered to have *who* do this?"

Rattan nodded and grinned. "Yeah, that's a question, isn't it? He's a fucking military project." He snorted. "Yeah, those bastards. Trying to see what kind of killing machines they can make out of human beings."

"How do you know all this?"

"I had a long conversation with the guy. A couple, actually. He liked to talk." Rattan shrugged. "I don't make a habit of seeing all my customers personal, but this guy, he was buying quantity. He was a good customer, I want to give a little personal service, right? Besides, I want to see what's going on with him. I mean, he's buying a *lot* of expensive shit, hard to believe he's doing it all himself. He's paying my prices, why should I care, right? Except I like to know what he's doing with it all, if anything weird's going on. Good business. So I go see him."

"What was he doing with the stuff?" Tanner asked.

"Shit, the guy's using it all himself. I mean, here I go see this guy, turns out he's half machine, and it turns out he's pumping all this stuff into himself. He's living in a flat in the Euro Quarter, which is where I go see him. First time he won't let me into the back rooms, and the front room and kitchen are practically empty. Front room's got a couple chairs and a bunch of electronic shit, which he tells me he hooks up to his cyborged parts.

"I get the feeling right off he doesn't have any friends, and he wants to talk, but he's got no one to talk to, and maybe it makes him crazy, I don't know, but he wants to talk to me. Doesn't hardly shut up, which is when he tells me about volunteering to be cyborged, how he's a big military project trying to see about making killing machines. Could be a load of shit, but he looks the part, right? So I ask him where are they now, the military, why isn't he on some army base somewhere, in some lab or whatever. He says he changed his mind, he didn't want to be a killing machine for the army, he didn't want to work for anyone. He was special now, he said. He said a lot of stuff like that, being special and powerful, and he wasn't going to take orders from anyone, he wasn't going to do anything he didn't want to do himself. So he escaped from wherever it was they had him. He didn't say where."

Rattan paused, adjusted his position in the chair. Tanner asked if he could do anything, but Rattan shook his head. He popped open the chair cabinet, took out a container of water, and drank deeply from it.

"Like I said," he continued, "could be a lot of crap, but I believe him. He says he hooks up a lot of this electronic stuff to himself, it does all kind of weird things to his body and his head, and then he pumps in the drugs, and he's like in another universe. I don't know, I hear that, it makes a lot of sense to me. I don't want to try it myself, but I can see it could be the ultimate rush.

"Still, something's off with this guy, I'm not sure what it is. I believe him about being a military project, and that he's using all the drugs himself, but there's something else, I have this gut feeling. So I ask can I come see him again, next time he needs a delivery, and he says sure. I think he likes the company, someone to talk to. So I go see him again, and this time I bring a few tick-ears, you know?"

"Listening bugs."

"Right. This time he trusts me some more, I guess, he takes me into one of the back rooms and shows me his special things. Now I know there's something weird about this guy. The room's full of angels and wings. Pictures of angels, some sculpture things. Lots of paintings and drawings, even a couple of things that look like photographs. And on the back wall is an actual set of wings, damned if they don't look like real angel wings. Made of something like feathers, but not real feathers, something else. I don't know if I can describe them, except they really looked like angel wings. As unreal as angel wings must be. I mean, I've never actually seen an angel, right, but . . .

"Now, here's where it gets good. He's showing me all this stuff, and then he takes off his shirt. His body's all crisscrossed with bands of metal, and he turns around so I can see his back. His back's *all* metal, from his neck down to his waist, real flexible and segmented or whatever, and up around his shoulder blades is some special device, all the way across his shoulders, with all kinds of slots and flanges and things, I don't know. What he does then, he goes to the back wall, where the angel wings are. I see now they have something that looks like it might hook up with what's on his back. He backs up to them, and I hear these clicking sounds, and then he steps away from the wall. The angel wings come with him, they're attached now. Somehow he's able to control the wings, they spread out, I don't know, maybe nine or ten feet across. Big fuckin' wings. He stands in the middle of the room, holding out his hands and arms, one metal, one human, remember, with the wings spread out behind him, rising a little. And then he says, 'When I'm wearing my wings, I am an angel. Destroying Angel.'

"So he's standing there, and he's smiling. He says the wings were his price for letting the military turn him into a cyborg. They had to give him wings." Rattan paused, shook his head. "That point, I'm glad I brought the tick-ears and dropped them around the place. This guy seems pretty fucking psycho to me now, and I'd like to know what's going on in his head."

Rattan stopped again, shook his head. "The next few days I listen to the tick-ears whenever I can. I mean, turns out I'm right about he has no friends or anything, no one comes to see him. But the guy likes to talk, right? So he talks to himself a lot. Most of the time he doesn't make any sense, I can't understand *what* the fuck he's talking about. But it's all pretty weird, and enough of it *does* make sense that after a few days I'm getting a pretty good idea that this guy's the fucking Chain Killer. I keep at it, I spend a lot of time listening, and when I'm pretty sure, I send you the message. I figure this is going to make me a lot of money."

"How did you know about the angel wings on the victims?"

Rattan smiled. "I didn't, really. It was a guess. He kept saying so much weird shit about angel wings, after a while I had the feeling he was doing something with angel wings to the bodies. So I was right?"

Tanner nodded. "He tattoos angel wings inside the nostrils of the victims."

"The nostrils? Why the hell does he do that?"

Tanner shook his head. "No idea." He paused. "So then what?"

"Then nothing. After a few days, I don't hear anything more. I think maybe he's found the tick-ears, so I send someone around to check on the building, see if she can pick up the guy and follow him around, see what he does, where he goes. Nothing. Do some more checking, the guy's gone. The flat's empty, and I mean stripped and cleaned out, not a damn thing left. I sort of bide my time, put out some feelers, see if this guy's showing up anywhere else, buying from my competitors, maybe. Nothing. After a while I realize the killings have stopped. I'm wondering what the hell's going on, the guy's gone, the killings stopped, I haven't heard a word from you or Freeman. I wonder has he been caught, but no, there's no way you guys wouldn't make a big deal catching that guy. Then I heard about Freeman being killed and you in the hospital, I realize why I haven't heard from you. Time goes on, the guy never shows, the killings never start again. I wonder if he's moved to some other city, but the killings don't start up anywhere else, near as I can figure. He's just gone."

"What do you think happened?"

"He didn't die, right, we know that now." Rattan nodded slowly to himself. "I think the military found him. They figured out he was the Chain Killer, and they found him and his angel shit, and they hauled him off and locked him up, and covered up everything." He turned to look at Tanner. "You don't think they were going to let anyone know that one of their pet projects had been running around killing people?"

Tanner shook his head. "No, I guess not. So what's happened now? He escape again?"

Rattan nodded. "Escaped, and picked up right where he left off two and a half years ago."

"And you know where he is."

Rattan nodded again, but did not say anything.

"Where?" Tanner said. "That's part of the deal."

"Yeah. Just remember, when there's bad news there's no use killing the messenger."

Great, Tanner thought. "All right, so what's the bad news?"

"He's in the Core."

The Core. Jesus. "You've seen him?"

"Oh no," Rattan said. "I don't go in there. Besides, I've been in this damn chair since he showed up again. But I've got a business, right, and I've got a few customers in the Core. I hear things from inside. Most things I don't care about, and most of what comes out of there you can't believe anyway. But when I started hearing that some half-metal freak with wings had shown up in the Core, I knew. I *knew*."

"Jesus," Tanner said. "Why the Core?"

"Hey, his kind of place, way I see it. Besides, he got found in the Tenderloin. He's trying to stay hidden from the military guys. How much deeper can you go than the Core? And who knows what the hell he's been doing in there? I heard about him several weeks before the first bodies showed up. Setting up shop, maybe. Who the fuck knows?"

Tanner did not say anything for a long time. The Core. Christ. They were going to have to go into the Core to find the bastard.

Rattan *had* come through. Tanner did not doubt his story at all, did not doubt that this man, Albert Cromwell, *was* the Chain Killer. The Destroying Angel.

"Now do you understand?" Rattan asked.

"Understand what?"

He wiggled his left arm stump. "Why I won't get cyborged prosthetics. I want to stay human. Look at that bastard, he's half-machine and look what he's doing, killing all these people."

"There have been serial killers before," Tanner said, "and they've all been completely human."

Rattan shook his head. "I don't care, I've seen this guy, and getting cyborged, shit, that's *done* something to him. Destroying Angel, complete with the fuckin' wings. I mean, just look at what he does to them, fusing metal chains to their bodies, to their skin. I mean, what *is* that?"

"You think it's connected to him being cyborged."

"Shit, don't you?"

"How? Why do you think he's doing it?"

"How the fuck should *I* know?"

"You've talked to him."

"He didn't tell me he was killing people. He didn't tell me why. But I tell you, I've been dealing drugs for a lot of years, and as far as I can see, wanting to turn yourself into a machine is a lot worse than taking drugs. At least when you're doing drugs you're still human. Bad shit, this cyborg crap. And it's not just this bastard. It's the fucking future, Tanner, and I don't like it at all."

There was another silence, Tanner trying to decide what else he should ask Rattan. He could not think of anything. He knew who it was, and where he was.

"I gave you what you wanted, didn't I?" Rattan asked.

Tanner nodded. Neither spoke for a long time. Tanner gazed at the lights of the shuttle and the gantry, the moving lights of vehicles snaking across the tarmac. Rattan would soon be going into space, leaving all this behind. Leaving it for Tanner.

Was Rattan right, that being cyborged had turned Albert Cromwell into the Destroying Angel? A madman, a monster, a killer? He could not believe it was that simple, but that did not mean there was nothing to it. And what about Rattan's other comment, that a transition from human to machine was the future? What the hell did *that* mean, if there was any truth in it?

"What would you have done?" Rattan asked. "If I hadn't actually known who it was? If I hadn't known a damn thing?"

Tanner looked down at Rattan's unrecognizable face, at the strange sacks over unhealed stumps. "I probably would have let you go anyway." He paused, thinking about it a minute, then smiled and shook his head. "No, actually, I wouldn't have. I probably would have ripped every goddamn tube out of your miserable body."

Rattan laughed. "What I like about you, Tanner. You're an honest man. Could use a few more like you in the drug trade."

"Which you're getting out of."

Rattan laughed again, and nodded. "And which you're already into in your own way. Smuggling from the rich and giving to the poor." He shook his head. "Let's go back inside. It's time."

Tanner followed him back around the corner of the building, up the ramp and through the automatic doors and back into the station. The processing teams had already run Paul and Britta through the system and were waiting for Rattan. Tanner kept back and watched as they put him through.

First was the most important—identity confirmation. Rattan laid his right hand over the reading plate and put his head into the retinal scanner. The security man punched it through, Rattan pulled out of the scanner, and they all waited. A minute later the confirm came up on the screens, and they moved Rattan down the line.

The security inspection took the longest as the teams worked over Rattan's wheelchair, running scanners over and through it, opening accesses, taking sections of it apart. No one really thought he was smuggling anything aboard, no one thought he was bringing weapons or explosives, but they were thorough nonetheless.

When they were done, the teams escorted Rattan, Britta, and Paul out of the station and onto a loading van, which then headed out toward the shuttle.

There was still a long time until liftoff, so Tanner went to the viewing lounge in the upper floor and sat at a table beside the dome window. He drank a beer and watched the activity on the field. He tried not to think about much, tried to empty his mind. The final stage, he hoped, was about to begin. With the information from Rattan, they finally had a direction to go, a place to look. He thought he should feel happy and excited, but instead he only felt vaguely depressed. He did not know why.

Sirens blasted, announcing imminent launch. Tanner turned his attention to the shuttle. Wisps of smoke, strangely illuminated by the gantry lights, curled away from the ship, disappearing into the night. The countdown began, broadcast throughout the station.

First came the rush of smoke pouring out and away from the shuttle, along with silent explosions of flame, quickly followed by the muted roar and the vibrations rumbling through the station. The shuttle began to rise, quite slowly at first, then

picking up speed, rising above the gantry, trailing smoke and
flame, climbing into the night. Tanner watched it rise, fading
into the darkness so that only the flame itself was visible, and
he continued to watch the flame as it rose and grew smaller
and smaller until it was only a star moving slowly across the
night sky. Rattan was gone.

Footsteps approached the table, and Tanner turned to see
Carlucci. Carlucci hesitated a moment, then sat across from
him. Tanner did not know what to say.

"Didn't expect to see me here, did you?" Carlucci said.

"No." He was half-tempted to ask Carlucci if this was just
a coincidence, but he knew Carlucci had been following him.
How much did he know? Did it matter?

"Who was that guy in the wheelchair?" Carlucci asked.

There was no point avoiding it now, Tanner decided. It was
too late for Carlucci to do anything. "Rattan," he said.

Carlucci nodded. "I was afraid of that. But I didn't know,"
he said, staring at Tanner. "It could have been anybody."

He had deliberately waited until it was too late, Tanner
realized. Carlucci must have been here since Tanner and the
others had arrived.

Carlucci looked out the window and up at the night sky as if
he could still see the shuttle carrying Rattan up to New Hong
Kong. "This the price for the info?"

"Yes," Tanner said.

"Was it worth it?"

"Yes."

Carlucci nodded, then stood. "Then let's go get the motherfucker."

It was not going to be that easy, Tanner thought. But telling
Carlucci could wait. He nodded, stood, and they headed out of
the station.

THIRTY-FOUR

THEY DROVE BACK into the heart of the city in
Carlucci's car, headed for the Tenderloin. On the way, Tanner
related everything Rattan had told him. Carlucci asked only a
few minor questions for clarification, and did not ask Tanner
why he had not told him about any of the arrangements with
Rattan. Neither of them even mentioned it.

When Tanner was finished, Carlucci pulled off to the side of
the road and parked. He called into the department, got patched
through to Info-Services, and a woman's voice came over the
speakers.

"Diane?" Carlucci said.

"Yes. That you, Frank?"

"Yeah, it's me. I need two things. First, get someone to make
a formal request to the Defense Department for information on
Albert Cromwell. My guess is that'll draw zeroes, so get one
of the free-lance demons to make 'informal inquiries.' "

"You want to wait for a response from DOD before sending
out the demon?"

"No, get the demon started right away."

"Sure thing. Frank, this have anything to do with . . . ?"

"Not a word, Diane. Not a word."

"I'll get right on it."

"Thanks."

Carlucci replaced the comm unit and stared out the windshield for a minute, silent. The car's headlights lit up a metal
drum lying on its side, liquid leaking through two holes onto

186

the concrete. Tanner waited, also silent. He had nothing more
to say at the moment.

"Do we go in now, or wait until morning?" Carlucci eventually said. It did not really sound like a question he expected
Tanner to answer.

"Into the Core?" Tanner asked.

Carlucci nodded. "That's something we ask Koto." He looked
at Tanner. "*Now* we use him."

"Yeah?"

"Yeah. That's why he's in there. He knows the Tenderloin,
better than most, but the real reason we've got him in there is
the Core."

"He doesn't live in it, does he?"

"No. But he knows it. He knows the ways in and out, he
knows some of the people. He's *our* way in. Without him,
we wouldn't have much of a chance. With him . . . With him
maybe we find this fucker."

"So we go see Koto."

Carlucci nodded. "We go see Koto." He put the car in gear
and pulled out into the street.

Koto lived in the Asian Quarter, in a building just two blocks
from the Core. It was close to two in the morning when Tanner
and Carlucci arrived at the building. They had left Carlucci's
car in Chinatown, entered the Tenderloin through Li Peng's
Imperial Imports, and walked in from there.

They stepped into the small lobby of Koto's building, looked
around for a minute, then approached the security desk. The
guard was a big, beefy man wearing a T-shirt that said KOREAN
AND DAMN PROUD. He also had a palm gun in his right hand.

"Don't like the looks of you two," the guard said, glaring
at them. He gestured at the front door with the palm gun.
"Good-bye."

"We're here to see Ricky Toy," Carlucci said.

The guard did not respond. He kept the gun pointed at
the door.

"Just buzz Toy," Carlucci said.

The guard hesitated, scowling, then said, "Names and IDs."

Tanner and Carlucci laid their driver's licenses and city
residential IDs on the counter. The guard scrutinized them,
then punched some buttons on his console. A voice came
through the console speaker.

"Yes, Bernie."

"Frank Carlucci and Louis Tanner to see you, Mr. Toy."

"Punch up the video."

Bernie punched more buttons and said, "Look into the cameras," nodding at the two small swiveling cameras mounted on the wall behind him.

There was a long pause, then, "All right, Bernie, let them up. I'll buzz you if I need to kick them out on their asses."

Bernie grunted, then gestured toward the elevator. "Fourth floor, number four oh one."

They had to wait several minutes for the elevator, and when it did arrive, three short older women dressed in identical purple body suits got off. Only their leather headbands varied in color—one white, one black, one gray. Tanner and Carlucci got on and rode to the fourth floor without a stop. Apartment 401 was the first door on the right.

Carlucci knocked, and the door opened. Though Tanner had heard about Koto over the years, he had never met him, never even seen a picture of the man, and he was surprised to see a tall, very handsome, and well-built man answer the door. For some reason he had always imagined Koto as a small, skinny guy who shunned the light. Koto was nothing like that, and even his stance, the way he held himself, exuded a sense of strength and confidence.

Carlucci took care of introductions, then Koto led them into a room with two huge windows looking out onto the Tenderloin night. The room was furnished with several comfortable chairs, a couple of small tables, and a huge, complex audio and video system. The walls were lined with cabinets holding hundreds of disks and tapes, even two racks of old vinyl recordings.

Koto offered food and drink, both of which Carlucci and Tanner declined, then they sat in chairs near the two picture windows. Tanner remained silent while Carlucci laid things out for Koto, condensing the information Tanner had received from Rattan, adding any other background info he thought would be helpful. When he was done, he turned to Tanner.

"I leave anything out?"

Tanner shook his head.

"You don't doubt that Rattan's information is accurate?" Koto asked.

Tanner shrugged. "There are always doubts, but in this case, not really. I'm convinced. This guy is the Chain Killer, and he's living in the Core."

Koto nodded. "And you think that's the best way to find him, go into the Core."

"Far as I can tell," Carlucci said, "it's the *only* way."

"I don't suppose we could set up posts on all the ways in or out of the Core?" Tanner asked. "Then just wait for him?"

Koto smiled and shook his head. "No one knows all the ways in and out. I only know a few. And even if you did, everyone in the Core and anywhere around it would know what was happening within hours. He wouldn't come near you."

"Then what do you think?" Carlucci said.

"How many to go in?"

"Just the three of us."

Koto nodded. "That's a max. Any more causes real logistical problems. Also, you shouldn't tell anyone what we're doing. Not even Boicelli." Boicelli was a deputy chief, Carlucci's immediate superior, and his longtime friend.

"Fine with me."

Koto looked away from them, out the window. Some kind of flashing lights were going off in the distance, bursts of white and blue.

"I'm willing to do it," Koto said. "But you should both understand, it's a real risk. The Core is a funny place. It's not really quite as bad as most people think, but it can be a disaster. You don't watch it, it's easy to get killed or worse. I don't go inside much myself, and only when I'm convinced everything's right for it. Call it superstition, whatever you want, but different ways apply in there. I'm willing to push it a bit for this, but not much, which means maybe we don't even go in right away. Or maybe not far. Once inside, we go by my gut feelings. If I have the slightest doubts, we get back out fast, no matter where we are. You have to be willing to be patient, move at my pace. Maybe it'll take several trips in to find this guy, maybe more. I know you want to find him before he kills anyone else, but you can't push it or you're likely to end up dead. You have to accept those conditions, or I won't go."

Carlucci shrugged. "Hey, whatever, let's just do it. So when's the best time to go?"

"Dawn or dusk," Koto said. "It's a transition time, day and night people shifting, starting up or running down."

"Can we go at dawn, then? Today?"

Koto smiled. "I love your patience, Carlucci." Then he nodded. "We can try, feel things out. I won't promise any more than that."

"Good enough." Carlucci turned to Tanner. "This time, I want no arguments. You'll carry a gun."

"I'll insist on something," Koto added. "Even if it's only a blade or handjet."

Tanner nodded. "I'll carry a gun."

An hour before dawn, they left Koto's apartment. Koto had come up with several weapons for Tanner to choose from, and he had selected a nine-millimeter Browning. The gun felt cold and hard against his side.

Koto led them out of the building and onto the street. He carried a small knapsack over his shoulder. The sky was still dark, and the street was noisy and crowded and brightly lit. They walked one block closer to the Core, then Koto led them into a restaurant called Mama Choy's. The restaurant was packed, noisy and hot and smoky; the aroma of Chinese food hung thickly in the air. Koto spoke a few words in Chinese to the head waiter, then headed toward the back of the restaurant. Tanner and Carlucci followed him, working their way in a zigzagging path through the tables.

In the rear of the restaurant was a narrow extension with a single row of half a dozen booths, the seats covered in bright red vinyl. Most of the booths were empty. Koto continued on to the last booth, right up against the back wall. An old woman sat in the booth. She was small and thin, and looked quite dignified, Tanner thought, until she grinned at Koto with a mouth empty of teeth. Koto made introductions. The woman was Mama Choy, and she invited them all to sit with her. Koto sat beside her, while Tanner and Carlucci sat on the opposite bench.

After the initial introductions, Koto and Mama Choy pretty much ignored Tanner and Carlucci. They spoke to each other in Chinese, laughing and nodding, Mama Choy occasionally slapping Koto's hand with a loud smack. Tea was brought— a pot and four cups—and then a few minutes later four small bowls of egg flower soup. The laughter and talk between Koto and Mama Choy continued as all four drank tea and soup.

Tanner tried to relax, tried to block out the sounds around him. The soup was good, and he tried concentrating on that, on the heat and flavor. He could sense Carlucci's impatience. He did not know what they were doing here with Mama Choy, but he did not care. He trusted Koto, even though he didn't know him.

When the tea and soup were gone, the laughing and talk ceased, and Mama Choy got very serious. She pulled the teapot close to her, and a waitress took away the cups and bowls. Mama Choy and Koto spoke a few more words, softly now, without laughter. Then Mama Choy removed the lid from the teapot and, grinning widely, looked inside. She studied the bottom of the pot, tapping at the sides a few times with her silver fingernails.

The grin faded and she pushed the pot away with a gesture of dismissal. Then she took Koto's hands in hers and closed her eyes. She and Koto remained silent and unmoving for a minute. Tanner looked at Carlucci, who just shrugged. Then Mama Choy smiled, released Koto's hands, and opened her eyes. She and Koto talked a little more, then Koto nodded. He said something, Mama Choy laughed, then he leaned forward and kissed her on the cheek. She slapped his hand again, and Koto, smiling broadly, slid out of the booth and stood.

Koto nodded to Tanner and Carlucci, and they got up from the booth, thanking Mama Choy, who smiled and nodded, clicking her silver nails on the table. Koto said a few more words, then headed toward the front. Tanner and Carlucci followed him out of the restaurant and onto the street.

"I never go without Mama Choy's blessing," Koto told them when they were outside. "If she says I shouldn't go, then I don't go." He shrugged, smiled. "She says we will have good fortune this morning."

"What?" Carlucci said. "She reads tea leaves?"

"No, she doesn't believe in that nonsense. She just does that with the teapot as a kind of personal joke."

"Then what does she do?"

Koto shook his head, but would not say any more.

Just down the street from Mama Choy's, Koto went into a store and bought three large packages of cheese and put them in his pack. He did not explain that, either, but no one asked him about it. Tanner was content now to just follow and wait. Patience, Koto had said. Wise counsel, Tanner decided.

They continued down the block, went left at the corner, then entered an alley halfway down the next block. The alley was narrower than most, the air filled with fire escapes and metal balconies jammed together, the ground filled with trash cans, wooden platforms, and deep potholes. A few people wandered through the alley, most with faces turned to the ground.

Not far along the alley was a flight of concrete steps descending to a basement door. They went down the steps and Koto opened the door, which was not locked. They entered and closed the door behind them. The basement was dark. A bright, narrow beam from a flashlight in Koto's hand appeared. He had the pack open, and took out two other flashlights, handing one each to Tanner and Carlucci.

The basement was empty. Koto led the way to the far corner and another door, also unlocked. "The Core doesn't exactly need any security," Koto said. Behind the door was another flight of steps, descending one more level. At the bottom of the steps, a long corridor—walls of stone, floor of dirt—stretched out before them. A metal sign hung from the ceiling a few feet away, big letters etched into it with color acid pens.

ABANDON ALL HOPE
ABANDON EVERYTHING
WE ARE ALL SUCH SORRY MOTHERFUCKERS

"Someone's a philosopher," Carlucci said.

Koto turned to face them. Their lights crisscrossed one another, shining in three directions, creating a strange web of light and shadow on their faces.

Carlucci nodded. Koto nodded back, then said, "Let's go."

They started forward.

THIRTY-FIVE

SOOKIE LOST THEM almost immediately. She blundered around in the darkness for a while, no idea where she was, where she was going. Then she stopped, tried to figure out what to do. She was kind of scared.

She'd had no trouble following them to Mama Choy's, then around the corner and down the alley. She'd seen them go down the stairs. Through a small, grimy window she'd seen flashlight beams and shadowy figures moving around the basement, going through another door.

She'd almost backed off going into the basement, it was so dark, too much like that other basement. But she'd gone in, felt around and found the door in the back, and gone down more stairs in darkness. Up ahead in the corridor she could see the thin, moving lights and the dark forms walking along. Easy to follow, she'd thought. But somehow, after making a few turns, taking a couple of side passages, the lights disappeared, and she'd lost them.

It was dark. Silent. Sookie lit a cigarette, used the match to look around. Nothing except stone walls. She kept the match going until the flame burned her fingertips, then dropped it to the floor. Dark again. She had to work hard to keep herself from breathing too fast. Where was she? She had the bad feeling she was under the Core. Or was that the same as being *in* the Core?

Think, think, *think*. Light another match? What was the point? She pressed herself back against the cold stone wall. Dragged in deep on the cigarette. Which direction? Forward or back? Back, but would that really get her out? She was lost, turned around. Now she just wanted to find the basement again, get out of here. Mixer was right. Following Tanner was a bad idea.

Sookie crushed out the butt and breathed in slowly, deeply. She had to do *something*. She didn't know where she was, so any way was as good as any other. Staying put was pointless. Just *move*.

Sookie started walking, keeping her right hand on the wall for guidance. Whenever she came to a break in the wall she lit a match to see the choices. She gave herself just until the match went out to make a decision, then went with it.

An hour passed. She was running out of matches. She was tired. Sometimes she felt real calm about everything, but sometimes she got real scared. She went up and down like that, and didn't have much control over it. If she didn't find a way out soon, she thought, she was going to be a mess. She kept on.

Gray light ahead. She hurried forward, came to a low, slanting passage leading up toward dim light. Sookie squeezed into the passage and started up the slope on her hands and knees. Strange noises grew louder as she climbed: slapping sounds, choked cries, gurgling.

Sookie slowed down as she got close to the end of the passage. She crept forward real slow, listening to the sounds. Then she was at the end. It came out about six feet above the floor of a room with half a dozen windows letting in the morning light. But what she saw made her sick. Sick, and scared again.

A man and a woman, both naked, circled each other, each holding leather whips, which they periodically swung at one another. Their bodies were covered with huge red marks and streaks of blood. On the floor nearby was a small, crushed form, so mashed Sookie could not tell if it was human or not. From the smell, though, she knew it had been dead a long time.

Sookie could see only one way out of the room, a doorway on the opposite side. She'd have to go past the man and woman, around the crushed body. The windows were too high. No, she decided. She was not going into the room with those two people. She flinched as the woman struck the man hard and loud across the face, knocking him to the ground. The woman stopped moving, waited until the man got back to his feet, then they began circling each other again. Sookie, feeling dizzy and sick, started crawling backward down the passage.

Back into the dark. Sookie staggered along for a while, no longer using matches, just bumping from wall to wall, down one passage or another. She felt kind of numb, hardly even scared anymore.

She came to a passage lit by coils of fuzzy green light. The walls were covered with graffiti, but the passage was a dead end. She didn't read the graffiti, she didn't want to know what any of it said. She just pushed on, leaving it behind.

She thought she heard footsteps behind her. She stopped, listened hard, but didn't hear anything. It might be anything, it might be nothing, she was so tired. When she resumed walking, though, she thought she could hear them again. Sookie stopped again, and this time they kept on, getting closer. Someone was following her.

The numbness left her, and she was getting scared again. She kept thinking about the woman in white who had tried to get her before. Someone was after her, somebody was trying to catch her.

Sookie ran. She was blind in the dark, and she crashed into walls, but she kept running. She tripped over stones and chunks of wood, scraping her skin, bashing her elbows and knees. She splashed through water, slipped on mud, fell over a ditch, got to her feet, ran on.

She ran headlong into a wall and crashed backward to the ground, stunned. She didn't move for a minute, unsure of what had happened. Then she scrambled awkwardly to her feet, and a metal hand grabbed her shoulder.

Sookie tried to scream, but another hand, flesh, clamped over her mouth. She struggled, kicked and squirmed as the hands and arms pulled her back, crushed her against the hard chest and legs of her pursuer.

"I know you, girl."

No! It was that voice, the thing from the basement with all the machines. Sookie went crazy, flailing legs and arms, but the thing was too strong, it kept wrapping her tighter, cutting off her movement. She tried to bite the hand over her mouth, but its grip was too strong, she couldn't move her jaw.

"Don't struggle, girl. It changes nothing."

The metal hand let go of her shoulder, then the fingers dug into her neck. A funny pain went up into her head, sharp and cold and hard, and she started to feel very strange. She stopped moving, just hung there. Things were getting even darker, but spotted with glittering lights, and she suddenly wondered if she was going to die.

"Sleep now," the machine said.

Sleep or die, Sookie wondered. Sleep or . . .

Then nothing.

THIRTY-SIX

"UNDERGROUND TO GET into the Core," Koto
said, "and to move between blocks. But it's not a good idea to
stay down here any longer than necessary."

They were still underground, though they had switched passages several times through nearly invisible doors and light
baffles. So far they had encountered few people: a group of
three men wearing shocker suits and carrying flaming torches,
the men sweating profusely, their bodies giving off electric
blue sparks; a woman with two parrots on her shoulder and
two cats on leashes; a man who charged them with a pair
of handjets until he got close enough to recognize Koto, then
gave Koto a tremendous hug and ran off screaming.

Soon after they encountered the man with the handjets they
passed a lighted alcove dug out of the rock. Inside, seated on
a folding chair and working a laptop, was a man wearing a
tattered business suit, including a striped tie; thick-rimmed
glasses reflected the flashlight beams as he glanced up at
them. But he did not say anything, and he turned his attention
back to his laptop. The man's fingers frantically worked the
keyboard, but there was nothing at all on the screen, no power
hook-up, and Tanner wondered how long ago the batteries had
gone dead. Days? Weeks?

Just past the alcove, Koto led the way up a metal ladder
mounted in the stone. Several feet above the passage ceiling, Koto leaned away from the ladder and stepped across
the gap, as if into the stone itself, to the floor of another
passage that Tanner figured must be near ground level. He

and Carlucci followed, flashlight beams showing the way. The passage curled to the right, slanting steeply upward, then opened into a concrete stairwell.

They continued upward, climbing one flight of stairs after another. There were no windows, no illumination except for their flashlights, and the doors at each floor appeared to be welded shut.

Tanner had not counted, but he thought they were seven or eight floors up when the stairwell ended at a small platform with a door. Koto took out the cheese packages, unwrapped them, and handed one each to Tanner and Carlucci.

"When the rats appear, just feed them. You'll be fine."

Koto turned off his flashlight, and Tanner and Carlucci did the same. Then Koto pushed open the door, letting in light from the room on the other side. Tanner heard scurrying sounds, glimpsed large dark shapes moving across the floor. Koto broke off several chunks of cheese and tossed them far into the room. More scurrying, and hisses. Tanner did not realize rats could hiss.

Koto moved into the room, followed by Carlucci, and finally by Tanner. Tanner blinked at the harsh light, but he could see several dozen rats swarming over the floor, sticking close to shadow whenever possible. Tanner and Carlucci broke their cheese into chunks and tossed them into the room, and watched the rats scramble.

The room was empty except for the rats. Light came in through several large windows in one wall and from an opening in the ceiling. A makeshift ladder of wood and plastic and metal led up to the opening.

"Hey! Sunrat!" Koto called. "It's Ricky Toy."

Scuffling noises came through the opening in the ceiling, then a few moments later a long, thin face appeared, eyes covered by tiny plastic goggle-shades. The man's skin was deeply tanned, his black hair short but wild and streaked with gray.

"Hey, Sunrat," Koto said.

"Who's that with you?" Sunrat asked.

"Two friends. We want to talk to you."

Sunrat squinted, looking back and forth between Tanner and Carlucci. "You two look like cops," he said.

"*I* am," Carlucci said. He pointed at Tanner. "He's not."

Sunrat turned his face toward Tanner, cocking his head. "You *look* like a cop."

"I'm not," Tanner said.

"You sure?"

Tanner smiled and nodded. "I ought to be sure."

Sunrat sniffed. "I guess. Maybe you *should* be a cop."

"And maybe not."

Sunrat grinned, then turned his gaze to Koto. "You sure these two are okay? Even the cop?"

Koto nodded.

Sunrat nodded in return, said, "Give me a minute to power down the grid." The face pulled back, and there were more scuffling sounds, then some clicks and loud knocks.

"You'd do a complete fry in about five seconds if you tried to climb the ladder with the grid up," Koto said. "He doesn't like surprise visitors."

"All right, come on up!"

Koto went first. As Tanner climbed, he looked back and watched the rats. All the cheese was gone and now they were settling down, hissing and nipping at each other, fighting for spots in the shade.

Tanner came up inside a room with no ceiling and the walls in ruins. Sunrat lay in a lounge chair, directly in line with the blazing sun. He wore only a tiny racing swimsuit, and his skin, except for his face, was incredibly pale. A shining, oily substance covered his skin, thick and clear. Twenty or twenty-five plastic bottles surrounded him, most of them filled with colored liquids, but a few already empty.

"Have a seat, anywhere," Sunrat said. He reached for one of the bottles, drank deeply from it, and set it back down. "Help yourself to a cooler."

Koto looked at Tanner and Carlucci and subtly shook his head. There were no chairs, so they all sat on the floor. Tanner could not figure out how, lying exposed like that, Sunrat could manage to get only his face tan and keep the rest of his skin so white. Maybe the oil, some kind of sun block. Why would he want to do that? Then it occurred to him that it might not be by choice, that it might be a result of some very strange genetic mutation; but when he thought about it further, that seemed pretty unlikely.

"So what is it?" Sunrat asked.

"We're looking for someone," Koto said.

Sunrat shrugged and snorted. He wasn't looking at any of them. He kept his face directed at the sun. "Don't know why you're here, I don't know anyone. I'm a social outcast." He grinned.

"He's being modest," Koto said. "Sunrat knows a lot of people, don't you, Sunrat?"

Still grinning, Sunrat said. "Nah. I don't know no one. And yeah, I know that's a double negative, I'm an educated man. So sue me." He took another long drink from one of the bottles.

"Do you know the woman who sings at dawn on Saturdays?" Tanner asked.

Sunrat's grin vanished, and he sat up, frowning. He pointed at Tanner, his hand shaking. "You looking for *her*? Then you just get the hell out of here right now. I mean *now*, before I throw you over the wall and . . ."

Tanner put up a hand and shook his head. "No, no, you don't understand. We're not looking for her. I was just asking. I heard her sing a few days ago, I was just curious."

Sunrat kept his hand pointed at Tanner, and said, "You're sure you're not looking for her?" He looked at Koto. "Toy?"

"He's telling the truth," Koto said. "We're not looking for her. You know me, Sunrat. I wouldn't run anything over you. He didn't know, that's all. He's an outsider."

Sunrat turned back to Tanner. "You heard her sing?"

Tanner nodded.

"What did you think?"

"She has a beautiful voice. It was something, listening to her sing."

Sunrat lowered his hand, and his expression softened somewhat. "All right," he said. "But I don't want to hear you mention her again. Not a single word. Got it?"

"Got it."

Sunrat lay back down, shook himself, and directed his face at the sun once again. "So then, who you looking for?"

"A freak," Koto said.

Sunrat laughed. "Hey, wrong place, Toy. No freaks here. Not a single freak in the Core. All normal people."

"A real freak," Koto said. "He's something like three-quarters cyborged. Showed up a couple months ago, maybe?"

Sunrat turned toward Koto. "Cyborged. Anything else about this guy?"

"Well. Maybe he's got wings."

Sunrat's expression hardened, and he stared at Koto for a few moments, then turned his gaze to Carlucci, then to Tanner. He reminded Tanner of Max, since Tanner couldn't see his eyes behind the goggle-shades.

"Wings," Sunrat said.

"Wings."

Sunrat grinned, shrugged, then lay back down. "Nope. Never heard of any freak like that."

He finished off a bottle of blue liquid, then threw the empty bottle hard at Tanner's head. Tanner ducked, and the bottle clattered across the floor behind him. Tanner and Carlucci both looked at Koto, who just shook his head again.

"Sun's rising," Sunrat said, "but we'll get rain soon. You should think about getting an umbrella. Before you get *drenched*."

"That sounds like a good idea," Koto said. He stood, nodded at Tanner and Carlucci. "We'd better go now."

"Yes," Sunrat said. "You'd better."

Tanner and Carlucci stood.

"See you, Sunrat," Koto said.

"Not too soon, I hope."

Koto turned, walked over to the floor opening, and started down the ladder, with Carlucci and Tanner behind him. When they got to the bottom of the ladder, they moved toward the door, and the rats shifted positions to open a path for them.

"Later," Koto whispered, before Tanner or Carlucci could ask him a question. "Let's get out of here now while we can."

He reached the door, opened it, held it for Tanner and Carlucci, then closed it tightly. "Down, quickly now."

They turned on the flashlights and hurried down the stairs. From above, screeching laughter sounded, punctuated by a series of popping explosions.

"Just keep going," Koto said.

They hurried on.

At the top of the ladder leading back down to the underground passage, Koto stopped. "Wait here a minute," he said. "I want to check something. What Sunrat said, about getting drenched. Probably means someone's planning to flood the tunnels." He shrugged, smiling slightly. "Happens."

Koto climbed down the ladder, stood in the passage, and played the flashlight beam back and forth, checking both directions. Then he closed his eyes and cocked his head from one side to the other. He opened his eyes and looked up.

"Come on down," he said. "We get the hell out of here now." He nodded. "Everything's just fine."

THIRTY-SEVEN

SOOKIE WOKE IN pain. Her eyes ached, and her arms and legs burned. Burned like they were on fire. She choked out some sounds, opened painful eyes to see if she was burning up.

Chains. Silver chains were burned onto her, melted to her skin. Her *skin* was melted. Metal bands on her wrists, bands on her ankles. Bracelets. Chains between them.

No.

"No," she said.

"Yes." The machine voice.

Sookie blinked her eyes, looked around. She was in that basement room again, lying on the floor, surrounded by machines. Chains and bands on the walls. Windows and gray light. Everything hurt. And there was something strange on her eyelids, she thought, dark smudges when she closed them. Something. She didn't know what.

Where was he?

She didn't see him. All she saw were the machines. The machines were silent, unmoving. Sookie worked herself up into a sitting position, her back against the stone wall. Every motion was painful. Every movement burned. But the rock was cool, almost soothing. Where *was* he? The Chain Killer.

No.

A rumble, and the machines came to life. All at once— spinning, whining, rumbling, groaning. The ground shook, the stone behind her shook.

A blue, glowing light appeared in the midst of the machines. It hovered motionless for a minute, then slowly moved forward. Sookie could not move—the chains held down her arms and legs with their weight and the burning pain. She thought her skin was tearing free from her bones. She had to get away, but she couldn't move. The blue light kept moving forward.

The figure took form in flashes appearing between the machines. Sookie saw bits of feathers first, then reflecting strips of metal. A head half-metal, half-flesh, no hair. Face half-metal, too. Then the figure and the glow disappeared. Sookie couldn't see or hear anything except the machines. She stared hard into them, but still didn't see anything, not even a glimpse.

Light again, and he stepped out from behind a machine, now in full view just a few feet away. Wings of shining feathers lifted and spread out behind him. He wore no clothes, and as far as Sookie could see he didn't need any. Both legs were metal, up to his waist, and there was nothing between them. Sexless. His body was a crisscross of metal and flesh. One arm and shoulder was normal, but the other was metal, steel fingers flexing. Metallic bands went up the side of his neck. More metal covered half his face, but she thought both eyes were real.

"I know you," the angel said.

Sookie shook her head. "No," she whispered.

The angel nodded, said, "I know you," again. "You were here before. You ran away."

No, Sookie thought, but she couldn't even manage a whisper this time.

"I am . . . Destroying Angel," he said. The wings flexed, moved slowly forward, then back.

"Leave me alone," Sookie whispered.

The angel took two steps forward, looking down at her. He reached toward her with the metal arm, curled and uncurled the metal fingers.

"This is the future," the angel said. "Man's future. The fusion of metal to flesh, flesh to metal. The organic with the inorganic. Man with machine."

Sookie was so scared now she didn't think she could take any more. She thought her chest was going to explode, her heart was going to come apart on her. He's going to kill me, she thought, and she closed her eyes.

"What do you *see*?" The angel's voice boomed, shaking inside her head. A bright light came on just in front of her closed eyes. "What do you see?"

"Nothing," she said. There was bright orange from the light, and dark smudges in her eyelids.

The light brightened, hot and painful, and then the angel's fingers gently touched her eyelids, the metal cool and soothing. "What do you see here?"

"Nothing," Sookie said again. "Orange light and dark shadows."

"Wings," the angel said. He took his fingers away. "Wings," he repeated. "The wings of death. *My* wings. *Your* wings." He paused. "And you can't see them."

The light faded, and Sookie slowly opened her eyes. The angel was only a foot away, gazing down at her.

"Angels . . . angels are the breath of God," he said. He breathed deeply, slowly shook his head. "The future is here," the angel said. "Those who refuse to join it must be destroyed. *I* must destroy them."

And then Sookie knew, way deep inside, that she was going to die. The fear went away, replaced by a terrible numbness that went completely through her. She suddenly felt so tired she knew she couldn't have moved an inch even without the chains. She *knew*.

The angel knelt before her, his two real eyes staring hard into her own. Maybe they weren't real, she now thought. How could they be? How could *he* be a human being? She didn't know, and now it didn't matter. She was all cold and numb inside, even her brain seemed cold and numb, and so it didn't matter. She thought maybe she was already dying.

The angel reached forward with his human hand and gripped her throat, pressing hard and tight. It surprised her, the feel of warm flesh. She thought it would have been the metal hand.

The fingers dug deep into either side of her throat, and the awful fear rose up again inside her, shooting through the numbness. She tried to struggle now, reaching up with her hands, trying to push him away. But she had no strength. It was hopeless, and the fingers dug in still harder.

Pain drove up into her head, and silver glitter fell in front of her eyes, blocking out the angel's face. She tried digging her fingers into his arm, but the pain drove the last of her strength away, and she stopped struggling. I'm dying, she thought. I'm dying.

The glitter rushed across her sight, a storm of it now, then exploded into a ball of dark, hot red, blinding her to everything. There was nothing but the flaming red now, and the pain driving up into her head and behind her eyes. The red brightened, blending into orange, then yellow, then finally a blazing white. The pain exploded, shooting all through her, bursting with the white light, and the light and pain grew brighter . . . and brighter . . . and brighter . . . and . . .

THIRTY-EIGHT

TANNER AND CARLUCCI were sitting in the Carrie Nation Cafe, drinking coffee, when the spikehead found them. It was the day after their trip into the Core, and it was noon—the day was extraordinarily hot and muggy, suffusing the Tenderloin with stagnation and lethargy. The streets were nearly empty, and many of those few people who *were* on the streets looked half-asleep or half-zoned.

The two of them were talking about when to take another shot at the Core. Koto had admitted that Sunrat probably knew something about the Chain Killer, but it was obvious that Sunrat was not going to tell them a thing about it. He had said he might go back to see Sunrat alone; maybe in a couple of days he would go see Mama Choy again, see what she had to say.

Carlucci had wanted Koto to go see her again right away, at least to ask her, but Koto had refused, insisting it didn't work that way. The two of them had gone back and forth awhile, Koto digging in, Carlucci getting more and more pissed.

Tanner had the feeling Carlucci was arguing more for form's sake than anything; despite their concerns about time, and the possibility of another killing, Carlucci knew better than to really push Koto. Carlucci was just frustrated. The DOD request was being stonewalled, and the demon hadn't gotten anywhere yet, and they all felt that even though they now knew who the killer was, and *where* he was, they hadn't made any real progress.

So Koto had gone off to think about things, and Tanner and

Carlucci had gone to the Carrie Nation. They were drinking coffee and trying to sort things out when the spikehead came in through the door and walked up to their booth. The spikehead put his hands on the table, stared at Tanner, and said, "I've been looking for you."

"Mixer, right?" Tanner said.

The spikehead nodded.

"Okay, you've found me."

Mixer gestured toward Carlucci, said, "You're Carlucci. Homicide."

"Shit," Carlucci said. "You want to just shout it?"

Mixer shrugged. "Your problem, not mine."

"What *is* your problem, then?" Tanner asked.

Mixer did not seem too sure he wanted to say anything. "It's about the Chain Killer," he eventually said.

They were silent a few moments, looking at Mixer, then Tanner finally said, "So tell us."

Mixer shrugged, shifted from one foot to the other, then slid onto the bench next to Tanner. "I think I know where he does the shit with the chains. You know? Melting them to the bodies?"

"Yeah?" Carlucci said. He sounded skeptical.

"Yeah."

"Where is it?" Carlucci asked.

"In the Tundra."

"Not in the Core?" Tanner said.

Mixer shook his head. "You gotta be out of your fucking head you think I'd go in there. No, it's in the Tundra. A big basement room under a building."

"How do you know that's what it is?" Carlucci asked.

"It's full of a whole bunch of strange old machines, which means I don't know what, really. Maybe just that it's weird. But there are silver chains hanging all over the walls. The same fucking chains, I'm telling you."

No one said anything for a few moments, then Tanner asked, "How did you find it?"

Mixer shrugged, looked directly at Tanner. "I didn't. Sookie did."

"Who the hell is Sookie?" Carlucci asked.

"A girl," Tanner replied. Then, to Mixer, "*Sookie* found it?"

Mixer nodded. "She showed me where it was, couple days ago. I've been trying to find you two ever since." He looked at Carlucci. "I knew you were head guy on this thing, figured you two were working together on it. Thought you guys would want to know."

"Where's Sookie now?" Tanner asked. "She didn't stay there, did she?"

Mixer snorted. "Not a chance. I don't know where she is, but I know she's not there. I had to drag her just to get her to show me where it was. She's too damned scared of the place." He paused. "She said she saw the guy there that time, when she found it."

"She *saw* the Chain Killer?"

"She thinks that's who it was. He scared the hell out of her. She said he was some weird guy with a metal skull." He paused, cocking his head. "And get this. She thinks the guy had wings."

"Jesus Christ," Carlucci said. "That's him."

They got into Carlucci's car—Carlucci and Tanner in front, Mixer in back. Carlucci called in, made arrangements; several other Homicide detectives would be waiting for them on the street.

The late-afternoon rain began soon after Carlucci pulled onto the road. It burst upon them, obscuring their vision until Carlucci managed to get the wipers going.

"Shit," Carlucci said. He rolled up the windows and turned on the air conditioning, which hissed and sputtered at them, dripping fluids to the car floor. The heat had not dissipated much from its early-afternoon peak.

Tanner turned and looked back at Mixer. "How long ago did Sookie find this place?" he asked.

"Two weeks ago, something like that."

"And she didn't say anything to you, anyone else?"

Mixer shrugged. "You know Sookie. I don't think she really thought about it." He tapped the side of his head with one finger. "She's all right, you know, but she doesn't think the same way as most people. I doubt it ever occurred to her that telling someone about it might help get this guy."

Tanner nodded. That sounded right. He wondered where she was now. Holed up somewhere, still afraid?

They hadn't gone more than a few blocks when Carlucci got a call on the radio. Another location had come up on Homicide's computers—the lagoon by the Palace of Fine Arts—which meant more bodies. Carlucci said he was on his way, then pulled over to the side of the road. He looked at Tanner.

"You want to go with me?" he asked.

Tanner nodded, feeling a little sick. "Time, I think."

Carlucci nodded his head at Mixer. "What about him?"

"We still need him to show us the basement. We've got to see it."

Carlucci shrugged. "All right." He turned to Mixer. "Just stay the hell out of our way."

"Hey," said Mixer.

Carlucci turned back, pounded once on the air conditioner, which only spat out more fluids. "Fuck this thing." He pulled away from the curb and shot out into traffic.

The lagoon was on their left, large and expensive houses on their right. Tanner could see several cops standing in the rain at the water's edge, down at the far end of the lagoon. Two of them were uniforms—called in to do the shit work, Tanner imagined. He wondered what the residents here were going to think of the Chain Killer's victims being dumped in their exclusive neighborhood.

When they were even with the group of cops, Carlucci pulled over and parked. He and Tanner got out and started across the grass, the rain drenching them. Mixer followed just behind them, and when Carlucci told him to stay in the car he just shook his head. Carlucci grimaced, said, "Then stay back, out of the way. Got it?" Mixer nodded, and they continued toward the water.

Incredibly, when they were halfway to the lagoon, the rain stopped. But they were still wet, hot and sticky, and even the rain had not cooled down the air. The sun was a dim, orange glow in the west, barely visible through the dissipating cloud cover.

The grass ended several feet from the water's edge, and Tanner and Carlucci had to carefully work their way through the strip of mud that circled the lagoon. When they reached the group of cops, there was no round of hand shaking, no chorus of hellos and greetings. One of the uniforms, a big blond woman, pointed at the water and said, "There it is."

Tanner could see the top of the spike a few inches above the water, and the rope tied to it. Carlucci looked around the empty streets.

"Coroner's men should be here soon," he said. He turned back to the uniform. "Go ahead and pull them in."

The woman nodded, glanced at her partner, a tall skinny guy with a mustache; he frowned, then nodded back. They got down on their knees in the mud and shallow water, took hold of the rope, and started pulling.

It looked too easy, Tanner thought; the two uniforms were hardly straining. The woman confirmed that when she said, "Mother, this must be a solo. There's hardly any weight."

Another solo? Tanner wondered for a few moments if it might be a phony, a sack or something, not a body at all. But that hope quickly faded as chained wrists appeared, tied to the end of the rope, and a mass of swirling, dirty blond hair.

It *was* a solo, a small, naked body facedown. The two uniforms backed up and pulled the body the rest of the way out of the water, onto the mud slope.

"Aw, shit," the woman said. "It's just a kid. That fucking son of a bitch."

A terrible, sick feeling went through Tanner as he looked down at the body still lying facedown in the mud, bound at the wrists and ankles by silver bands and chains. A kid, yes, a girl. He did not want them to turn her over.

He took a few steps back, so he was just behind and to the side of Carlucci, but he still could see the body. The two uniforms slowly turned her over, and even though her face was mostly covered by wet hair and mud, Tanner recognized her.

Sookie.

Tanner felt dizzy, and his vision went funny on him, twisting slightly. The two uniforms carefully pulled the hair away from her face, then gently washed away the mud with lagoon water. Christ. Angel wings had been tattooed onto her eyelids. Tanner thought he was going to lose his balance and he reached out, grabbed Carlucci's shoulder to keep from falling.

Carlucci turned, said, "What is it?" Then he stared into Tanner's eyes for a few moments. "What, Tanner, do you know her?"

Tanner nodded, still staring at the body. He could not quite accept that he was seeing her. "It's Sookie," he said.

"Sookie? The girl who found the basement?"

Tanner nodded again. He thought he should stop looking at her, but he couldn't. He wasn't sure he was breathing. The cops were moving around, but he didn't really hear anything, little more than a background hum. He felt Mixer push past him, heard the spikehead say her name, saw him kneel down at Sookie's side until one of the cops pulled him back to keep him from touching the body. And then, as Tanner took in a deep breath, as he thought he was starting to pull everything back together, as he was about to let go of Carlucci's shoulder, the vertigo got worse, and a paralyzing ache went through him.

It was like seeing Carla dead all over again. As if she had been reincarnated, and now had died again, and he had to see her dead body once more. It was like seeing two dead people, both of whom meant something to him, both of whom he cared for in different ways—Sookie and Carla, he was seeing both of them. And then a third, as Connie's face superimposed itself over Sookie's. They weren't that different in age, just two or three years. It occurred to him that it could have been Connie lying there, dead and chained. It could have been both of them, Sookie and Connie, dead, face to face in chains.

"You all right?" Carlucci asked.

Tanner shook his head and finally pulled his gaze away. He released Carlucci's shoulder and took a few steps back, almost losing his footing on the slick mud. He looked around for a place to sit—a bench, a stump, a rock, anything—but there was nothing except mud and grass and water nearby.

He stood motionless, feeling somehow stupid and lost. A phrase came into his mind, from a movie or a book, he couldn't remember. "Catch the killer, and save the girl." Something like that. They had definitely failed at the second part of that, and it was still uncertain whether or not they could even manage the first.

He saw the coroner's van pull up, the men getting out and starting across the grass toward the lagoon and Sookie's body. Tanner finally moved, making his way through the mud and onto the grass, then walking slowly, unsteadily toward Carlucci's car. He could not really figure out what was happening to him. As he walked he kept sensing the ground coming up at him as if he were pitching forward, crashing face first into the grass; but he was moving along just fine, maintaining his balance, walking upright.

He reached Carlucci's car, opened the passenger door, and dropped onto the seat. He glanced toward the lagoon, saw Carlucci talking to the coroner's men, then looked away. He leaned his head back against the seat and closed his eyes.

Tanner breathed slowly and deeply. He tried to concentrate exclusively on his breathing, blocking out all other thoughts. In, long and deep . . . then slowly out. In . . . hold . . . out . . . in . . . hold . . . out. . . . He managed to induce a kind of trance; he focused on his breathing, the way it eased the pressure in his head, his chest.

Carlucci's voice intruded, breaking the trance. Tanner opened his eyes. Carlucci stood a few feet away, looking at him.

"What did you say?" Tanner asked.

"You going to be all right?"

Tanner nodded. He sat up, swung his legs outside the car. "I'll be fine."

"Have you known her a long time?"

"No. But it's not just her." He shrugged. "It's complicated."

Carlucci nodded, and did not say anything. They both were silent for a minute, and Carlucci looked back toward the lagoon. He ran his hand through his hair twice, then jammed it into his pocket.

"Why do you think the angel wings were on her eyelids?" Carlucci finally asked.

Tanner shook his head. "I don't know. Maybe because she had seen him before? It could be that simple, I suppose. I don't know. Right now I feel like I don't understand this guy at all."

"Did you ever?"

Tanner shrugged, then shook his head once more.

Tanner looked back toward the lagoon. The coroner's men were strapping Sookie's body to the stretcher. Mixer stood nearby, watching them. They cinched the straps, checked them, then lifted her and started back toward the van. One of the men slipped and fell, dropping his end of the stretcher into the mud. Tanner half expected Sookie's body to slide off the stretcher, but it remained secure. The man got to his feet, picked up his end, and they started again. They moved more slowly, carefully, until they reached the firmer footing of the grass. Mixer watched them for a minute, then headed back for the car. He seemed to be having as much difficulty walking back as Tanner had.

When Mixer reached the car, he did not say a word. He and Tanner looked at each other, but neither spoke.

"You feel up to going into the Tundra?" Carlucci said to Tanner. "I assume you want to be part of this."

Tanner turned to look at Carlucci. "Christ, yes, let's just get this over with."

Carlucci nodded, then walked around the car and got in behind the wheel. Tanner got back into the car and closed the door. Mixer climbed into the back, still silent. Carlucci started the engine.

"Wait a minute," Tanner said.

The coroner's men had reached the van. They loaded Sookie's body into the back, secured the stretcher inside, then backed out and shut the doors.

"All right," Tanner said. "Let's go."

Carlucci put the car into gear and swung out into the street.

THIRTY-NINE

THEY CAME AROUND a corner, and Tanner saw
four people standing on the sidewalk, talking to each other.
He recognized the woman—Fuentes—and one of the men—
Harker. The other two were probably Homicide detectives as
well. Carlucci pulled the car up onto the sidewalk and cut the
engine. He dug two flashlights from under the seat, handed
one to Tanner, and then they got out.

Mixer led the way into a narrow gap between two buildings. Fuentes and Harker joined them while the other two
detectives remained out in the street. About twenty feet into
the alley, Mixer headed down a flight of concrete steps to
a basement. It was a lot like the way they'd gone into the
Core, Tanner thought. He and Carlucci followed him down;
Fuentes and Harker remained in the alley at the top of the
steps.

"Used to be this vent screen was open," Mixer said. "How
Sookie got in the first time. But the other day when she brought
me here, it was boarded over. Solid. I had to bust my way in
through the door."

He opened the door, and they went inside, Tanner and
Carlucci switching on the flashlights. The room was nearly
empty. A few rickety shelves hung from one wall, a steel
cabinet was propped against another, and broken glass lay in
two piles next to the cabinet. There was a hatch in the floor,
and in the far right corner was a wooden door.

"Through there," Mixer said, pointing at the door. "She only
found it by accident. She'd wanted to get to the underground

215

lines, but the hatch was stuck or sealed or something, so she'd gone through the door."

"All right," Carlucci said. "Fuck this room, let's get right to it."

Carlucci led the way, and Mixer joined them. There were no locks on the door, and they entered a short, narrow passage, the room at the other end dimly lit but partially visible through an open door.

One at a time they emerged from the passage and into a huge room filled with machines. The ceiling was high, and windows near the top, though grimy, let in light from outside. On the walls hung sets of silver bands and chains.

Carlucci approached the wall and closely examined the chains without touching them. "Jesus," he said. "This is the place."

Tanner stood and looked around the room. The machines were old, but clean and dust free. There were some he did not recognize, but most he did. A drill press, a grinder, two band saws, a router, a polisher. Toward the back he thought he saw a mold press and a die cutter. Sookie had been here. The Chain Killer had brought her here. He sniffed the air, smelling something odd, and wondered if it had anything to do with the machines. A kind of burnt odor.

"Anyone else smell that?" he asked. He watched the others draw in sharp, deep breaths.

"Yeah," said Mixer. "Stinks, but what?"

"Burned flesh," Carlucci said. "I know that smell. Jesus," he said again. "I wonder how recently that bastard's been here."

No one answered him. Tanner wondered if any of them really wanted to know.

"I'll get Porkpie to come in and go over this place," Carlucci said. Porkpie was one of the senior crime-lab techs. "Don't know if he'll be able to get anything that'll help us, but I guess you can't ever tell." He shook his head and looked at Tanner. "He's still in the Core, that motherfucker. But maybe, just maybe . . ." He shrugged. "Think about this, will you? Do we keep taking runs at the Core, or do we wait here instead and hope he shows up before he does the next one? I suppose it's possible this isn't the only place he's got."

Tanner shook his head. "I don't know. How likely is it, though, that he's got another setup like this? Posting teams here around the clock just might catch something."

"Why not just bust your way through the hatch?" Mixer said. "That's gotta be the way he comes and goes. Follow the way back, maybe to where he lives."

They looked at Mixer. What he said made sense, Tanner thought. "Might be something to that," he said. "He's probably got any alternate ways in sealed off, to keep people out of here, so maybe there's only one place to end up. Like working a maze backward, from the finish to the start."

Carlucci grunted, said, "Worth thinking about, I guess."

Tanner and Carlucci wandered among the machines, working their way through them toward the back of the large room. Tanner wondered what the Chain Killer did with all these machines. Anything? He could not see a connection with most of them. Maybe they were just for effect. But then for whose benefit?

In the rear of the room, the machines gave way to a large open area occupied primarily by an operating table. Beside the table were smaller machines and tools, including gas canisters, welding torches, and other tools he did not recognize. This was where he did it, Tanner realized, noticing the restraints attached to the table. This was where he fused the chains to his victims.

Sookie had been on this table. Sookie had . . .

He turned away from the table. "Carlucci," he said. Then, "Something you should see."

He waited for Carlucci to work his way through the machines, scanning the area for anything else that might be significant. He felt numb again, slightly sick.

"Jesus," Carlucci said when he reached Tanner's side. He stared at the table and tools, then said, "Jesus Christ, look at that." He pointed to the floor, at something Tanner had not noticed—small pieces of what appeared to be melted or burned skin. "Something for Porkpie to sink into." He sighed heavily and turned to face Tanner. "The spikehead's right," Carlucci said. "No more fucking around. We bust through the hatch, we get this fucker now, whatever it takes."

Tanner nodded, silent and still numb. There was nothing else to say, there was nothing else to do.

Tanner stood in the Tundra basement and watched the two techs working on the floor-hatch locks; he did not much care about this anymore. Sookie was dead. Yet it was Sookie, however unintentionally, who had made this possible; it was Sookie who had led them here.

Four people would be going through the hatch: Tanner, Carlucci, Fuentes, and Harker. More than that in the close, underground confines would make for too many potential problems. Mixer was *not* going, if only because Carlucci had proved to be more stubborn than the spikehead.

Tanner himself was ambivalent. His part of this was over, it seemed to him. He had made his contribution. He had found, or been found by, Rattan, and had learned who and where the Chain Killer was. It no longer mattered if Tanner was along. Carlucci and the other cops would either find the Chain Killer or not, it made no difference whether or not Tanner was with them.

He wondered if Sookie's death should have enraged him, made him eager for revenge and justice, eager to be part of the Chain Killer's capture. But it had always seemed to him that revenge was vastly overrated, and justice was far more complicated and far less easily attained than most people wanted to admit.

Seeing Sookie's dead, mutilated body had depressed him more than anything else. She had very likely saved his life after he'd gone out that window, saved him from Max, but he had not come close to saving hers. He had not even known she had needed saving. What the hell did that mean? Anything?

Still, here he was, waiting with Carlucci for the techs to do their work. Why? If nothing else, he felt a need to see it through.

He felt for the trank pistol jammed into his back pocket. They were all armed with tranquilizer weapons in addition to their guns. The other weapons were to be a last resort. They wanted the Chain Killer alive. The mayor and the chief of police, in particular, wanted to see him tried, convicted, and publicly executed. One more thing Tanner did not really care much about.

"Got it," said one of the techs. Lights were trained on the hatch as the techs raised it, swinging it open on its hinges. "It's all yours."

Tanner and Carlucci crouched at the edge of the opening, aimed their lights through it. A metal ladder led down to a

platform beside a set of rail tracks. The platform was empty, and the tunnel in both directions was silent. "Let's go,"
Carlucci said.

Carlucci went first, then Tanner, and the other two followed.
There was barely enough room on the platform for all four of
them, and the ceiling was only a few inches above their heads.
Tanner had the urge to duck as he moved, though it was not
actually necessary. The walls were part stone, part concrete,
part solidly packed dirt. The ground along the tracks was a
mix of dirt, gravel, and rock.

The tunnel leading to the right, away from the Tenderloin
and the Core, was sealed just a hundred feet or so beyond the
platform—a brick and concrete wall filled the tunnel, blocking
the tracks. Not even a rat could have found a way through
it.

Carlucci led the way in the other direction, stepping off the
platform and walking along the side of the tracks. Tanner and
the others followed, single file, flashlights casting wide, shaky
beams through the dark.

They spent the next hour slowly following the tracks. It was
a relatively straightforward path, necessitating little discussion
and no decisions of significance. During that hour they came
across several passages branching away from the main tunnel
and the tracks, and they investigated each one; but in every
case, as expected, they found the branching passages sealed,
usually quite close to the main tunnel.

Graffiti covered the walls in some stretches of the tunnel,
and they even came across several large and beautiful paintings done on the stone walls, preserved by clear fixatives:
an abstract done in yellows and black, framed in white; a
machine with a man-shaped head and dozens of mechanical
arms, hovering above a deserted city square; a portrait of a
dark-haired woman.

Tanner trudged on, just behind Carlucci, still quite numb.
The air in the tunnel was not as cool and fresh as it should have
been, as most underground tunnels were in the city. Too many
passages blocked off, too much natural venting and circulation
eliminated. Stagnant and tepid, like death.

The tracks ended.

The ceiling rose, and the tunnel widened into a closed
chamber. Two large carts that apparently ran on the tracks

were mounted against one wall. A large door was the only
other way out.

They spent a couple of minutes checking the room, but did
not find anything. No one spoke, and they moved with hardly
a sound. Carlucci stepped up to the door, tried the handle.
Unlocked. At his signal, all lights were extinguished. The
darkness was complete; Tanner could not see a thing.

A slight cracking sound as Carlucci opened the door. A
faint slash of light appeared, slowly widened, cut across the
room. A wide passage lay beyond the door, dimly lit from
an unidentifiable source. The passage appeared to be empty.

Carlucci swung the door completely open and Tanner joined
him in the doorway, gazing down the passage. There was
nothing to be seen except blank walls. The passage extended
nearly fifty feet, then ended at another door. There were no
sounds except a faint, humming vibration that seemed to roll
smoothly through the air around them.

Carlucci and Tanner started down the passage, and the others
followed at ten-foot intervals. When they reached the door,
Tanner and Carlucci drew the trank guns. Carlucci gripped
the door handle, slowly pushed it down. This door, too, was
unlocked. He turned, checked to make sure everyone was
ready; the others all had their trank guns out. He pressed
down on the door handle, there was a quiet click, then he
pushed open the door.

The door opened into a huge room fifty feet across with
a thirty-foot-high ceiling. Standing in the center of the room,
illuminated by blue, shimmering light from a dozen spirals of
phosphor strings hung about the room, was the Chain Killer.
Destroying Angel.

He appeared much as Tanner had expected—both legs and
one arm cyborged, no clothes, part human, part machine,
with large, beautiful wings of glistening silver spread high
above and behind him. Fifteen or twenty cables ran from
his artificial limbs and across the floor, where they were
plugged into electronic consoles that lay against the walls.
The floor around him was littered with drug vials and injectors. The man's eyes were rolled back into his skull, and
his body and wings quivered as he stood in the middle of
the room.

The hum was loud in here. Tanner and Carlucci entered the room, Tanner moving right, Carlucci moving left, and the others came in behind them.

"Mother . . . fuck." It was Harker.

The man's eyes rolled back down so he was looking at Harker, who still stood in the doorway. Fuentes had joined Tanner on the right and they continued moving farther in along the wall, Carlucci doing the same on the other side of the room. Everyone had their trank guns aimed at the man.

Wings flexed, swinging forward then back. Tanner imagined the movements as preparation for takeoff, though he knew the man couldn't fly. The wings flexed again, but otherwise the man did not move.

"Albert Cromwell," Carlucci said.

The man's head turned, slowly, stiffly, until he was facing Carlucci.

"We've found you," Carlucci said. "Why don't you just make things easier for everyone, get down on the floor, arms and legs spread."

The man—machine, Destroying Angel—still did not move except to slowly shake his head.

"We don't want to kill you," Carlucci said. "So get down on the floor. And disconnect the wings."

The man opened his mouth, and a harsh, stuttering sound emerged. But no words. The wings flexed one more time, then the man staggered toward Carlucci, trailing cables, his motions stilted and slow. Why? Tanner wondered. He was outnumbered four to one, he had to know he didn't stand a chance, cyborg or not.

"Watch the crossfire," Carlucci shouted. "But shoot. Take this fucker down."

Suddenly the man began to move toward Carlucci with great speed. Tanner aimed and fired, heard the muffled bursts of the other guns, then heard the clanking sounds of pellets striking metal. He wondered if any of the shots were hits. He saw Carlucci fire twice and run to his left. The man turned and tried to follow, hampered by the wings and the cables. Tanner and the others fired again, Tanner aiming more carefully for flesh—the arm, upper chest, neck, face.

This time he was sure there were hits, the man jerked twice, though he kept after Carlucci. Carlucci dashed across the center of the room, avoiding the cables, leading the man toward Tanner and Fuentes. More shots from the trank guns, more hits.

The man staggered, dropped to his knees, got to his feet, then fell again, wings folding up around him, crumpling in a heap. He tried once more to get up, the wings spasmed, then he finally collapsed. He did not move.

Carlucci approached him first, then Fuentes, and Harker. Tanner kept back, watching from a few feet away, watching the three cops standing silently over Albert Cromwell. No one seemed to know what to say, what to do. Finally, Carlucci knelt beside the man, checked his pulse and breathing.

"All right," he said. "We've got him. Now let's get him out of here alive."

Tanner and Carlucci watched the paramedics load Albert Cromwell into the ambulance. It was difficult to think of him as Destroying Angel now. Night had fallen, and half the lights around them were flashing. There probably hadn't been this many cop cars inside the Tenderloin in years.

The senior paramedic walked over to them. "Can't guarantee anything," she said, "but all his vitals are strong. We'll be running toxics on the way over, and we're already countering the tranks. He looks a lot worse than he actually is. He should be fine."

"Thanks," Carlucci said.

She nodded, walked back to the ambulance, and got in the back with Cromwell. Doors were pulled shut, sirens and lights came on, and the ambulance pulled away, police escort in front and back as it headed out of the Tenderloin. There were still several other police cars nearby, one of which would be taking Carlucci to the hospital so he could stay on top of things.

They had found a quick, simple way out of the Chain Killer's place. The room *was* in the Core, but right at the edge. They had managed to get out and into the Tenderloin proper—the four of them carrying Cromwell between them—where Carlucci called in extra forces and the paramedics. The paramedics had arrived in less than five minutes.

"You want to go to the hospital with me?" Carlucci asked.

Tanner shook his head. "I can't think of one good reason I should," he said.

"Neither can I." Carlucci breathed in deeply, then slowly let it out. "It's over, I guess."

"I guess."

Neither spoke for a minute. Tanner watched the police cars loading up, pulling away.

"You'd better go," he said.

Carlucci nodded. "You going home?"

"Yes," Tanner said. "I could use a good night's sleep."

"Me too." Carlucci shrugged. "But I'm going to have to finish things up at the hospital. Who knows what time I'll get home. I'll be happy if it's still dark." He grunted, shrugged again. "I'll talk to you."

"Sure. Go on."

They shook hands, then Carlucci walked over to the last waiting car and got in. The siren kicked on, and the car pulled away.

Tanner stood and watched it move down the street, lights flashing, until it turned a corner three blocks up. People on the streets hardly paid it any attention. Within a couple of minutes all the sirens were barely audible, nearly drowned out by the normal sounds of the Tenderloin at night. Everything back to normal, Tanner thought.

Time to go home. He had been ready to do just that for a long time. He glanced back at the Core, then turned away and started walking down the street.

FORTY

THAT NIGHT TANNER slept long and deep, and did not awaken until almost noon. Over twelve hours. If he dreamed, he did not remember anything.

He lay in bed awhile without moving, listening to the sounds of the city coming in through the open window. There was a slight breeze, and although the air was hot it was not stifling. He did not know what day it was. Whatever day, he was in no hurry to start it.

Tanner finally got up, and wandered aimlessly about the apartment for a few minutes before finally going into the bathroom. He relieved himself, then stood and looked at his reflection in the mirror above the sink. About two weeks' growth of beard. He decided he did not like it.

He spent fifteen minutes carefully shaving off the beard, bringing his face back to normal. Afterward, he took a long shower, using all the hot water, then standing under a stream of cold for several minutes until he finally felt like moving again.

He dressed and ate a single piece of toast. He was not hungry, but he thought he should put something in his stomach. Then he left the apartment for coffee and the newspaper.

On Columbus Street he stopped in front of a newsrack, struck by the morning headline: CHAIN KILLER CAUGHT, KILLED. Killed? The paramedic had said he was going to be fine. What the hell was going on?

He bought a newspaper, but did not immediately read it. He went into a cafe, ordered coffee, then sat at a table with the coffee and the newspaper.

Tanner avoided the article on the Chain Killer. He drank his coffee and went through the rest of the paper, section by section. Only when he had read everything he would normally have read, and was halfway through a second cup of coffee, did he read the headline story.

According to the article, a man named Albert Cromwell, whom the police had finally identified as the Chain Killer, had been captured and arrested deep inside the Core after a long investigation and search. Although the police had used tranquilizer weapons in an attempt to capture the Chain Killer alive, the Chain Killer's metabolism had reacted adversely to the huge doses that had been used to subdue him, and he had died en route to the hospital. There were no pictures of Albert Cromwell, and no mention that he had been a cyborg.

Tanner left the cafe and searched out a phone booth. He tried calling Homicide, but was told that Carlucci was on vacation. No one would give him Carlucci's home number, and he finally had to get it from Lucy Chen.

Tina, Carlucci's daughter, answered the phone. At first she said Carlucci wasn't around, but when Tanner identified himself she said that her father had been waiting for his call. A few moments later Carlucci came on the line.

"I expected to hear from you a lot sooner," he said.

"I just saw the newspaper," Tanner replied.

"You sleep in?"

"Yes, as a matter of fact. What the hell is going on?"

"Let's meet somewhere," Carlucci said.

So, Tanner thought, nothing over the phone. "All right."

"Any preference?"

Tanner did not answer right away, but it didn't take him long to decide where he wanted to talk to Carlucci. "Yes," he said. "You know the Carousel Club?"

"South of Market somewhere, isn't it?"

"Yes, near the slough."

"I'll find it. Half an hour?"

"Make it an hour," Tanner said.

"Fine. See you then."

"Right." Tanner hung up the phone.

Tanner arrived at the Carousel Club a half hour early and went up to the second floor. All three balcony tables were occupied, so he had to take one just inside, near the wide doors. He ordered a bottle of lime-flavored glacier water— just for the hell of it—and kept an eye on the balcony. A few minutes after the waitress brought the glacier water, the two women at one of the balcony tables left, and Tanner moved out to it.

There must have been a slight breeze blowing away from the club because he could not smell the stench of the slough. The breeze, if it indeed existed, did not help much with the heat, however. Though there were no clouds visible, the humidity was high and Tanner was already sticky with sweat.

He drank the glacier water and gazed across the slough at the junkyard. This was where it had all started, he thought. At least for him. He pictured Sookie sitting cross-legged on a wrecked car, waving strange hand signals at him. It was still difficult to believe she was dead, and Tanner could not shake the feeling that he was at least partially responsible for her death.

When the glacier water was gone, he switched to regular mineral water. The glacier water had not tasted any better, but it had cost three times as much.

As he sat and sipped at the water, the other two tables emptied, and soon he was alone on the balcony, gazing across the slough, watching the light reflect off the water. He was still looking at the junkyard and thinking about Sookie when Carlucci arrived. He sat across from Tanner, ordered a beer, and looked down at the slough.

"This where you were?" Carlucci asked. "When we pulled the bodies out?"

Tanner nodded. "That day was the first time I saw Sookie," he said. "She was sitting on top of a car in the junkyard. By the time you showed up she was hidden—in one of the cars, I guess. She told me she watched you pull the bodies out of the water." He paused, a sharp ache driving through his chest. "Three weeks later she ends up being pulled out of the water herself." He turned to look at Carlucci. "So tell me what the hell is going on?"

"Let me explain something first," Carlucci said. "I've been officially ordered not to say anything about this to anyone, period. Anyone asks me about it, newshawkers, official investigators, whoever, I say nothing. I don't lie, I don't confirm or deny anything, it's just 'no comment' and refer all questions to my superiors. Which means Boicelli. I say anything, I lose my job, my pension, and any shot at working in this city again. Okay? I told them I would talk to you, tell you the same thing, but without any explanations. Just tell you that it's in your best interest not to say a thing. Nothing else." He sat back in the chair, shrugged. "So what I'm going to tell you now, well, I'm going to be way out of line. Thing is, you risked your life in all this, damn near lost it, and I figure I owe you. You deserve to know. But I want you to understand the situation."

"I understand," Tanner said. "And I appreciate the risk you're taking. So tell me how the hell he died."

Carlucci shook his head. "He didn't. The bastard's still alive." He continued to shake his head. "The military's got him back."

"What's with the newspapers then?"

"Official story. The company line. Given to us by the feds. I don't know how those bastards got onto it so fast, but they were at the hospital, waiting, when the ambulance arrived. Cromwell never actually got into the building. The military guys kept him in the ambulance, kept things hung up until they got their own transport on the scene. Lots of shouting and arguing, believe me. We tried to hold on to him, get him inside the hospital, but they wouldn't budge. They had their own doctor go in and work on him. *They* didn't want him dead, either." Carlucci shook his head, drank from his beer. "Pretty much a standoff, until McCuller, Vaughn, and Boicelli arrived. They told us to hand him over. I don't know about the other two, but I know Boicelli wasn't too happy about it. No choice, he said. Said word had come down 'from so high up it'd give you nosebleeds.' So they took him away. Everybody who knew anything was given orders: none of us knows a damn thing. I got a mandatory, fully paid two-week vacation, effective immediately. And that's supposed to be the end of it. Case closed."

"Why?" Tanner asked, though he had a few ideas already floating around in his head.

"*Their* official word," Carlucci said, "is that they want him in custody so they can examine and study him, figure out what went wrong so it won't happen again." Carlucci snorted. "I'd guess there's *some* truth to that, they probably *do* want to figure out what the hell this guy's all about, why he went over the edge."

"But what they're really worried about," Tanner said, "is bad publicity. They don't want any of this public."

Carlucci nodded. "You got it. They can't afford to have him go to trial. *Everything* would come to light, any half-assed attorney would make sure of that. And if this went public, kiss off the program, whatever the hell it is they've got going. So he's dead. He's not, and they've got him locked away somewhere, but officially he's dead. Albert Cromwell, deceased."

"So everything we did was for nothing," Tanner said. He slowly shook his head, returning his gaze to the slough and the junkyard on the other side of the water. "It's all so goddamn futile."

"No," Carlucci said. "We caught him. He would have killed again if we hadn't, who knows how many more?"

"He still could if he escapes again."

"That's pretty unlikely," Carlucci said. "They can't afford that happening, so they'll pretty much make it impossible. If it ever happened again, they know the shit would fly. All agreements would be void, and we'd blow them out of the fucking water over it."

Tanner just shook his head. "You may be right, but it's still shit." He looked at Carlucci. "You know, this is one fucked-up world we live in."

Carlucci gave him a short, hard laugh. "Big surprise, Tanner. Look, I won't argue that. But there's something you ought to keep in mind."

"Yeah? What's that?"

"This is the only world we've got."

Tanner did not reply. They sat in silence for a few minutes, both of them gazing out over the slough, the junkyard, the other ramshackle buildings and overgrown lots lining the water. The waitress came by for reorders, but Carlucci shook his head, saying, "I need to go soon." Tanner ordered another mineral water. He wanted to stay awhile and think some more.

After the waitress came back with the mineral water, Carlucci got up from the table.

"I'm on vacation," he said. "I'm going to spend it with my family. I don't know, maybe we'll take a trip somewhere. Where it doesn't rain so damn much."

He put out his hand, and Tanner gripped it with his own. "Thanks for talking to me," Tanner said.

Carlucci nodded, then said, "Sure thing." He released Tanner's hand and stepped back.

"Enjoy the vacation," Tanner said.

"I will. You might want to take one yourself."

"I may do that."

"I'll see you, Tanner."

"Yeah."

Carlucci turned and walked inside, made his way through the tables, then headed down the stairs and out of sight.

Tanner remained on the balcony a long time, thinking and watching the shadows lengthen across the surface of the water. People's faces shifted around in his thoughts, making appearances, then shifting away to reappear again later: Sookie, Carla, Valerie and Connie. Carlucci. Albert Cromwell. Destroying Angel. Sookie and Carla were dead, but they were still there with him. Maybe Carla too much so. Was that what Hannah had tried to tell him? Maybe Hannah was right. Could it be that he still had not let her go? And what about Valerie? Was Hannah right about her, too? He had not known what else to do.

And there was Albert Cromwell, Destroying Angel. Back with the military, who knew what was happening with him. Gone, missing again. But Carlucci's words came back to him: 'This is the only world we've got.' It seemed to Tanner now, sitting here thinking and gazing out over the slough, that Carlucci was absolutely right.

It was late afternoon when Tanner finally left the Carousel Club. He had to walk three blocks before he could find a working telephone. He picked up the receiver, then put it back down and walked off. Two blocks farther on he stopped at another phone booth and again picked up the receiver. This time he ran his card through and punched up Valerie's home number.

As he listened to the ringing, he thought about Connie and hoped she wouldn't answer. He still wasn't sure what to say to her; he still had not worked all that out. He wasn't sure he even wanted Valerie to answer, so when the phone kept ringing, he felt relieved. Finally, he hung up.

He hesitated before trying the hospital, almost walked away from the phone, then finally punched up the number. When his call was answered, and he asked for Valerie, he was switched up to ICU, and the nurse who answered said Valerie was busy. Tanner left the phone booth number and hung up.

He was unsure about this, wondering if it was a mistake, wondering if it was worth trying. But it seemed like something he had to do. Something he needed.

The phone rang.

Tanner stared at it, again nearly turned and walked away. His heart was beating hard. The phone kept ringing. Then, something inside him released, and he let out a breath he had not realized he'd been holding in. He knew what he wanted to do. He knew. Tanner breathed in deeply once again, put out his hand, and picked up the phone.